John Stevens Cabot Abbott

Captain William Kidd, and Others of the Pirates

Or buccaneers who ravaged the seas, the islands, and the continents of America

two hundred years ago. Vol.1

John Stevens Cabot Abbott

Captain William Kidd, and Others of the Pirates
Or buccaneers who ravaged the seas, the islands, and the continents of America two hundred years ago. Vol.1

ISBN/EAN: 9783337083397

Printed in Europe, USA, Canada, Australia, Japan

Cover: Foto ©Andreas Hilbeck / pixelio.de

More available books at **www.hansebooks.com**

DEATH OF BLACK BEARD.

CAPTAIN WILLIAM KIDD,

AND

OTHERS OF THE PIRATES OR BUCCANEERS WHO RAVAGED THE SEAS, THE ISLANDS, AND THE CONTINENTS OF AMERICA TWO HUNDRED YEARS AGO.

BY

JOHN S. C. ABBOTT.

ILLUSTRATED.

NEW YORK:
DODD & MEAD, No. 762 BROADWAY.
1874.

PREFACE.

THERE can scarcely anything be found, in the literature of our language, more wild and wonderful, than the narrative contained in this volume. The extraordinary career of Captain Kidd, a New-York merchant, the demoniac feats of those fiends in human form, Bonnet, Barthelemy, and Lolonois; the romantic history of the innocent female pirate Mary Read, and of the termagant Anne Bonney; the amazing career of Sir Henry Morgan, and the fanaticism of Montbar, scarcely surpassed by that of Mohammed or Loyola, combine in creating a story, which the imagination of Dickens or Dumas could scarcely rival.

And yet these incidents seem to be well authenticated. The writer has drawn his facts from Esquemeling's *Zee Roovers*, Amsterdam, 4to, 1684; Oexemelin's *Histoire des Aventuriers*, 12mo, Paris,

1688 ; Johnson's *History of the Pirates*, 2 vols., London, 1724 ; Thornbury's *Monarchs of the Main*, 3 vols., London, 1855 ; *History of the Buccaneers of America*, 1 vol. 8vo, Boston, 1855 ; with many other pamphlets, encyclopædias, and secondary works.

In exploring this hitherto almost unknown field of research, the writer has been as much surprised at the awful scenes which have opened before him, as any of his readers can be. There are but few thinking men who will peruse this narrative, to whom the suggestion will not arise, "What a different world would this have been, and would it now be, were all its inhabitants conscientiously, prayerfully, with brotherly love striving to do right." And this is the religion of Jesus. He has taught us to pray, "Thy kingdom come on earth as in heaven."

JOHN S. C. ABBOTT.

FAIR HAVEN, CONN.

CONTENTS.

CHAPTER I.

Origin of the Buccaneers.

CHAPTER II.

William Kidd becomes a Pirate.

CHAPTER III.

Piratic Adventures.

CHAPTER IV.

Arrest, Trial, and Condemnation of Kidd.

CHAPTER V.

Kidd, and Stede Bonnet.

CHAPTER VI.

The Adventures of Edward Teach, or Blackbeard.

CHAPTER VII.

The Close of Stede Bonnet's Career.

CHAPTER XVIII.

A New Expedition Planned.

CHAPTER XIX.

Capture of St. Catherine and Chagres.

CHAPTER XX.

The March from Chagres to Panama.

CHAPTER XXI.

The Capture of Panama.

Captain Kidd.

CHAPTER I.

Origin of the Buccaneers.

Renown of Captain Kidd.—Wild Legends.—Demands of Spain.—
Opposition of the Maritime Powers.—The Rise of the Buc
caneers.—The Pirates' Code.—Remonstrance of Spain.—Reply
of France and England.—Confession of a Buccaneer.—Adven
tures of Peter the Great.

THERE are but few persons, in the United
States, who have not heard the name of the renowned pirate, Captain Kidd. There are also but
few to be found who have any intelligent conception
of his wild and guilty career. The banks of the
Hudson, the islands scattered through the Sound
which skirts the southern New-England coast, and
the wild rivers and craggy harbors which fringe the
rugged shores of Maine, are all rich with legends of

1*

the exploits and hiding-places of this notorious buccaneer.

Thousands of fanatical people have employed themselves in digging among the rocks and sands, in search of treasure of gold and jewels supposed to have been buried, in iron-bound chests, by this chief of outlaws. It was well known that he had plundered many a rich Spanish galleon, laden with golden coin, bound to or from the colonies. Many a Spanish lady had been compelled to walk blindfolded the awful plank, until she was jostled into the sea, while her chests of golden ingots and diamonds fell into the hands of brutal assassins.

It was not always easy for the pirates to dispose of these treasures. They were sometimes pursued by men-of-war. Doubtless, as a measure of safety, they did at times bury their spoil, intending at a convenient hour to return and reclaim it. And it can hardly be questioned that, in some cases, pursued, harassed, cut up, they never did return. Therefore it may be that there is treasure still hidden in some secluded spot, which may remain, through all coming ages, unless by some accident discovered. This belief has, in bygone days, nerved many a treasure-seeker to months of toil, all along our northern coast, from Passamaquoddy Bay to the Jerseys.

Half a century ago, when superstition exerted

much more powerful sway than now, the wildest stories were told, around the fireside, of the complicity of the robber with the Archfiend himself, and of the agency of the Prince of the Power of the Air in protecting his subjects. Hundreds of parties, equipped with hazel rods, whose dip should guide them to the treasure, and with spades to dig, have gone to the most lonely spots at dead of night, in search of these riches. It was believed that not a word must be spoken, and particularly that Satan was so jealous, that if the Divine name were uttered, some terrible doom would befall them.

The writer remembers hearing, sixty years ago, at the kitchen fireside, many of these wondrous stories. One or two may be given in illustration of them all. A fortune-teller had told some men where Captain Kidd had buried a chest. They were to go to the spot, in the darkness of a moonless midnight. Not one word was to be spoken. A lantern, dimly burning, was to guide their steps. One carrying a hazel rod was to lead the party of four. When they reached the precise spot the hazel rod would bend directly down to indicate it. By digging they would find, five feet beneath the surface, an oaken chest, bound with iron, filled with doubloons.

They obeyed all the directions implicitly. The spot was found. In silence and with energy they plied their spades. At the depth of five feet they struck the chest. There it was, beyond all question, in its massive strength of oak and iron. The size of the chest and the difficulty with which it could be moved, proved that they had come upon an amount of treasure which would enrich them all beyond the dreams of romance. One thoughtlessly, in the excess of his excitement, exclaimed, " Thank God ! " In an instant there was a flash of lightning which blinded them all ; a peal of thunder which stunned them all. Those in the pit were violently thrust out, and every one was thrown helpless and senseless upon the ground.

After a time they recovered one by one. The darkness was like that of Egypt, which could be felt. The rain was falling in torrents. Their pit was entirely closed up, and replaced by a ledge of solid granite. Terrified, they crept to their homes, fearing ever again to seek the treasure which the pirate, as an emissary of Satan, had seized with bloody hands, and with bloody hands had buried.

Again, there was a young woman who had a sacred stone into which she looked and saw whatever she wished to have revealed. She could read the fortunes of others. She could foresee all future events. She could reveal any secrets of the past. Into this mysterious crystal she gazed, and saw a small vessel, under an immense cloud of canvas, flying before a huge man-of-war. But the smaller vessel was the fleetest. The larger vessel was firing upon it with heavy cannon, and the balls were bounding over the waves. She looked upon the deck of the little schooner, and it was crowded with the fiercest-looking armed men. Among them stood a man, in rich uniform, with drawn sword, and pistols in his belt, who was evidently their leader. She at once recognized him as Captain Kidd.

It was in the evening twilight. The pirate ran in at the mouth of the Kennebec River. The man-of-war could not venture to follow amid the rocks and shoals. The commander, however, felt that the pirate was caught in a trap and that he could not escape. He decided to lay off and on until morning, carefully watching the mouth of the river. Then he would send his war-boats thoroughly manned, and the pirates would soon swing at his yard-arms, and their treasures would be transferred to his chests and his ship's hold.

Captain Kidd had a large amount of treasure on board his vessel, which he had plundered mainly from the rich argosies which carried on the commerce between Spain and her colonies. At the same time he was not at all particular in his inquiries as to what nationality the ship belonged to, if the cargo of goods or coin were valuable. His adventurous sail ran along the shores of both the Indies, and all richly freighted ships he encountered were doomed.

The swift-sailing schooner which had run into the mouth of the Kennebec was heavily laden with gold and silver coin, rich silks, and others of the most precious fabrics of the two Indies. To save these from capture, so the story goes, and to lighten his vessel, so as to be able to creep away over the shallow waters out of reach of the man-of-war, he threw the heaviest and least valuable articles overboard. Then landing a portion of the crew in the night, he searched out a secluded spot, where he dug a deep hole, and placed in it an immense iron-bound hogshead. Here he carefully packed away his gold and silver coin in strong canvas bags. His silks and satins were wrapped in canvas envelopes, and then protected with tarred cloth, impervious to both air and moisture. Thus the cask soon held treasure amounting to countless thousands. This was carefully covered up and concealed, Captain Kidd taking notes which would enable him to find the place without difficulty.

Then in the darkness he again spread his sails, and stealing out of one of the unfrequented mouths of the river, crept along the shore unseen, and turning his course south, was soon again engaged in his piratic cruise among the islands of the West Indies. He never returned to regain his treasure.

The next morning the man-of-war sent up three boats well manned and armed to capture the pirate. But not the slightest vestige of his vessel could be found. It was believed that Satan had aided them to escape. Some of the sailors declared that in the night they had seen the schooner under full sail in the clouds, passing over their heads, and that they had heard shouts of merriment from the demoniac crew.

The girl, looking into her enchanted stone, saw all this. She informed those inquiring of her, of the precise spot where the treasure was buried. To obtain it they must go at dead of night, and work in perfect silence. The utterance of a single word would bring disaster upon all their efforts.

They went, and worked with a will, in the darkness, by dim torchlight. Not a word was spoken. They reached the cask, spaded away the earth around it, and were just ready to open it and rifle it of its contents, when to their astonishment a little negro boy was seen sitting upon the head of the cask, entirely naked. One of them in his surprise thoughtlessly exclaimed, " Who are you?"

The spell was broken. Instantly one of the

blackest of thunder-clouds enveloped them, with a tornado which wrecked the skies. Carousing fiends were seen with bat-like wings through the gloom. Shrieks of derisive laughter were heard. Every man was seized, and whirled through the air to distances several miles apart. Awaking from stupor, terror-inspired, they with difficulty found their way to their homes. Upon subsequently revisiting the spot they found no traces of their labor.

Such was the general character of the legends which were floating about very freely half a century ago. Captain Kidd was the hero of all these marvellous tales. It is not easy to account for the fact that his name should have attained such an ascendency over that of all other buccaneers. Though there was nothing so very remarkable in his achievements, there was something strange in the highest degree, in his partnership with men in England occupying the most exalted position in rank and power.

After the discovery of the New World, Pope Alexander VI. issued a proclamation dividing all the newly discovered lands, in both the East and West Indies, between the crowns of Portugal and Spain, to the exclusion of all other powers. This *bull*, as it was called, excited great discontent throughout all Christendom. This was nearly two hundred years ago. France, England, and the Netherlands, the three remaining great maritime nations, combined against Spain and Portugal. These courts would give any man a commission to take a ship, fill it with armed men, and prey upon the commerce of Spain and Portugal. There was no court to decide upon the validity of prizes. The captors were responsible to nobody. They decided for themselves whether the prize they had taken was their legitimate booty. The whole spoil was divided among them according to their own agreement.

Very soon all seas swarmed with these adventurers. They sailed in fleets. In armed bands they landed and ravaged the coasts, battering down forts and capturing and plundering cities. They did not deem themselves pirates, but took the name of buccaneers. Though often guilty of great enormities, they assumed the air of legitimate privateersmen. With heads high uplifted they swaggered through the streets of England, France, and the Netherlands, with lavish hand scattering their ill-gotten gold. They were welcomed at every port they entered, for they proved very profitable customers. They sold their booty very cheap. They purchased very freely, regardless of price. In drunken frolics they had been known to scatter doubloons in the streets to see men and boys scramble for them. The merchants all welcomed them, not deeming it necessary to ask any questions for conscience' sake. Their numbers became so great and their depredations so audacious, that no ship could sail in safety under any flag. The buccaneers were not careful to obtain any commission. Assuming that they were warring against the enemies of their country, even when there was no war existing between the two nations, they ravaged the seas at their pleasure.

Generally their bands were well organized and under very salutary discipline. The following articles of agreement, signed by the whole crew, were found on board one of these ships:

" Every man is entitled to a vote in affairs of importance, and to an equal share of all provisions and strong liquors which may be seized. Any man who defrauds the company in plate, jewels, or money, shall be landed on a desert island. If he rob a messmate, his ears and nose shall be slit, and then he shall be landed on a desert island. No man shall play at cards or dice for money. The lights are to be put out at eight o'clock at night. No woman is to be allowed on board. Any man who brings a woman to sea disguised shall be put to death. No man shall strike another on board, but quarrels shall be settled on shore with sword or pistol.

" Any one deserting, or leaving his quarters, during an engagement, shall be either landed on a desert island or put to death. Every man losing a limb or becoming crippled in the service shall have, eight hundred dollars. The captain and quartermaster shall receive two shares of every prize; the master, boatswain, and gunner, one share and a half, and all other officers one and a quarter. Quarter always to be given when called for. He that sees a sail first is to have the best pistols and small arms on board of her."

Thus it will be seen that these buccaneers were regularly organized bands, by no means ashamed of their calling. They were morally scarcely inferior to the robber knights and barons of the feudal ages, from whom the haughtiest nobles of Europe are proud to claim their lineage. They were not petty thieves and vulgar murderers. They unfurled their banners and waged open warfare on the sea and on the land, glorying in their chivalric exploits, and ostentatiously displaying, in all harbors, the trophies of their wild adventures.

These freebooters assumed the most gorgeous and extravagant dresses. Their favorite ornament was a broad crimsom sash, of bright scarlet, passing round the waist, and fastened on the shoulder and hip with colored ribbons. This was so arranged that it formed a belt into which they could thrust three or four richly mounted pistols. These pistols were often sold at auction, on shipboard, for two hundred dollars each. Cocked hats, with a showy embroidery of gold lace, formed a conspicuous feature of their costume.

The captain, in time of battle, was invested with dictatorial power. He could stab or shoot any one who disobeyed his orders. His voice was generally decisive as to the treatment of prisoners. The large cabin was appropriated to his exclusive use. Often the freebooters combined, in several armed vessels, to attack some richly freighted fleet under convoy. Occasionally they landed, and captured and plundered very considerable cities.

These buccaneers were generally, as we have said, Englishmen, Frenchmen, or Germans. Still, adventurers from all nationalities crowded their decks. The Spanish Court remonstrated with the several Governments of Europe against these outrages. France replied:

" The people complained against act entirely on their own authority and responsibility, not by any commission from us. The King of Spain is at liberty to proceed against them according to his own pleasure."

Elizabeth, England's termagant queen, with characteristic tartness replied:

"The Spaniards have drawn these inconveniences on themselves, by their severe and unjust dealings in their American commerce. The Queen of England cannot understand why her subjects, or those of any other European prince should be debarred from traffic in the West Indies. As she does not acknowledge the Spaniards to have any title to any portion of the New World by the donation of the Bishop of Rome, so she knows no right they have to any places other than those of which they are in actual possession. Their having touched only here and there upon a coast, and given names to a few rivers or capes, are such insignificant things as can in no ways entitle them to a property in those parts, any further than where they have actually settled and continue to inhabit."

Some curious anecdotes are told illustrative of the great respect some of these adventurers entertained for religion and morality. In many cases all bolts, locks, and fastenings of any kind were prohibited, as implying a doubt of the honor of their comrades. Not a few men of noble birth became buccaneers. A captain of one of these bands shot one of his crew for behaving irreverently in church. Sir Raveneau de Sussan, being deeply involved in debt, joined the freebooters because, he said, "he wished, as every honest man should do, to have withal to satisfy his creditors."

The French called the buccaneers *nos braves*. The English papers were filled with admiring accounts of their unparalleled exploits. A French buccaneer, Francois l'Olonnais, at the head of six hundred and fifty men, captured the towns of Maracaibo and Gibraltar, in the Gulf of Venezuela. and extorted half a million dollars for the ransom of those places. A French priest extolled the deed as one of chivalric heroism.

The pirates seized the Island of Tortuga, built a town there, and erected a strong fort on an eminence which commanded a view of the encircling sea to the horizon. This island is situated a few leagues north of the magnificent Island of San Domingo, then called Hispaniola. It is long and narrow, running east and west, and is about sixty miles in circuit. It is mainly a mountainous island of rock, but at that time was densely covered with a gigantic forest. The western part of the island was uninhabited. It was very rugged and barren, and had no harbor or even cove into which a vessel or boat could run. On the southeastern shore there was one good harbor, so landlocked that it could be easily defended. The island abounded with wild boars, and at some seasons, the very air seemed darkened with the flocks of pigeons which frequented its groves.

The buccaneers seized this island, and sent to the French governor of St. Christopher's to furnish them with aid to fortify it. The governor sent them a ship full of men, with all needful supplies. With this assistance they built a fort on a high rock, which perfectly commanded the harbor. There was no access to the fort but by climbing a narrow passage, along which but two persons could pass at a time. With great difficulty two guns were raised and mounted. There was a plentiful supply of fresh water on the summit, from an abundant spring gushing from the rock.

One of these buccaneers, John Esquemeling, has given quite a minute account of the achievements of himself and comrades. His narrative, which is deemed authentic, was written in Dutch, but was translated and published in London in the year 1684. He had sailed from Havre-de-Grace, in France, for the New World, in the year 1666, to seek his fortune. He gives the following reason for joining the buccaneers:

"I found myself in Tortuga like unto Adam when he was first created by the hand of his Maker; that is, naked and destitute of all human necessaries. Not knowing how to get a living, I determined to enter into the wicked order of pirates or robbers of the sea. Into this society I was received by common consent both of the superior and vulgar sort. I continued among them six years, until the year 1672. Having assisted them in all their designs and attempts, and served them in many notable exploits, of which I here give the reader a full account, I returned to my own native country."

We will give one incident illustrative of the mode in which these buccaneers operated.

There was at Tortuga a man born in Dieppe, Normandy. From his gigantic stature and his bold carriage he was familiarly called Peter the Great. He took a large boat, and with twenty-eight companions, desperate men, thoroughly armed, set out from the harbor in search of booty. For a long time they sailed over those tropical seas, keeping a vigilant watch from the mast-head, but no vessel appeared in sight. Their food was rapidly disappearing, and they began to be in despair.

At length they espied, one afternoon, in the distant horizon, a sail. As they approached it, they found, somewhat to their alarm, that it was a huge Spanish galleon laden to the gunwales with treasure. It probably contained passengers and crew, and perhaps soldiers, three or four times outnumbering the buccaneers. The sagacious Peter immediately surmised that the galleon was one of a merchant fleet which had recently sailed from Spain under a strong convoy, and being heavily laden, had, in some storm, got separated from the squadron. It was one of the most desperate of enterprises to attack such a ship with their little boat. The ship, though a merchant-man, had, without any doubt, some heavy guns, and the crew was well armed.

But they were desperate men; their provisions were exhausted; they were in danger of actual star-vation. The captain assembled them all around him, and addressed them in a very glowing and inspiring speech. We cannot quote his identical words. But we have a record of the motives he urged to rouse his men to a frenzy of courage.

"Our cruise," said he, "has been thus far a fail-ure. We have no money. We have no food. We must soon perish by the most miserable of all deaths, lingering starvation. In that ship there is food in abundance, wine in abundance, gold in abundance. We are now beggars. Let us take that ship, and we are princes. We can revel in luxury. Our for-tunes are made for our lives. We can sail to any land we please, and there live in independence. Even if some of us must die, it is better to die sud-denly than to starve. We can take the ship if we all do our duty. I call upon every one now to take a solemn oath either to capture the ship or to die in the attempt."

To this appeal the piratic crew responded with cheers, and the oath was promptly taken. The captain of the Spanish ship had been informed that there was a boat in sight, and that it probably was manned by pirates. He came upon deck, examined it carefully with his glass, and then, turning upon his heel, said contemptously :

" We need not care for such a pitiful concern as that. It is a mere cockle-shell. If you wish, you may rig the crane out, and we will hoist the whole thing, crew and all, on board. We need fear no ship which is not bigger and stronger than our own."

The pirates had the advantage of the wind. They kept away until dark. Peter, or Pierre as they called him, informed them of his desperate plan. He would, in the gloom of night, put on all sail, and run his boat directly alongside of the galleon. Grappling-irons were immediately to be thrown over the gunwale of the ship, with ropes attached, by which the boat's crew were instantly to leap on board. The carpenter was to have tools ready and bore a large hole in the bottom of the boat, so as to sink it at once. He was then to leap on board.

Every man was to have three or four loaded pistols in his belt, and a sabre in his hand. Escape ·

was impossible. If they failed to capture the ship, and were captured themselves, their inevitable doom was death by hanging. The programme was carried out in full. The night was dark. There was no vigilance, no suspicion of danger on board the ship. The boat came alongside the huge bulk of the galleon so noiselessly that it was not perceived.

The pirates rushed pell-mell on board. With their sharp sabres they cut down the terrified crew on the right hand and on the left. Pierre, leading a party, plunged into the cabin. The captain with several of his officers was playing cards. He sprang from his seat exclaiming:

"Lord Jesus; are these devils?"

Pierre, presenting a pistol at his breast, demanded the surrender of the ship. Had the captain or any of his officers raised a hand in self-defence, death would have been their immediate fate. They were all disarmed and bound. Another party, sweeping the decks with sword and pistol, drove all whom they did not kill into the hold, and shut the hatches upon them. They then seized the gun-room, where all the arms and ammunition were stored.

In almost less time than it has taken to describe the scene, this majestic ship with its vast treasures was captured. Not a single pirate was killed or wounded. With three cheers the pirates proclaimed

their astounding victory. They were nearly all seamen, and familiar with those waters. They turned
the ship to sail to Europe. Coming in sight of an
island, they landed the captain and all the ship's
company in a cove, and giving them a small supply
of provisions, left them to shift for themselves.
Several of the crew remained on board the ship, en-
listing in the service of the pirates. This being done,
they set sail for France, where they sold their ship,
divided their immense booty, scattered, and were
heard of no more.

The inhabitants of Tortuga soon received tidings
of this brilliant achievement. It seemed to inspire
them all with the intense desire to go and do like-
wise. All Tortuga was in an uproar. Every one
applauded a deed which they deemed so glorious as
well as so profitable. They saw that by a single enterprise, Pierre had made his fortune for life. In a
few months, more than twenty piratic vessels were
fitted out at Tortuga.

CHAPTER II.

William Kidd becomes a Pirate.

Ravages of the Pirates.—The King's Interview with Earl Bellomont.
—William Kidd, the New York Merchant.—His Commission.—
Sailing of the Adventure.—Recruiting in New York.—Circuitous Trip to Madagascar.—Perils and Sufferings.—Madagascar
the Pirates' Home.—Murmurings of the Crew.—Kidd reluctantly
turns Pirate.—His Repulses, and his Captures.

IN the year 1695, the King of England, William
III., summoned before him the. Earl of Bellomont,
who had been governor of Barbadoes, and whom he
had recently appointed governor of New York, and
said to him:

" The buccaneers have so increased in the East
and West Indies, and all along the American coast,
that they defiantly sail under their own flag. They
penetrate the rivers ; land in numbers sufficient to
capture cities, robbing palaces and cathedrals, and
extorting enormous ransom. Their suppression is
vital to commerce. They have possessed themselves
of magnificent retreats, in Madagascar and other
islands of the Indian Ocean. They have established
their scraglios, and are living in fabulous splendor

and luxury. Piratic expeditions are fitted out from the colonies of New England and Virginia; and even the Quakers of Pennsylvania afford a market for their robberies. These successful freebooters are making their homes in the Carolinas, in Rhode Island, and along the south shore of Long Island, where they and their children take positions among the most respectable in the community.

"The buccaneers are so audacious that they seek no concealment. Their ships are laden with the spoil of all nations. The richest prizes which can now be taken on the high seas are the heavily laden ships of the buccaneers. I have resolved, with the aid of others, to fit out a private expedition against them. We have formed a company for that purpose. By attacking the pirates we shall accomplish a double object. We shall in the first place check their devastating operations, and we shall also fill our purses with the proceeds of the abundant spoil with which their ships are laden."

This second consideration was doubtless the leading one in the movement. The king was in great need of money. His nobles were impoverished by extravagance. They were ready to resort to any measures to replenish their exhausted treasuries. This royal company was therefore organized, not as a national movement, sustained by national law, but as a *piratic* expedition against the *pirates*. The reclaimed treasure was not to be restored to its owners, nor to be placed in the treasury of the kingdom, but to be divided among the captors, as their legitimate spoil. And still the king was to give the commission in his kingly name.

The king informed the Earl of Bellomont that he was about to invest him with the government of New York, and wished him to suggest the name of some suitable person, who was familiar with the North American coast and the West Indian seas, to whom he could intrust the command of the frigate they were then fitting out. It so chanced that an illustrious Englishman, Mr. Robert Livingston, the first of that name who had emigrated to the New World, was then in London. The earl consulted with him. He was informed that just the man he needed had accompanied him from New York to London, leaving his family behind. He was a merchant, by the name of William Kidd, a man of tried courage and integrity.

In the last war with the French, Captain Kidd had commanded a privateersman, and had gained signal honor in many engagements. He had sailed over all the seas frequented by the buccaneers, and was familiar with their haunts. The commission which the king gave to Captain Kidd is a curious document. It is here given abridged of its excessive verbiage :

"William the Third, by the grace of God King of England, Scotland, France, and Ireland, to our true and well-beloved Captain William Kidd, commander of the ship Adventure. Whereas divers wicked persons commit many and great piracies, robberies, and depredations on the seas, upon the coasts of America and other parts, to the hindrance of trade and the danger of our subjects, we have thought fit to give to the said William Kidd full authority to seize all such pirates as you may find on the seas, whether our subjects or the subjects of other nations, with their ships, and all merchandise or money which shall be found on board, if they willingly yield themselves. But if they will not yield without fighting, then you are, by force, to compel them to yield. We do also require you to bring, or cause to be brought, such pirates, freebooters, or sea rovers, as you shall seize, to a legal trial, to the end they may be proceeded against according to the law in such cases.

"We enjoin you to keep an exact journal of your proceedings, giving the names of the ships you may capture, the names of their officers and crew, and the value of their cargoes, and stores. And we command you, at your peril, that you do not molest our friends or allies under any pretence of authority hereby granted.   Given the 26th of January, 1695."

Captain Kidd at the same time received another document, which was called a commission of reprisals.   This authorized him, as a privateersman, to take any French merchant ships he might chance to meet ; for there was then war between France and England.

A ship was purchased, for thirty thousand dollars, called the Adventure.   Of this sum, Captain Kidd and Mr. Livingston furnished three thousand each.   The remainder was contributed by the Earls Bellomont and Romney, Lord Chancellor Somers, the Lord High Admiral, the Duke of Shrewsbury, and Sir Henry Harrison.   The king, rather ingloriously, paid nothing.   He purchased his share in the enterprise by the royal patronage.

It seems that Captain Kidd was a man of high reputation at that time.   It was a large amount of property to be intrusted to his hands ; for the vessel and its outfit must have cost at least fifty thousand dollars.   Mr. Livingston became Kidd's security that he would faithfully discharge his duties and account for all his captures.   It is said that Kidd was not pleased with this arrangement, as he was very unwilling that Mr. Livingston should be his bondsman.   He probably, even then, felt that it might

2*

prove an obstacle in his future course. The operations of the human mind are often inexplicable. He might wish to *steal* the ship and turn *pirate* on his own account. And he could not *honorably* do this while his friend was his bondsman. Such pressure was put upon him that he was constrained to yield.

Armed with the royal commission, and in command of the Adventure, Captain Kidd sailed from Plymouth, England, in May, 1696. The frigate had an armament of thirty guns, and a crew of eighty men. He was ordered to render his accounts to the Earl of Bellomont in New York. He sailed up the Narrows, into New York harbor, in July. His wife and children were in his home there. In crossing the Atlantic, Captain Kidd came across a French merchantman, which he captured. The prize was valued at but seventeen hundred dollars. This was considered a legitimate act of war.

Captain Kidd knew full well that the enemy he was to encounter would fight with the utmost desperation, and that he might meet a fleet of piratic ships, or a single ship, more powerful in men and armament than his own. He therefore sent out recruiting officers through the streets of New York, to enlist volunteers. The terms he offered were that every man should have an equal share of every prize that was taken, after reserving for himself and the owners forty shares. With these offers he soon increased his crew to one hundred and fifty-five men.

Sailing from the harbor of New York, he made first for Madeira, to lay in a stock of wine. Then he directed his course to the Cape de Verd Islands, for a supply of salt and provisions. Having obtained these, he spread his canvas for a long voyage around the Cape of Good Hope, to the Island of Madagascar, on the eastern coast of Africa. This island had become renowned as one of the most important rendezvouses of the pirates.

Madagascar is larger than Great Britain. The pirates, by aid of their firearms, their desperate courage, and their superior intelligence, had gained possession of a considerable portion of the island. The natives were an inefficient race, copper-colored, with long, black hair. The pirates had treated them with such enormous cruelty, that the savages fled before them as if they had been demons.

In this retreat, so far distant from the abodes of civilization, the buccaneers had reared forts, and built mansions which they had converted into harems. From their voyages they returned here enriched with the plundered commerce of the world, to revel in all sensual indulgence. They made slaves of their prisoners; married, in their rude way, any

number they pleased of the most beautiful of the
native females; " so that every one," writes one of
their number, "had as great a seraglio as the Grand
Seignior at Constantinople. At length they began
to separate from each other, each living with his
own wives, slaves, and dependants, like independent
princes. As power and plenty naturally beget contention, they sometimes quarrelled, and attacked
each other at the head of their several armies. In
these civil wars many of them were killed."

These reckless men used their power like tyrants.
They grew wanton in cruelty. Nothing was more
common than, upon the slightest displeasure, to
cause one of their dependants to be tied to a tree
and shot through the heart. The natives combined
for their extermination. The plan would have succeeded but for betrayal by a woman. They trembled in view of their narrow escape, and combined
for mutual defence.

These ruffians assumed all the airs of the ancient
baronial nobility. Their dwellings were citadels.
They generally chose for their residence some dense
forest, near running water. The house was surrounded by a rampart and a ditch. The rampart
was so high that it could not be climbed without
scaling-ladders. The dwelling was so concealed, in
the dense tropical forest, that it could not be seen

until you were very near it. The only approach
was so narrow that two could not pass it abreast.
It was contrived in so intricate a manner that, to all
not perfectly familiar with it, it was a perfect laby-
rinth, with cross paths where one might wander for
hours, lost in the maze.

All along these narrow paths, large and very
sharp thorns, which grew in that country, were planted in the ground, so as to pierce the feet of the un-
shod natives. If any should attempt to approach
the house by night, they would certainly be pierced
and torn by those cruel thorns.

It was a long voyage to Madagascar. Before he
reached the island nine months had elapsed since
leaving Plymouth. Captain Kidd had expended all
his money, and his provisions were nearly exhausted.
Not a single prize had they captured by the way.
This ill luck caused a general feeling of murmuring
and contention on board. The most amiable are in
danger of losing their amiability in hours of disaster. Rude seamen, but one remove from pirates, in
such seasons of disappointment and chagrin become
almost demons in moroseness.

One morning the whole ship's crew were thrown
into a state of the most joyous excitement by the
sight of three ships in the distant horizon. They
had no doubt that it was some buccaneer, with two

prizes, heavily laden with the treasures of the Orient. Suddenly all became very good-natured. Eagerly they prepared for action. They had no fear that the pirate, with his prizes, could escape their swift-sailing frigate. The supposed pirate was apparently conscious that escape was impossible ; for he bore down boldly upon them.

Terrible was the disappointment. Captain Kidd, gazing upon the approaching vessels through his glass, exclaimed, with an oath, "They are three English war-ships."

Captain Warren was in command of the men-of-war. Meeting thus in mid-ocean, the two captains interchanged civilities, visited each other, and kept company for two or three days. It was in the month of February, 1666, that Captain Kidd, coasting along the shores of Madagascar, approached the harbor upon the island frequented by the pirates. Here he expected to find treasure in abundance. He had very decidedly exceeded his orders in leaving the waters of America for the distant shores of Africa and Asia. Triumphant success, which he was sanguine of achieving, might cause the disobedience of instructions not only to be forgiven but applauded. Failure would be to him disgrace and irretrievable ruin.

Again Captain Kidd and his crew were doomed

to disappointment. It so happened that they arrived at the island at a time when every vessel was out on a piratic cruise. There was not a single vessel there. All were growing desperate. Captain Kidd had but very little money left, and nearly all his provisions were consumed. As hastily as possible he replenished his water-casks, and taking in a few more stores, weighed anchor, and voyaged thirteen hundred miles farther east to Malabar, as the whole western coast of Hindostan was then called, from Cape Comorin to Bombay.

He came within sight of these shores in June, four months after his arrival at Madagascar. For some time he cruised up and down this coast unavailingly. Not a single sail was to be seen on the boundless expanse of ocean. There was universal discontent and murmurings on board the Adventure. The situation of the ship's company was indeed deplorable. One-half of the globe was between them and their homes. Their provisions were nearly all gone, and they had no means with which to purchase more. It was clear that unless Providence should interpose in their favor, they must either steal or starve.

And Providence did, for a time, singularly interpose. As they were one day sailing by a small island, called Joanna, they saw the wreck of a ship on shore. Captain Kidd took a boat, and was rowed to the land, where he found that it was a French vessel. The crew had escaped, having saved quite a quantity of gold. The ship and cargo were a total loss. The Frenchman, so the narrative goes, *loaned* this gold to Captain Kidd. Perhaps he did. It is more probable that it was a forced loan. Captain Kidd had, as we have mentioned, a double commission, one against the pirates, and the other a regular commission as a privateersman against the French. Had he captured the ship before the wreck it would have been his lawful prize. It is hardly probable that he had any scruples of conscience in seizing the doubloons when transferred to the shore.

. With this gold he sailed to one of the ports on the Malabar coast, where he purchased food sufficient for a few weeks only. There was, at that time, in Asia, one of the most powerful nations on the globe, called the Mongols. The emperor, who was almost divinely worshipped, was titled the Great Mogul. His gorgeous palaces were reared in the city of Samarcand, in the province of Bokhara. This magnificent city, thirty miles in circumference, glittered with palaces and mosques of gorgeous architecture, constructed of white marble. The empire was founded by the world-renowned Gengis Khan, and extended by the equally celebrated Tamerlane. The sails of Mongol commerce whitened all the East-Indian seas. Piracy then so abounded that this commerce was generally carried on in fleets under convoy. Upon this cruise of disappointment and anxiety, Captain Kidd passed several of the ships of the Great Mogul. He looked upon them with a wistful eye. They were merchantmen. With his force he could easily capture them. There could be no doubt that they contained treasure of great value.

There was loud murmuring among the crew. They could not understand those scruples of conscience which would allow them to plunder a few shipwrecked Frenchmen, and yet would turn aside from the rich argosies of the East.

But Captain Kidd, a respectable New-York merchant, held in high esteem by the community, and who had been sent on this expedition expressly to capture and punish the pirates, was not then prepared to raise himself the black flag, and thus join the robbers of the seas.

The struggle, in his mind, was probably very severe. He was daily growing more desperate. Starvation stared him in the face. His crew was growing mutinous. He had reason to fear that they would rise, throw him overboard or land him upon some island, and then, raising the black flag of the pirate, scour the seas on their own account, and join the riotous band defiantly established at Madagascar.

He had no doubt that the powerful company, who had sent him on this cruise, would overlook any irregularities in plundering wrong vessels, and would make no troublesome inquiries into his mode of operations, if he would only bring them home an abundance of gold. On the other hand, should he fail, he would be dismissed from their service in disgrace, an utterly ruined man.

He had learned that the Great Mogul was about to send from the Red Sea, through the Straits of Babelmandel, a richly freighted fleet of merchantmen, under convoy, bound to China. The Straits are but about fifteen miles wide. Consequently there could be no difficulty in intercepting the fleet.

Captain Kidd had probably, in his silent thoughts, decided to turn freebooter. Though as yet he had divulged his secret to no one, and had committed no overt act, he had passed the Rubicon, and was in heart a pirate. The change was at once perceptible. He ran his ship in toward the shore, and coasted along until he came in sight of a village of the natives, where herds were seen in the fields, and harvests were waving, and the boughs of the groves were laden with the golden fruit of the tropics. Doubtless he would have been glad to purchase these stores. But he had no money. He had reached that point in his career at which he must either steal or starve.

He sent several armed boats to the land, and robbed the unresisting natives without stint. He was not a man to pursue half measures. Having well revictualled his ship, he turned her bows toward the entrance to the Red Sea. Summoning his crew before him, he informed them of the change in his plans.

"We have been unsuccessful hitherto, my boys," he said; "but take courage. Fortune is now about to smile upon us. The fleet of the Great Mogul, freighted with the richest treasures, is soon to come out of the Red Sea. From the capture of those heavily laden ships we will all grow rich."

This speech was greeted with shouts of applause by the desperate men whom he had picked up in the streets of London and New York. He sent out a swift-sailing boat well manned to enter the Red Sea, and run along its eastern coast on a voyage of discovery. The boat returned after an absence of a few days, with the rather alarming intelligence that they had counted a squadron of fifteen large ships just ready to sail. While some of them bore the flag of the Great Mogul, at the mast-head of others floated the banners of England and of Holland.

England was in alliance with Holland, and on the most friendly terms with the Great Mogul. In the commission given to Captain Kidd by the king it was written:

"We command you at your peril, that you do not molest our friends or allies, under any pretence of authority hereby granted."

Captain Kidd must have pondered the question deeply and anxiously before he could have made up his mind to become an utter outlaw, by attacking a fleet composed of ships belonging not only to England's friend, and to England's ally, but also containing England's ships. Neither did he yet know how strong the convoy by which the fleet was guarded.

He, however, while weighing these thoughts in his anxious mind, sailed to and fro before the mouth of the Strait, keeping a vigilant watch at the masthead. After the lapse of four days the squadron hove in sight, far away on the northern horizon. As the vessels approached, Captain Kidd carefully scrutinized them through his glass. His experienced eye soon perceived that the fleet was convoyed by two men-of-war, the one English, the other Dutch. This added to his embarrassment, and greatly increased his peril in case he should attempt an assault.

The fleet was much scattered; for, strong in its guard, no danger was apprehended. Kidd's vessel was concealed from the general view behind a headland. His ship was a swift sailer, and he had an immense amount of canvas, which he could almost instantaneously spread to the breeze. There was a large, bulky. Mongol ship, laden to the gunwales, slowly ploughing its way through the waves, approaching the point where the pirate lay concealed. The guard ships were at the distance of several miles.

Captain Kidd darted out upon the galleon like an eagle upon its prey. He probably hoped to capture it, plunder it, and make his escape before the war-vessels could come to its rescue. He opened fire upon the ship. But the convoy, instantly taking the alarm, pressed all sail, and bore rapidly down upon him, opening a vigorous fire from their heavy guns. Kidd could not think of contending with them. His chance was gone. He sheered off, and soon his cloud of swelling canvas disappeared beyond the southern horizon. The armed frigates could not pursue him. They were compelled to remain behind to protect the slowly sailing fleet.

Captain Kidd, imbittered by constant failure, was now a disappointed, chagrined, exasperated, desperate man. He was ready for any enterprise, however atrocious, which would bring him money. He ran back to the coast of Malabar. Cruising along, he soon came in sight of a native vessel. Kidd captured it without a struggle. It was called the Maiden, belonged to some merchants of Aden, but was commanded by an Englishman by the name of Parker. The mate, Antonio, was a Portuguese, familiar with the language of the country.

There was nothing of value on board. Kidd, having resolutely embarked on a piratic cruise, impressed the captain, Parker, as pilot in those unknown waters. The mate he retained as an interpreter. Vexed in finding no gold, and believing that the crew had concealed it, he treated them with the utmost cruelty to extort a confession of where they had hid the coin. They were hoisted up by the arms and beaten with terrible severity. But all was in vain. No amount of torture could bring to light gold which did not exist.

The pirate, having robbed the poor men of a bale of pepper and a bale of coffee, with a few pieces of Arabian gold, contemptuously turned them adrift, bleeding and almost helpless in their exhaustion. After continuing his cruise for some time without any success, Kidd ran into a small port, on the Malabar coast, called Carawar. There were several English merchants residing in that place.   The tidings had already reached them of the capture of the Aden vessel, the impressment of the English captain and the Portuguese mate, and the cruel treatment of the crew.

As soon as Captain Kidd entered the port, it was suspected that he was the pirate.   Two English gentlemen, Mr. Harvey and Mr. Mason, came on board, and charged him with the crime, asking him what he had done with his two captives, Captain Parker and the Portuguese mate.   Kidd assumed an air of injured innocence, denied that he had any knowledge of the event, showed them his commission from the King of England as the head of a company of the most illustrious nobles to pursue and punish the pirates.   Triumphantly he submitted the question if it were reasonable to suppose that a man who enjoyed the confidence of the king and his nobles, and was intrusted by them to lead an enterprise so essential to the national honor, should himself turn pirate.

The gentlemen were silenced, but not convinced. All this time Parker and Antonio the Portuguese were concealed in a private place in the hold. There he kept them carefully guarded eight days, until he again set sail.   Just after he had left the port, a Portuguese man-of-war entered.   The English merchants communicated to the commander their suspicions. He immediately put to sea in search of the Adventure, resolved, should he overtake her, carefully to examine the hold, hoping to find the captives on board, or at least some evidence of their having been there.

The two ships met. Kidd was by no means disposed to have his vessel searched. A fierce battle ensued which lasted for six hours. Neither vessel was disposed to come to close quarters until the other was disabled. Kidd at length, finding the Portuguese ship too strong for him, spread all his sails and escaped. With his vast amount of canvas he could run away from almost any foe. Ten of his men were wounded in this conflict, but none killed.

Again these desperate men found it necessary to run into the land for provisions. They entered a small port called Porco. Here they filled their water-casks, and "bought," Kidd says, a sufficient number of hogs of the natives to victual the company. As it is known that Kidd had no money, it is probable that the swine were obtained by that kind of moral suasion which is found in the muzzle of a pistol and the edge of a sabre.

This suspicion is confirmed by the fact that the natives, in their exasperation, killed one of his men. The retaliation was characteristic of the crew and the times. Captain Kidd brought his guns to bear upon the village. With broadside after broadside he laid their huts in ruins. The torch was applied, and in an hour the peaceful village was converted into mouldering ashes.

One of the natives was caught. They bound him to a tree, and then a whole boat's company, one after another, discharged each a bullet into his heart. Having achieved this exploit, which they probably thought chivalric, but which others may deem fiendish, Captain Kidd again spread his sails for a piratic cruise.

The first vessel he came across was a large Mongol ship richly freighted. Kidd gave chase, unfurling the French flag. The captain was a Dutchman, by the name of Mitchel. Seeing that he was pursued under French colors, he immediately ran up the banner of France. Captain Kidd at once spread to the breeze the flag of England. He was very exultant. He could lay aside the odious character of a pirate, and seize the ship in the less disgraceful capacity of a privateersman. He exclaimed with an oath, "I have caught you. You are a free prize to England."

A cannon-ball was thrown across the bows of the ship, and she was ordered to heave to. The ship was hailed in the French language, and some one replied in the same tongue. They were then ordered to send their boat on board. The boat came bearing the captain of the ship, who was a Dutchman, by the name of Mitchel, and a French gentleman by the name of Le Roy.

Kidd received them in his cabin, and upon inquiry ascertained that the ship and cargo belonged to Mongol merchants; that they had intrusted the command to a Dutch captain, as was not unfrequently the case in those days, and that the French gentleman was merely a passenger accidently on board, passing from one port to another.

These tidings, to use a sailor's phrase, "struck him all aback." Holland, as we have mentioned, was England's ally. The Great Mogul was England's friend. Kidd must release the ship, or confess himself a pirate and an outlaw, and run the imminent risk of being hanged should he ever return to England. For a moment he seemed lost in thought, bewildered. Then his wicked mind, now rapidly descending into the abyss of sin and shame, rested in a decisive resolve.

AUDACITY OF KIDD.

CHAPTER III.

Piratic Adventures.

CAPTAIN KIDD, with a piratic frown upon his
brow, and piratic oaths upon his lips, turned to Mr.
Le Roy and said :

" Do you pretend that this is not a French ship,
and that you are but a passenger on board ? "

" It is so," Mr. Le Roy politely replied. " I am
a stranger in these parts, and have merely taken
passage on board this native ship, under Captain
Mitchel, on my way to Bombay."

" It is a lie," said the pirate, as he drew from
his belt a pistol and cocked it. " This is a French
ship, and you are its captain ; and it is my lawful
prize. If you deny this, you shall instantly die."

The features of Kidd, and his words blended
with oaths, convinced Mr. Le Roy that he was in

the, hands of a desperate man, who would shrink from no crime. He was silent. Kidd then added:

"I seize this ship as my legitimate prize. It belongs to a French subject, and is sailing under the French flag. I have a commission from his majesty the King of England to seize all such ships in his name."

It seems strange that Kidd, after the many lawless acts of which he had already been guilty, should have deemed it of any consequence to have recourse to so wretched a quibble. But the incident shows that the New-York merchant, formerly of good reputation, still recoiled from the thought of plunging headlong into a piratic career. By observing these forms he could, in this case, should he ever have occasion to do so, claim the protection of the royal commission authorizing him to capture French ships.

Kidd took his prize, which he called the November, because it was captured in that month, into one of the East-Indian ports, and sold ship and cargo for what they would fetch. What the amount was, or how he divided it, is not known. Again he resumed his cruise. It was evident that he had become anxious to renounce the career of pirate, upon which he had barely entered, and resume that of privateersman. They soon came across a Dutch ship, unmistakably such, in build and flag and rig-

ging. The crew clamored for its capture ; Kidd resolutely opposed it. A mutiny arose. A minority
of the ship's company adhered to the captain. The
majority declared that they would arm the boats
and go and seize her.

The captain, with drawn sabre in his hand, and
pistols in his belt, and surrounded by those still
faithful to him, stood upon her quarter-deck and
said to the mutineers, firmly :

"You may take the boats and go. But those
who thus leave this ship will never ascend its sides
again."

One of the men, a gunner by the name of William Moore, was particularly violent and abusive.
With threatening gestures he approached the captain, assailing him in the most vituperative terms,
saying:

"You are ruining us all. You are keeping us in
beggary and starvation. But for your whims we
might all be prosperous and rich."

The captain was by no means a meek man. In
his ungovernable passion he seized an iron-bound
bucket, which chanced to be lying at his side, and
gave the mutineer such a blow as fractured his skull
and struck him senseless to the deck. Of the wound
the gunner died the next day Not many will feel
disposed to censure Captain Kidd very severely for

this act. It was not a premeditated murder. It was perhaps a necessary deed, in quelling a mutiny, in which the mutineers were demanding that the black flag of the pirate should be raised, and which demand the captain was resisting. And yet it is probable that this blow sent Kidd to the gallows. Upon his subsequent trial, but little evidence of piracy could be adduced, and the death of Moore was the prominent charge brought against him.

Kidd ever averred that it was a virtuous act, and that it did not trouble his conscience. It was done to prevent piracy and mutiny. He also averred that he had no intention to *kill* the man. Had he so intended he would have used pistol or sabre. In the ballad which, half a century ago, was sung in hundreds of farm-houses in New England, the lull-aby of infancy, the event is alluded to in the following words :

> " I murdered William Moore, as I sailed, as I sailed,
> I murdered William Moore as I sailed ;
> I murdered William Moore, and left him in his gore,
> Not many leagues from shore, as I sailed."

We will give a few more verses to show the general character of this ballad of twenty-five stanzas, once so popular, now forgotten :

> " My name was William Kidd, when I sailed, when I sailed,
> My name was William Kidd when I sailed,
> My name was William Kidd, God's laws I did forbid,
> And so wickedly I did when I sailed.

> " Thus being o'ertaken at last, I must die, I must die,
>   Thus being o'ertaken at last, I must die ;
>   Thus being o'ertaken at last, and into prison cast,
>   And sentence being pass'd, I must die.
>
> " To Newgate now I'm cast, and must die, and must die,
>   To Newgate now I'm cast, and must die,
>   To Newgate now I'm cast, with sad and heavy heart,
>   To receive my just desert, I must die.
>
> " To Execution Dock I must go, I must go,
>   To Execution Dock I must go ;
>   To Execution Dock will many thousands flock,
>   But I must bear my shock, and must die.
>
> " Come all ye young and old, see me die, see me die,
>   Come all ye young and old, see me die ;
>   Come all ye young and old, you're welcome to my gold,
>   For by it I've lost my soul, and must die."

The Dutchman had no consciousness of the peril to which he had been exposed. The two ships kept company for several days, and then separated. Is it possible that all this time Kidd was hesitating whether to raise the black flag and seize the prize ? It looks like it ; for a few days after the Dutch ship had disappeared, quite a fleet of Malabar boats were met with, laden with provisions and other articles which Kidd needed. Unscrupulously he plundered them all. Probably he had no fears that tidings of the outrage would ever reach England. And even if a rumor of the deed were ever to reach those distant shores, he had no apprehension that England would trouble herself to punish him for a little harsh treatment of semi-savages on the coast of Malabar.

A few days after this robbery a Portuguese ship hove in sight. Kidd's moral nature was every hour growing weaker. He could no longer resist the temptation to seize the prize. He robbed the vessel of articles to the estimated value of two thousand dollars, and let her go, inflicting no injury upon the ship's company.

For three weeks they continued to cruise over a sailless sea, when one morning, about the middle of December, an immense mass of canvas was seen rising over the distant horizon. It proved to be a native ship of four hundred tons burden. The ship was called the Quedagh Merchant, was very richly laden, and was commanded by an Englishman, Captain Wright. The wealthy merchants of the East were fully aware of the superior nautical skill of the English seaman, and were eager to intrust their important ventures to European commanders.

Kidd unfurled the French flag, chased the ship, and soon overtook it. A cannon-ball whistling over the heads of the crew was the very significant hint with which the ship was commanded to heave to. Kidd ordered the captain to lower his boat and come on board the Adventure. The captain obeyed, and informed the pirate that all the crew were East-

Indians, excepting two Dutchmen and one Frenchman, and that the ship belonged exclusively to
East-Indian merchants.

Kidd took piratic possession of the ship. He
had not the shadow of a claim to it on the ground of
his commission as a privateersman. He landed the
officers and the crew, in boatload after boatload,
upon the shore, and left them to shift for themselves.
One or two of the merchants who owned the ship
and cargo were on board. They offered the pirate
twenty thousand rupees, which was equivalent to
about fifteen thousand dollars, to ransom the property. Kidd declined the offer.

His own ship, after such long voyaging, was
leaky and much in want of repairs. The Quedagh
Merchant was far superior to the Adventure. He
therefore transferred all his stores to his prize.
The torch was applied to the Adventure; and the
ill-fated ship soon disappeared in a cloud of smoke
and flame. Kidd, now a confirmed pirate, directed
his course toward the great rendezvous of the pirates at Madagascar. Here the prize was valued at
sixty-four thousand pounds, or about three hundred
and twenty thousand dollars.

Still this strange man assumed that he was acting under the royal commission, in behalf of the London company; and these treasures were the legiti-

mate plunder of a piratic ship. He therefore reserved forty shares for himself and the company. There were about one hundred and fifty men composing this piratic crew. Each man received about two thousand dollars. Kidd's portion amounted to nearly eighty thousand dollars.

In the pirates' harbor at Madagascar, Kidd found a large ship, the Resolution, belonging to the East India Company, which the captain, a man by the name of Culliford, with the crew, had seized and turned into a pirate. It was clearly Kidd's duty, under his commission, at once to attack and capture this piratic ship. When Captain Culliford saw him entering the harbor with his powerful and well-armed ship, he was terrified. The pirates had heard of Captain Kidd's commission, and had not yet learned that he had turned pirate himself. Captain Culliford, with the gallows in vision before him, and trembling in every nerve, for there was no possibility of escape, sent some officers, in a boat, on board the Quedagh Merchant, to ascertain Captain Kidd's intention.

It was testified at the subsequent trial of Kidd, that he stood upon his deck and received with open arms the piratic officers as they came up over the ship's side; that he invited them to his cabin, where they had a great carouse in drinking and smoking ; and that in the frenzy of drink he offered for a toast :

" May damnation seize my soul if I harm a hair of the head of any one on board the Culliford."

It was declared that he received large presents of bales of silk from the piratic captain, and sold him some heavy ordnance, with suitable ammunition, for two thousand dollars ; and that he was on the most friendly terms with Culliford, exchanging frequent visits with him.

On the other hand, Kidd emphatically denied all these charges. He said, " I never stepped foot on board Captain Culliford's ship. When I entered the harbor and ascertained the character of the craft, I ordered my men to prepare for action. But the mutinous crew, who had already compelled me to resort to measures against which my soul revolted, peremptorily refused, saying that they would rather fire two shots into my vessel than one into that of Captain Culliford. The mutiny became so menacing that my life was in danger. The turbulent crew rifled my chest, stole my journal, took possession of the ammunition. I was compelled to barricade myself in the cabin. The mutineers held the ship, and being beyond all control, acted according to their own good pleasure. I was in no degree responsible for their conduct."

The captain's statement was not credited by the court. At the same time it was quite evident that he had lost the control of his crew. His testimony was, however, in some degree borne out by the fact that ninety-five of his men in a body deserted him, and joined the piratic crew of Captain Culliford. This would seem to prove conclusively that Captain Kidd was not sufficiently piratical in his measures to satisfy the demands of the mutineers.

For several weeks these guilty and wretched men remained in the " own place " of the pirates, indulging in every species of bacchanal wassail and sensual vice, amidst their palaces and in their harems. Their revelry could not have been exceeded by any scenes ever witnessed in Sodom or Gomorrah. There were between five and six hundred upon the island. They were continually coming and going. Some of them were so rich that they remained at home cultivating quite large plantations by slave labor. They amused themselves by hunting, and in the wide meadows and forests found abundant game. The arrival of a ship in the harbor was the signal for an universal carouse. They endeavored to magnify the charms of their women by dressing them gorgeously in silks and satins, with glittering jewelry.

Often a pipe of wine would be placed upon the shore, the head taken out, and the community would drink of it as they pleased, as freely as if it were water. Drunken pirates reeled through the streets. Oaths filled the air. Knives gleamed, and pistols were discharged, and there were wounds and death. In the midst of all their revelry and wantonness and brawls, it is evident from the record we have of those days, that a more unhappy, wretched set of beings could scarcely be found this side of the world of woe. There was not a joy to be found there. There were no peaceful homes; no loving husbands and wives; no happy children climbing the parental knee and enfolded in parental arms; and in death nothing but a "fearful looking for of judgment and fiery indignation."

These wretched pirates were hateful and hating. Satiated with vice, they knew not where to turn for a single joy. Their shouts of laughter fell discordantly upon the ear like the revelry of demons. Satan never allows his votaries any happiness either in this world or in that which is to come. Wisdom's ways only are ways of pleasantness, and her paths alone are those of peace.

How far Captain Kidd entered into these godless carousals is not known. But it is not probable that he was then able to throw off all restraint, and become hail-fellow with these vulgar, degraded, profane wretches, whom in heart he must have despised. Neither is it probable that one accustomed to the society in which an honored New-York merchant would move, could so soon have formed a taste for the drunken revelry of the lowest and vilest creatures on earth.

It is evident that these men had occasionally reproaches of conscience, and some faint sense of their terrible responsibility at God's bar. Four of them decided one day to make a little artificial hell for themselves, that they might see who could stand its pains the longest.

A cloudless tropical sun blistered the deck with its blazing rays. The cabin was heated like an oven. In addition to this, they built a fire in the stove, till the iron plates were red hot. They then with blaspheming oaths entered this furnace, and sprinkled brimstone upon the fire till the room was filled with its suffocating fumes. One of these wretches, apparently as fiend-like as a man could be, bore the pains of this little artificial hell for five minutes. None of the others could endure them so long. The victor came out very exultant. One would have thought that the idea would have occurred to their minds that there was some considerable difference between five minutes and eternity.

We do not learn that any of these men were made better by the brief endurance of their self-inflicted tortures. The mind is appalled by the thought that these same men, when transferred to the spirit land, *may* be as persistent in their hostility to all God's laws as they were here.

Captain Kidd found himself abandoned by nearly all his crew. He remained in port only long enough to recruit sufficient men to navigate his ship, and then, spreading the sails of his stolen vessel, the Quedagh Merchant, he set out for the West Indies, with his ill-gotten treasure of eighty thousand dollars. The news of Kidd's piratic acts had been reported to the home government by the East India Company. Orders had accordingly been issued to all the governors of the American colonies to arrest him wherever he should appear.

The voyage from Madagascar to the West Indies was long and tempestuous. Not a single sail appeared in sight. Day after day the ocean was spread out in all its solitary grandeur before these guilty, discontented men. At length, in a very destitute condition, the ship reached Anguilla, or Snake Island, so called from its tortuous figure. This is the most northerly of the Caribbee Islands, and there was a small English colony here.

As Kidd dropped anchor in the little harbor he was greeted by the intelligence that he had been officially, in England, proclaimed a pirate; that his conduct had been discussed in Parliament; that a committee had been appointed to inquire into the character of the company which had commissioned him, and into the nature of the commission he had received; that a British man-of-war, the Queensborough, had been dispatched in pursuit of him, and that a royal proclamation had been issued, offering pardon to all who had been guilty of piracy, eastward of the Cape of Good Hope, before the last day of April, 1699, excepting William Kidd, and another notorious buccaneer by the name of Avery.

This Avery had obtained great renown, and the most extravagant stories were reported and universally believed in reference to his achievements. It was said that this pirate had attained almost imperial wealth, dignity, and power; that he had become the proud founder of a new monarchy in the East, whose sceptre he swayed in undisputed absolutism. His exploits were celebrated in a play called, "The Successful Pirate," which was performed to admiring audiences in all the theatres.

According to these representations, Avery had captured a ship, belonging to the Great Mogul, and laden with the richest treasures. On board the imperial ship there was a beautiful princess, the daughter of the Great Mogul. Avery had married her. The father, reigning over boundless realms, had recognized the union, and had assigned to Avery vast territories in the East, where millions were subject to his control. He occupied one of the most magnificent of Oriental palaces, had several children, and was surrounded with splendors of royalty quite unknown in the Western world. He had a squadron of ships manned by the most desperate fellows of all nations. In his own name he issued commissions to the captains of his ships and the commanders of his forts, and they all recognized his princely authority.

His piracies were still continued on a scale commensurate with his power. Many schemes were offered to the royal council of England for fitting out a squadron to disperse his fleets and to take him captive. Others affirmed that he was altogether too powerful to be assailed in that way. They urged the expediency of sending an embassage to his court, and inviting him and his companions to come to England with all their treasures, assuring him of a hospitable reception and of the oblivion of all the past. They feared that unless these peaceful measures were adopted, his ever-increasing greatness would enable him to annihilate all commerce with the East.

These rumors were so far from having any foundation in truth, that at the same time that such wondrous tales were told, the wretch was a fugitive, wandering in disguise through England, trembling in view of the scaffold, and with scarcely a shilling in his pocket. His career was sufficiently extraordinary to merit a brief notice here.

Avery was born in one of the western seaports of England, and from a boy was bred to the hardships and the degradation of a rude sailor's life. He was educated only in profanity, intemperance, and vice. As he grew up to stout boyhood he became a bold smuggler, even running contraband goods onshore on the far-away coasts of Peru. The Spaniards were poorly provided with war-ships to guard from what they deemed illicit traffic their immense regions in the New World.

They therefore hired at Bristol a stout English ship, called the Duke. It was manned chiefly by English seamen. Captain Gibson was commander. Avery was first mate. The captain was a gambler, fond of his cups, and he often lingered many days in foreign ports, spending his time in haunts of dissipation.

Avery was a fellow of more cunning than courage. He despised the captain, and formed a conspiracy with the most desperate men on board, to get rid of the captain and any sailors who might adhere to him, run away with the ship, and crossing over to the distant waters of the East Indies, reap a harvest of wealth from the commerce which whitened those seas.

The ship was one day at anchor in a South American port. The plan had been, that night, when the captain was on shore, to weigh anchor, leaving the captain behind, and to set out on their cruise. But it so happened that the captain, that night, having drank deeply, did not go on shore as usual, but, at an early hour, went to bed. All the crew, excepting the conspirators, were either on shore or had retired to their berths.

At ten o'clock at night the long-boat of the Duke came to the ship's side, bringing sixteen stout desperadoes, whom Avery had enlisted from the vagabonds of all nations who thronged the port. They were received on board; the hatches were closed; and then, everything being secure, the anchor was leisurely weighed, and the ship put to sea.

The motion of the ship and the noise of the running tackles awoke the drunken captain, and he rang his bell. Avery, with two sailors, entered the cabin. The captain was sitting up in his berth, rubbing his eyes, and evidently much alarmed.

"What is the matter?" he exclaimed in hurried accents. "Something is the matter with the ship. Does she drive? What weather is it?"

"Nothing is the matter," said Avery coolly; "only we are at sea, with a fair wind and good weather."

"At sea!" said Gibson. "How can that be?"

"Don't be in a fright," Avery replied. "Put on your clothes, and I will tell you a little secret. *I* am now captain of this ship. This is my cabin, and you must walk out of it. I am bound to Madagascar, with the design of making my own fortune and that of all the brave fellows joined with me."

The captain was now completely sobered. In anticipation of immediate death his terror was pitiable. Avery endeavored to console him with the not very consolable words:

"You have nothing to fear, captain, if you will join us, keep sober, and do your duty. If you behave well, I may, perhaps, some time, make you one of my lieutenants. Or, if you prefer, here is a boat alongside, and we will put you ashore."

The terror-stricken man begged to be landed. The rest of the crew were brought up, and all who wished to go on shore with the captain were permitted to do so. But five or six availed themselves of the privilege. All the rest joined the piratic crew. The captain and his few adherents were placed in the boat and turned adrift, to make their way to the land as best they could. The carousing pirates directed their course to Madagascar. Here they found two piratic vessels, with whose crews they entered into close alliance. The three vessels, under Avery as admiral, set out on a cruise.

Upon the Arabian coast, near the mouth of the Indus, the man at the mast-head cried out, "A sail." They ran down upon her, and fired a cannon-ball across her bows. But the vessel, instead of yielding at once, hoisted the Mogul's colors, and cleared her decks for battle. Avery kept at a distance, cannonading her with his heavy guns, and not approaching within reach of the shot of his foe. He thus lost greatly reputation with his men, who regarded him as a coward. The crews of the two accompanying sloops, with their decks swarming with pirates, ran one upon the bow and the other upon the quarter, and clambering over the bulwarks of the heavily laden merchantman, took her by storm.

It is true, as the story had it, that the vessel belonged to the emperor, or Great Mogul, himself. His daughter was on board, as well as several of the most distinguished personages of his court. They were bound on a pilgrimage to Mecca, with the richest treasures to present at the shrine of Mohammed. They had costly silks, precious jewels, vessels of gold and silver, and large sums of money. The booty obtained from this prize was immense.

Having plundered the ship of everything they wanted, the pirates let her go. The Mogul, when he heard the tidings, was greatly enraged. He threatened to send an army, with fire and sword, utterly to exterminate the English in all their East-Indian colonies. The East India Company, in England, was greatly alarmed. They immediately dispatched an embassage to the Great Mogul to pacify him. They promised, in the name of the British Government, to pursue the pirates with the utmost vigor, and, if captured, to deliver them over into his hands.

In the mean time the successful buccaneers were making their way back to their rendezvous at Madagascar. There they intended to store their booty, erect a fortification for its defence, garrison it with men of desperate valor, and then to set out again on another cruise. As they were sailing along, with this design, each of the vessels having a portion of the plunder, the villanous Avery sent for the chief officers of each of the vessels to come on board the Duke. He then said to them :

"We have immense treasure, sufficient to enrich us all for life, if we can only get it to some secure place on shore. But we are in great danger of being separated by bad weather. In that case, should either of the sloops meet any ship of force, it would be captured. But the Duke, in build and armament, is superior to any ship to be encountered in these waters. My ship is so well manned that she can defy any foe; and moreover, she is such a swift sailer, that she can easily escape any other ship, if she does not wish to fight.

"I therefore propose, for our mutual safety, that we put all the treasure on board the Duke. We can seal up each chest with three seals, of which each vessel shall keep one. The chests shall not be opened until we open them together at the rendez-vous."

This proposal seemed so reasonable that they all agreed to it. All the treasure was transferred to the Duke. Avery then said to the villains who surrounded him:

"We have now the whole treasure at our own control. Let us, at night, give the rest a slip, and sail for unknown parts in North America. We can go ashore, divide our wealth, and with ample riches settle wherever we please."

We have heard that there is honor among thieves. Among these thieves there was none. Not a dissentient voice was heard. All agreed to the plan. In the darkness of the ensuing night the ship changed her course, and in the morning the crews of the two sloops searched the horizon in vain for any sight of her. They knew by the fairness of the weather, and the course they were pursuing, that the flight had been intentional. The reader must be left to surmise the scenes of confusion and profanity which must have been witnessed on board these piratic crafts.

The first land the Duke made in America was the Island of Providence. Here Avery sold the ship, pretending that it had been fitted out as a privateer, but having been unsuccessful, the owners had ordered her to be disposed of, as soon as any purchasers could be found. With a portion of the proceeds a small sloop was bought, and the buccaneers sailed for Boston, New England. Avery, thief as he was, had concealed the greater part of the diamonds, of whose great value the crew were ignorant.

At Boston they landed. Many of the men received their shares, and scattered throughout New England. Avery was afraid to offer his diamonds for sale there, where diamonds were so unusual a commodity, lest suspicion should be excited. He persuaded a few of his companions to accompany him to Ireland. They landed at one of the northern ports and there separated. Avery went to Dublin. He was still afraid to offer his diamonds for sale, lest inquiry should lead to the discovery of his manner of acquiring them. He thus found himself in poverty with all his wealth.

After remaining some time in Ireland under a feigned name, and ever trembling at his shadow, he crossed over to Bristol. Here he fell in with some sharpers, who, getting a hint of the treasures he had to dispose of, took him under their especial care. They wormed most of his secrets out of him, and then recommended that he should dispose of his jewels to an established firm of wealth and credit, who, being accustomed to great transactions, would make no inquiries as to the way he obtained his treasure.

Avery, not knowing what to do, assented to this proposal. The sharpers brought some men whom they introduced to Avery as gentlemen of the highest standing in the jewelry business. Avery exhibited to them his diamonds and pearls, and many vessels of massive gold. They took them to sell on commission. This was the last he saw of his stolen wealth. To his remonstrances he received only the reply :

"If you speak a word out loud, we will have you hung for piracy."

Utterly beggared, and terrified by these menaces, he again, in disguise, and under a feigned name, crossed over to Ireland. Here his destitution and distress became so great, for he was absolutely constrained to beg for his bread, that he resolved to go back to Bristol, and demand payment for his treasure at whatever hazard. He worked his passage in a small coasting vessel to Plymouth, and walked to Biddeford. Here, overcome with fatigue and suffering, both mental and bodily, he was seized with a fever, died, and, not one penny being found in his pockets, was buried at the expense of the parish as a vagabond pauper.

Such was the end of the pirate Avery, of whom such extravagant stories had been told. It was while he was in this extreme of poverty in England, and when it was supposed that he was rioting in successful piracy in the East, that the Government coupled his name with that of Captain Kidd, denouncing them as outlaws, and declaring that their sins were too great to be forgiven, and that, if arrested, the gallows was their inevitable doom.

CHAPTER IV

Arrest, Trial, and Condemnation of Kidd.

Appalling Tidings.—Trip to Curacoa.—Disposal of the Quedagh Merchant.—Purchase of the Antonio.—Trembling Approach toward New York.—Measures for the Arrest of Kidd.—He enters Delaware Bay.—Touches at Oyster Bay and Block Island.—Communications with the Government.—Sails for Boston.—His Arrest.—Long Delays.—Public Rumors.—His Trial and Condemnation.

CAPTAIN KIDD was greatly disturbed in learning at Anguilla that he had been denounced as a pirate, proscribed as an outlaw, and that he with the notorious Avery was expressly excluded from the pardon offered by the king to other buccaneers. He had thus far flattered himself with the hope that he could make it appear that all the prizes he had captured belonged to the French, and were legitimately taken under his commission as a privateersman. He also had placed much confidence in the support of the distinguished men composing the company by which he had been commissioned. The large wealth which he had expected to bring back to them, he thought, would unite their powerful influence in his support.

But instead of this, it now appeared that the company was disposed to make him their " scape-goat." They had been so severely condemned, as if responsible for the conduct of their agent, that in self-defence they became the loudest of his assailants, denouncing him in the severest terms, and clamoring most loudly that all seas should be explored to catch and hang the miscreant. It was these political complications, united with the renown of the company of king and nobles, which gave the name of Captain Kidd prominence far above anything which his achievements would warrant. It was known that he had been scouring the East-Indian seas with one of the most powerful of English ships, and it was surmised that he had accumulated wealth suffi-cient to found an empire. What became of this boundless wealth? This was the question which agitated England and America, and which set the money-diggers at work in so many different places.

Captain Kidd and his crew, at Anguilla, were greatly alarmed. They kept a careful watch of the horizon from the mast-head, fearing every hour that they should see the flag of an English man-of-war approaching to convey them to trial and the scaf-fold. About a thousand miles south of Anguilla, there was, on the coast of Venezuela, the little island of Curacoa. It was but about forty miles long, and fourteen broad, and, belonging to the Dutch, was quite outside of the usual course of the British ships.

To this place Kidd repaired to lay in supplies, of which he was greatly in need. Though he had heard of his proscription, he was not fully aware of the strength of hostility which was arrayed against him. He still clung to the hope that no evidence could be brought to prove that he had acted in any other capacity than that of a privateersman.

But the very ship in which he sailed was evidence against him. The Quedagh Merchant, the property of the Great Mogul, was undeniably an East-Indian ship belonging to a friendly power, whom Kidd was expressly prohibited from assailing. He could not safely approach any English port in this ship. He accordingly purchased at Curacoa the small sloop Antonio, from Philadelphia. In this he placed his most portable treasures of doubloons, gold-dust, jewels, and vessels of silver and of gold, and with a crew of forty men set sail for New York. He kept the Quedagh Merchant in company with him as far as the southern coast of San Domingo. There he left the bulky ship, with a crew of twenty-two pirates, under command of a man by the name of Bolton. The ship had a very valuable cargo of one hundred and fifty bales of the finest silks, eighty tons of sugar, ten tons of junk iron, fifteen large anchors, and forty tons of saltpetre. The ship was also well provided with ammunition, had thirty guns mounted, and twenty more in the hold.

This was the division of the piratic plunder. The share which fell to Bolton and twenty-two of the men was the ship and this portion of the cargo. These wretches are heard of no more. It is to be hoped that the next storm which rose engulfed them all. It is more probable that for months they continued to range the seas, perpetrating crimes over which demons should blush, until, in drunken brawls and bloody fights, they one by one sank into the grave, and passed to the judgment-seat of Christ. Unreliable rumor says that Bolton transferred his cargo and crew to a more swiftly sailing ship, and then applied the torch to the Quedagh Merchant. Many other rumors were in circulation, but none worthy of credence.

Earl Bellomont was then in authority at New York. Kidd was hoping for his protection. But the earl felt that very active measures were requisite to exculpate himself, the king, and the ministry from all responsibility for the robberies of Kidd. He therefore, so soon as he heard of Kidd's arrival upon the coast, ordered out an armed sloop in pursuit of him.

It is evident that Kidd was then one of the most

wretched of men. His reputation was ruined ; his prospects in life were all blighted ; his companions were bloodthirsty pirates, whom he could not but despise, and he was in imminent danger of an ignominious death upon the scaffold.

Tremblingly he approached New York. As his vessel needed some repairs, he ran into Delaware Bay, and tarried for a short time at Lewiston. This was early in June, 1699. It was from this place that Bellomont heard of his arrival. Here one of the pirates, a man by the name of Gillam, left, being in possession of a heavy chest, laden with the fruits of his robberies.

Kidd soon departed from the harbor, and thus escaped the sloop sent in pursuit of him. Instead of sailing directly to New York, in his perplexity he followed along the southern coast of Long Island, until he reached its eastern extremity, and then, turning into the Sound, crept cautiously along to Oyster Bay. From this place he wrote a letter to Bellomont, and also another very loving letter to his wife and children. In his letter to the earl he wrote :

" The reason why I have not gone directly to New York, is that the clamorous and false stories that have been repeated of me, have made me fearful of visiting or coming into any harbor, till I could hear from your lordship."

In response to these letters, a lawyer by the name of Emot came from New York, and visited Kidd on board the Antonio. He brought the captain tidings respecting his family, and also the important intelligence that the Earl of Bellomont was then absent in Boston. Kidd employed Emot to repair immediately to Boston, to secure from the earl the promise of safety if Kidd should visit him there.

"Inform the earl," said Kidd, "that unquestionable piracies have been committed by men nominally under my command. But this has never been by my connivance or consent. When these deeds have been performed, the men have been in a state of mutiny, utterly beyond my control. Disregarding my imperative commands, they locked me up in the cabin, and committed crimes over which I had no control, and for which I am in no sense responsible."

To this the earl replied, "Say to Captain Kidd that I give him the promise of my protection if his statement can be proved to be true."

Kidd was still in a state of pitiable agitation. It might not be easy to prove his declarations. There was no evidence which he could possibly bring forward but that of the pirates themselves. And it was not at all probable that they would be willing greatly to exaggerate their own guilt by exonerating him. He, however, ventured as far as

Block Island. From that place he wrote to Bellomont again, protesting his innocence, and dwelling
much upon the devotion with which he had conse-
crated himself to the interests of the owners of the
Adventure. He also sent to Lady Bellomont a present of jewels, to the value of three hundred dollars.
The earl's lady, for a time, retained these presents
from the proscribed pirate and outlaw. When subsequently reproached with this, they were surrendered to the general inventory of Kidd's effects.
The earl apologized for retaining them by saying
that he feared, if they were rejected, the giver would
be so offended that the earl would not be able to get
the developments he wished to obtain.

While at Block Island, Mrs. Kidd and the children joined Captain Kidd, under the care of Mr.
Clark. They were all received on board the Antonio,
and Kidd, with a pale cheek and a trembling heart,
set sail for Boston. As Mr. Clark wished to return
to New York, Kidd turned from his course and
landed him at Gardiner's Island. Captain Kidd did
not venture ashore at this place. But, for some un-
explained reason, he deposited with Mr. Gardiner,
the proprietor of the island, for safe keeping, a very
considerable portion of his treasures. He then sailed
for Boston, and entered the harbor on the first of
July, 1699.

4*

For nearly a week he remained in his vessel or traversed the streets unmolested. On the sixth of July, an officer approached him, placed his hand upon Kidd's shoulder, and said, "You are my prisoner." The pirate endeavored to draw his sword. It might have been an instinctive motion. It might have been that he deliberately preferred to be cut down upon the spot rather than undergo a trial. Others interposed. He was seized and disarmed, while his sword remained in its scabbard.

It is evident that there were very many chances that the trial might terminate in Kidd's favor. It is a maxim of law that every man is to be considered innocent until *proved* to be guilty. Kidd's piracies were perpetrated on the other side of the globe. None of his victims could possibly appear against him. There were none to be brought upon the witness's stand but his own sailors, who would be slow to admit that they had been engaged in a piratic cruise, which would condemn them to the gallows. It would seem, therefore, that there were insuperable difficulties in the way of his condemnation.

Mrs. Kidd, in coming from New York to Block Island with her children to join her husband, had brought with her a servant-girl, about three hundred dollars in money, and several valuable pieces of plate. These were all seized, together with all the effects on board the Antonio, and the treasure deposited at Gardiner's Island, which was brought to Boston by a vessel sent to the island for that purpose.

The whole amount proved much less than had been expected. There were eleven hundred and eleven ounces of gold, two thousand three hundred and fifty-three ounces of silver, fifty-seven bags of sugar, forty-one bales of goods, and seventeen pieces of canvas. Mrs. Kidd petitioned the governor and council to have her property restored to her, which was done.

The small amount of property found led to the suspicion, that as Kidd slowly passed over the waters of Long Island Sound, he must have buried, at Thimble Island and other places along the coast, a large amount of gold and jewels. And it is indeed difficult to account for what became of the vast treasures of that kind which it is supposed he found in the Quedagh Merchant. These rumors were intensified by the statement that while Kidd was at Block Island, three sloops came from New York and departed with a portion of his treasure. Kidd admitted this, but said that the goods belonged to his men and were shipped by them.

Immediately upon Kidd's arrival the earl sent

for him, and held quite a long interview, though he was careful to do so in the presence of witnesses. A narrative was very carefully drawn up of his alleged proceedings. Mrs. Kidd took up her residence in a boarding-house kept by Mr. Duncan Campbell. The earl kept a close watch upon Kidd, fully intending, as he said, eventually to arrest him. But he thought it expedient to dally with him for a while, in order to discover the extent of his adventures, and the disposition he had made of the property acquired. Kidd sent to the boarding-house some gold-dust and ingots, which he said were intended as a present for the earl's lady. They were valued at about four thousand dollars. When searching the house they were found between two feather beds.

As Kidd did not seem disposed to unbosom himself very freely, and as the earl feared that some stormy night he might escape, he decided to hold him secure in prison. This led to his arrest, which we have already alluded to, on the sixth day after his arrival. The arrest took place in the streets of Boston, near the door of the earl's residence. At the same time some commissioners took possession of his sloop. They seized and examined all his papers, and placed a guard over the property. Quite a number of his men were also arrested, twelve in

all, under charge of piracy and robbery on the high
seas.   It is supposed that the others escaped.

On the seventeenth of July, Captain Nicholas
Evertse arrived in Boston, with the statement to
which we have referred, that Bolton, who was left in
charge of the Quedagh Merchant, had transferred her
cargo to another vessel, conveyed the goods to Curacoa, and set the Merchant on fire.   He testified that
he saw the flames of the burning ship as he was
skirting the coast of San Domingo.

Kidd and his confederate pirates were held in
close custody in Boston for several months.   In the
mean time intelligence of their capture was sent to
London.   The home government dispatched a ship
of war to take them to England for trial.   The excitement throughout Great Britain and in this country was intense, in consequence of the rumor which
had so extensively prevailed of Kidd's partnership
with the king and several of the ministry.   Many
months had already elapsed since his arrest, and yet
he had not been brought to trial.   The ship sent to
transport him to London encountered a severe
storm and put back.   This caused an additional
delay, and increased the excitement.   It was said
that the ministry, out of regard to their own reputation, were determined not to bring him to justice.
Thus, throughout all England, he ceased to be

regarded as an ordinary pirate, and was raised to the dignity of one entitled to a state trial.

Immediately upon Kidd's arrival, the House of Commons addressed a petition to the king, praying to have his trial postponed until the next Parliament. The question of his guilt or innocence had become so involved in political issues, that there was a strong party ready to make the greatest exertions to secure his condemnation. They urged the postponement on the ground that this length of time was requisite to obtain, from the Indies, documents and affidavits in reference to his transactions. Kidd and his companions were consequently confined in Newgate prison for a whole year.

At that very time the House of Commons had impeached the Earl of Oxford and Lord Somers, for their connection with Kidd, and for the extraordinary commission which they had been instrumental in placing in his hands. It was said that commission and grants had been conferred upon him, which were highly prejudicial to the interests of trade and dishonorable to the king. In accordance with this commission, Kidd could capture any ship, and, without referring the question to any court of inquiry, could, of his own pleasure, declare the ship to be a pirate. He could then confiscate ship and cargo to his own use, and dispose of the crew in any way which to him might seem best. This was the course which, under the commission, he did pursue.

These were certainly very extraordinary powers. It was contended that they were contrary to the law of England and to the Bill of Rights. To these arguments it was replied, by the friends of the impeached nobles, that pirates were the enemies of the human race; that as such any person had a right to destroy them, and seize the property they had so iniquitously acquired, and to which they had no legitimate title. It was also declared, though perhaps the royal commission would hardly sustain the statement, that Kidd was authorized to seize only that property for which no other owner could be found. Certainly there was no provision made for searching out such ownership. It was, however, urged, and very truthfully, that the commission contained the all-important clause:

"We do also require you to bring, or cause to be brought, such pirates, freebooters, or sea-rovers, as you shall seize, to legal trial, to the end they may be proceeded against according to the law in such cases."

The fact that Kidd entirely ignored these instructions, constituting himself the court to try and condemn, could not justly be brought as a charge against the ministers who commissioned him.

Upon these questions popular feeling ran high. Parties took sides. Agitating rumors filled the air. It was confidently affirmed that the lords then on trial, with the connivance of the ministry, that they might escape the investigation which the trial of Kidd would involve, had set the Great Seal of England to the pardon of the pirate. This roused the anti-ministerial party to the highest state of exasperation. They resolved at all events to hang Kidd, hoping thus to prove that the ministers were alike guilty with him. And on the other hand, the ministers themselves had come to the conclusion that any attempt to shield Kidd would redound to their own ruin. It had become essential to their own reputation that they should manifest more zeal than any others to bring Kidd to the scaffold.

Thus the wretched pirate had no chance of a fair trial. Undoubtedly he was guilty. But it is very doubtful whether he were proved to be guilty when called before the court. The bill of impeachment against the lords was not carried. Though their participation with Kidd in the profits of an expedition which was authorized only by their own official acts was deemed very censurable, when the vote was taken there were but twenty-three in favor of the impeachment, while there were fifty-six opposed to the bill.

The Earl of Bellomont, harassed by the proce-
dure in the House of Commons, and knowing that
measures were about to be instituted against him,
for his recall from the provincial government, and
perhaps for his still more severe punishment, was
taken sick and died in New-York, in March, 1700.
Thus he escaped from the further troubles of this
ever-troubled world.

At the close of the year 1700, the papers which
had been sent for arrived from the East Indies. A
petition came from several of the East-Indian merchants, subjects of the King of Persia, giving a minute recital of the capture of the Quedagh Merchant,
and praying that the property of which they had
thus been robbed, and much of which had been conveyed to the North American colonies, might be restored to them. A very distinguished East Indian,
by the name of Cogi Baba, came to London in behalf
of the petitioners. He was summoned to appear
before the House of Commons. At the same time
Kidd himself was brought from his prison before the
bar.

After an examination, a motion was made to the
House to declare the grant made to the Earl of Bellomont and others of the company, of all the treasure
taken by Kidd, to be null and void. But this motion
was negatived. A vote was then taken requesting

the king to institute immediate proceedings against Captain Kidd for piracy and murder. He was accordingly brought to trial, under this indictment, at the Old Bailey, in the year 1701.

Several of Kidd's confederates were tried with him. Some of them pleaded the king's pardon, saying that they had surrendered themselves within the time limited in the royal proclamation. The governor of New Jersey, Colonel Bass, then in court, testified to the truth of this assertion, the surrender having been made to him.

To this it was replied, "There were four commissioners named in the proclamation, Thomas Warren, Israel Hayes, Peter Delanoye, and Christopher Pollard. These commissioners were sent to America to receive the submission of such pirates as should surrender. No other persons were entitled to receive their surrender. They therefore have not complied with the conditions of the proclamation."

They were condemned and hanged. One of the crew, Darby Mullens, made the following strong defence.

"I served under the king's commission. I could not therefore disobey my commander, without exposing myself to the most severe punishment. Whenever a ship goes out upon any expedition, under the king's commission, the men are never allowed to call their officers to account. Implicit obedience is required of them.   Any other course would destroy all discipline.   If anything unlawful is done, the officers are to answer for it, for the men, in obeying orders, only do what is imperiously their duty."

The court replied, " When a man is acting under a commission, he is justified only in doing that which is lawful, not in that which is unlawful."

The prisoner responded, " I stand in need of nothing to justify me in what is lawful.   But the case of a seaman is very hard, if he is exposed to being scourged or shot if he refuse to obey his commander, and of being hung if he obey him.   If the seaman were allowed to dispute the orders of his captain, there could be no such thing as command kept up at sea."

The court replied, " The crew, of which you were one, took a share of the plunder ; they mutinied several times ; they undertook to control the captain ; they paid no regard to the commission ; they acted in all things according to the customs of pirates.   You are guilty, and must be hanged."   He was hanged.

Kidd was tried for piracy, and for the murder of William Moore.   He was not allowed counsel, but was left to make his own defence.   On the whole, he appeared remarkably well while passing through this dreadful ordeal. In opening his defence, he said:

"I was a merchant in New York, in good repute and in good circumstances, when I was solicited to engage, under the royal commission, in the laudable employment of suppressing piracy. I had no need of embarking myself in piratic adventures. The men were generally desperate characters, and they rose in mutiny against me. I lost all control over them. They did as they pleased. They threatened to shoot me in my cabin. Ninety-five deserted at one time, and destroyed my boat. I was thus disabled from bringing the ship home. Consequently I could not bring the prizes before any court to have them regularly condemned. They were all taken by virtue of the commission, under the Broad Seal, and they had French papers."

When the jury was impanelled, and he was invited to find cause, if he wished to do so, for the exclusion of any of them, he replied:

"I shall challenge none. I know nothing to the contrary but that they are all honest men."

Kidd was greatly agitated during the trial, and frequently interrupted the court with his exclamations and explanations. He was first tried for the murder of William Moore. This indictment gave a very particular account of the event, stating that the gunner died of a mortal bruise received at the hands of the captain; that from the thirtieth day of October to the one-and-thirtieth day, he did languish and languishing did live, but that on the one-and-thirtieth day he did die; and that William Kidd, feloniously, voluntarily, and of malice aforethought, did kill and murder him."

To this Kidd replied, and probably with entire truth, as we have before said, that he had no intention of killing the man; that he struck him down to quell a mutiny, and to prevent the crew from engaging in an atrocious act of piracy; that his conscience never had condemned him for the deed, and that he then felt that for it he merited approb on rather than censure.

He told a very plain, simple story, which, if true, and its truth could not be disproved, would exonerate him in this affair from blame. The intelligent reader of this narrative will perceive that there were many corroborative circumstances to substantiate the accuracy of his account.

" I will inform the court," he said, " of the facts precisely as they occurred in this case. We were within about three miles of the Dutch ship, when I perceived that many of my men were in a state of mutiny, clamoring for her capture. Moore, addressing the mutineers, said that he could propose a plan by which the ship could be captured, and yet all who were engaged in the enterprise might be perfectly safe.

"'And how is that to be done,' I inquired?

"He replied, 'We will hail the ship, and have the captain and officers invited on board to visit our officers. While they are in the cabin with our captain, we will man the boats and plunder the ship. The captain will shut his eyes and close his ears, and then he and the officers can testify that the ship was not captured.

"To this I said, 'This would be Judas-like treachery, to rob the ship under the guise of friendship. I dare not do such a thing.'

"'We must do it,' Moore replied. 'We are already beggars. We have no other resource. You have brought us to utter ruin.'

"'Shall we be guilty of the crime,' I said, 'of capturing this ship because we are poor?'

"Upon this Moore and the mutineers were so violent that I seized a slush-bucket, which chanced to be at hand. With it I struck him in my passion, not intending to kill him. If I had premeditated his death, I should not have made use of so rude and chance-directed a weapon. I am heartily sorry that I killed him. And if the deed cannot be justified as a preventive of mutiny, it certainly should

not be adjudged anything more than manslaugh-
ter."

There was much force in these arguments. It
is at least doubtful whether an intelligent jury of
the present day would under such testimony have
brought in a verdict of guilty of murder in the first
degree. One who has carefully examined all the
proceedings of the court on this occasion, writes :

"Yet, it being determined to hang him at all
odds, the lawyers were given hints, the witnesses
were browbeaten, and the jury were instructed,
after tedious iteration, to bring him in guilty."

This was done. He was pronounced to be the
murderer of John Moore, and was, for that crime,
doomed to die.

The next day he was tried on the indictment for
piracy. Two of his crew, who, by their confession,
were sharers in his piratic adventures, turned state's
evidence. One of these was a deck hand, by the
name of Palmer. The other was a surgeon, Bradingham by name. Kidd closely cross-examined
them, but their stories perfectly agreed, being
straightforward and consistent.

Kidd's only defence was that he had acted only
as a privateersman, under his Majesty's commission.
He declared that he had never captured a ship
which he had not evidence was a French ship, be-

longing to French owners, and sailing under French papers. It scarcely admits of a doubt that this statement was utterly false. Kidd assumed of both of the witnesses against him that they were miserable vagabonds, whose testimony was unworthy of the slightest credence. In reference to the testimony of Bradingham, he exclaimed:

"This man contradicts himself in a hundred places. He tells a thousand lies. He knows no more of these things than you do. This fellow used to sleep five or six months together in the hold."

At another time, when the testimony was going strongly against him, he cried out bitterly:

"It is hard that the life of one of the king's subjects should be taken away upon the perjured oaths of such villains as these. Because I would not yield to their wishes, and turn pirate, they now endeavor to prove that I was one."

When the solicitor general asked if Kidd had any further questions to put to the witnesses, he despairingly replied:

"No! no. Bradingham is saving his life by taking away mine. I will not trouble the court any more, for it is a folly. So long as these men swear as they do, no oaths of mine will be of any avail."

The verdict of *guilty* was rendered. The judge pronounced the awful doom:

" William Kidd, the sentence that the law hath appointed to pass upon you for your offences, and which this court doth therefore award, is, that you, the said William Kidd, shall go from hence to the place from whence you came, and from thence to the place of execution, where you shall be hanged by the neck until you are dead.   And may the God of infinite mercy be merciful to your soul."

Kidd replied, " My lord, it is a very hard sentence.   For my part, I am the most innocent person of them all.   I have been sworn against by perjured persons."

5

CHAPTER V.

Kidd, and Stede Bonnet.

The Guilt of Kidd.—Rumors of Buried Treasure.—Mesmeric Revelation.—Adventures of Bradish.—Strange Character of Major Bonnet.—His Piracies.—Encounters.—Indications of Insanity.—No Temptation to Turn Pirate.—Blackbeard.—Bonnet Deposed.

Mr. Charles Elliot, in his History of New England, writes : " It seems to have been felt necessary by those who were charged, in England, with complicity with Captain Kidd, that a vigorous prosecution should be urged, and that an example should be made of him, to satisfy a clamorous public opinion. He was brought to trial, and was convicted and sentenced for the murder of William Moore, one of his own sailors, whom he had struck in an altercation.

" This appears to have been the only blood laid against him ; and the charge of piracy could hardly have been proved. As was the custom of that day, Kidd was not allowed counsel. He plead his commissions for what he had done, but was roughly treated by the court ; and Livingston, who was one of his partners and sureties, had got possession of his papers, and refused to give them up to him.

"Kidd probably had no idea of being charged with piracy, nor did he consider himself a pirate; and if there had been no charge made against his partners, he would not have died on the gallows. He was hanged at Execution Dock, May 12, 1701; and all England was agog with the doings of the pirate Kidd. It was a mere accident that Kidd was hanged as a pirate instead of being feasted as a victor."

These scenes occurred one hundred and seventy-five years ago. And yet, for some inexplicable reason, while hundreds of other events of vastly greater moment have passed into oblivion, the name of Captain Kidd, from that hour to this, has been almost a household word in both England and America.

Many believed that the Quedagh Merchant, instead of being burned at sea, was brought into the Hudson River at night, and sunk near the Highlands, with most of her treasure on board. Several circumstances seemed to corroborate this assertion. At the base of the Dunderberg, there could be seen sunk, deep in the bed of the river, and almost buried in its sands, the wreck of some large ship. A pamphlet was published, entitled:

"An Account of Some of the Traditions and

Experiments Respecting Captain Kidd's Piratical Vessel."

The traditions here referred to asserted that Kidd's vessel, the Quedagh Merchant, laden with the treasures of the East, was chased up the North River by an English man-of-war. Kidd, finding escape impossible, collected as much money as he could carry, and set fire to the ship, having left by far the larger part of the gold and silver on board. With a portion of the crew he ascended the river much farther, in boats, and then crossed the country, through the wilderness, to Boston.

These traditions are embellished with many romantic stories. It is said that as he and his piratic comrades were journeying along, they came to a log house in the woods. The man of the household was absent at his work. The woman, thinking that they were savages, in terror fled at their approach. In her fright she left one of her children behind. The bloodthirsty pirate, Kidd, in pure wantoness thrust his sword through the child.

An old Indian, who had wandered far away to Michigan, declared that he was on the river-bank when the pirates set fire to the ship and took to their boats. Very graphically he described the midnight scene as, buried in the glooms of the forest, he witnessed it in the brilliant illumination of the blazing vessel. He was induced to come all the way from Michigan to the Hudson to point out the spot of the sunken vessel. And deep in the water the charred timbers were to be seen. Another pamphlet was published, entitled:

"A Wonderful Mesmeric Revelation, giving an Account of the Discovery and Description of a Sunken Vessel, near Caldwell's Landing, supposed to be that of the Pirate Kidd; including an Account of his Character and Death, at a distance of nearly three hundred miles from the place."

This strange mesmeric revelation came from a Mrs. Chester, the wife of Charles Chester, of Lynn, Massachusetts. She declared that she had never heard anything about the sunken vessel; that never had she been upon the Hudson River; that she had never read or heard of the career of Kidd; and that she had never even been spoken to upon the subject, until, when placed in the magnetic state, the extraordinary revelation had been made to her.

While in this mesmeric condition, she saw, with clearest vision, the sunken vessel. Her eyes, with supernatural powers, pierced water, timbers, sand, and chests. There she saw bars of massive gold, heaps of silver coin, and precious jewels, including many large and brilliant diamonds. The jewels had been enclosed in shot-bags of stout canvas. The bags had decayed, and the jewels were clustered in brilliant heaps. She also saw "gold watches, like ducks' eggs in a pond of water," and the wonderfully preserved remains of a very beautiful woman, with a necklace of large and lustrous diamonds around her neck.

A man was seen just leaving the spot, who was preternaturally revealed to Mrs. Chester as Captain Kidd. He was a large, stout man, not very tall, with broad chest and shoulders, thick neck, aquiline nose, piercing eyes, and a head indicative of great power and all destructive qualities.

A very able writer in the Merchant's Magazine, of 1846, writes sarcastically of this mesmeric announcement:

"This most singular revelation, as it is corroborated by the traditions, presents us with another triumph of animal magnetism, and must serve not only to advance that science, but to demonstrate how much safer it is to rely upon tradition, than upon record evidence made in courts of justice held contemporaneously with the events, or official documents preserved in the public archives.

"In the present case, mesmerism has taken a progressive step; for it has not only disclosed what *is now* to be found in the waters of *Cocks-rack*, but also who *was there* one hundred and forty-five years ago. In this new application of the science we may hope not only to see the earth disembowelled, but the very forms and features of the ancient time brought up to our present view.

"What is more remarkable, if the traditions existed, as is pretended, is, that no individual or company should have undertaken, when the witnesses were living, to raise the vessel, especially as so many persons were found, near the time of the transactions of Kidd, credulous enough to ruin themselves in vain explorations after his money. But that perhaps was not an age of enterprise like the present, nor of humbug."

There is usually some ground for a tradition. Its basis is generally truth.

As we have mentioned, in the days of Captain Kidd the seas were swarming with pirates. It would require volumes to relate their adventures. Many of these lawless men performed deeds far more extraordinary and infamous than any perpetrated by Kidd. There was, however, at that time, a pirate by the name of Bradish, whose actions, in the popular mind, were blended with those of Kidd.

He was boatswain of a ship, of the same name with that in which Kidd sailed from New York, the Adventure. The ship was bound to Borneo, the largest island in the world, if Australia is recognized as a continent, and sailed from England in March, 1697. On the voyage the vessel stopped at the Island of Polonais for water. Bradish, a desperate man, had formed a conspiracy with several of the sailors to watch their opportunity, seize the ship, and set out on a piratic cruise.

At Polonais, the captain and several of his officers went on shore in one of the boats. Bradish assumed the command, silently raised the anchor, spread the sail, and ran out to sea. The wide world was before them to go where they pleased. The commerce of the seas spread its wealth for their plunder. There was the sum of about forty thousand dollars in gold on board. This money Bradish divided equally with his piratic crew. He then cleared his decks for action, placed a lookout at the mast-head, and commenced his cruise in search of additional treasure.

They directed their course toward the American coast. What vessels they captured on the way is not known. Upon reaching Long Island, Bradish went ashore and deposited with some confederate there a large amount of money and jewels. If pursued by a man-of-war, he could easily run his vessel ashore, and the crew could disperse through the woods. Much of his treasure would still be safe.

He ran along to Block Island. Here they pur-

chased two small vessels, and, dividing into two par-
tions, separated, each party taking its share of the
remaining treasure. It is said that there was enough
to load both of the small vessels. Many of the men
landed on the Rhode Island and Connecticut shore.
They behaved very civilly; called at the farm-houses,
and bought horses and food, for which they paid
abundantly. The rumor of the landing and disper-
sion of the pirates spread. A proclamation was
issued for their arrest. The captain and about
eighteen of the men were apprehended, sent to England, tried, and executed. What became of the
large ship, the Adventure, is not known.

By many it was supposed that she ran into the
North River, and was scuttled and abandoned when
near the Highlands.

We now bid adieu to Captain Kidd, leaving it
with our readers to form their own opinion, from the
facts here given, of the degree of praise or blame to
be attached to his character.

About the same time when William Kidd was
passing through his strange adventures, there was
another buccaneer appearing upon the stage, whose
character and career were still more astonishing.
There was a gentleman in Barbadoes, of wealth,
position, and education, by the name of Stede
Bonnet. He had a large fortune, and was highly

5*

esteemed for his intellectual culture and his honorable character. He seemed to be exposed to no temptation whatever to enter upon the guilty and perilous life of a pirate. His melancholy fate excited pity rather than condemnation, as it was generally believed that he was the victim of some strange mental hallucination, which, in some degree at least, exonerated him from moral responsibility.

Some domestic griefs rendered him unhappy in his home. He fitted out, entirely at his own expense, a sloop armed with ten guns, and manned by seventy sailors, desperate men, ready for any deeds of violence and crime. The sloop he named the Revenge. It was his avowed intention to prey upon the Spanish commerce, which none of the English courts would then punish as piracy.

But he immediately entered upon the career of a pirate, capturing and plundering every vessel he came across, without any regard to the flag under which she sailed. His first cruise was off the Capes of Virginia. The first vessel he encountered was the Anne, from Glasgow. A few cannon-balls thrown across her bows brought her to. His boats, filled with demoniac men armed to the teeth, boarded the ill-fated prize, and plundered her of everything the pirates desired, money, clothes provisions, and ammunition. The ship was then allowed to go on her way.

A day or two passed, and another sail was discerned in the distant horizon. She was soon overtaken by the swift-sailing sloop, which spread a wonderful cloud of canvas. It proved to be the Turbet, from his own island, Barbadoes. Instead of treating her kindly on that account, he plundered her mercilessly, put the crew in boats, to find their way to the shore as they best could, and set the vessel on fire.

Scarcely had the smoke and flame of the burning vessel vanished from their view, when another sail was descried. She proved to be the Endeavor, from Bristol. She was robbed of everything valuable. Another vessel soon underwent the same fate. It was the Young, from Leith.

Stede Bonnet was no sailor. He had no acquaintance with navigation. He, however, employed skilled seaman to manage the ship in obedience to his commands as owner of the whole concern. After this short and very successful cruise on the Virginia coast, he ordered the sloop to be taken to the shores of New England. As they were passing the eastern end of Long Island, they met a vessel bound from one of the New England colonies to the West Indies. It was promptly plundered.

Stede Bonnet stood in for Gardiner's Island, where he landed with a portion of his crew. He behaved in a very gentlemanly way, addressing all whom he met courteously, making many purchases and paying liberally for all he took. He then directed his course to South Carolina, and ran up and down before the harbor of Charleston. Two vessels, entering the harbor, he seized almost at the same time. One was a sloop from Barbadoes, laden with rum, sugar, and negroes. The other was a brigantine from New England. The hold of the Revenge was already packed full of plunder ; and they had no room for the negroes. Taking, therefore, such few articles as they needed, they landed the crew and the negroes on an island, and wantonly ran the Barbadoes sloop ashore, and set her on fire. The New England brigantine they plundered of all the money on board and such other articles of value as they needed, and let her go.

While on this cruise they met, in rogues' companionship, another piratic ship, commanded by a desperado, an Englishman, by the name of Edward Teach. From the mass of hair which covered his face he was known by the name of Blackbeard. His beard came up to his eyes, was intensely black, and so long that he was accustomed to braid it and twist it with ribbons into cues, or tails, which he would hang over his ears. It is said that in aspect he was a revolting monster. This villain had captured a large and very strongly built East-Indian ship, upon which he had mounted forty heavy guns. With this powerful armament he swept the seas, bidding defiance to all assailants. Upon one occasion he encountered a British man-of-war of thirty guns. After sustaining an action of some hours, the man-of-war fled before him, and took shelter in the harbor of Barbadoes, under protection of the guns of the fort.

As Teach continued his triumphant cruise, he came across Bonnet's piratic sloop. Finding that Bonnet understood nothing of maritime affairs, he, without difficulty, got up a conspiracy among his men, deposed him, and placed one of his own crew, a man by the name of Richards, in command of the Revenge. Thus he had two vessels with which to prosecute his lawless career. He took the deposed captain on board his own ship, saying to him with a sarcastic smile :

" I perceive, my dear sir, that you are not used to the cares and fatigues of commanding a vessel, and I will relieve you from them. It will be much pleasanter for you to live at your ease in my cabin. There you will have no duty to perform, and can follow your own inclinations."

The career of this most ferocious of pirates was so strange that we must leave Stede Bonnet for a time, and devote a chapter to that fiend in human form, called Blackbeard.

CHAPTER VI.

The Adventures of Edward Teach, or Blackbeard.

Seizure of the Protestant Cæsar.—The Piratic Squadron.—Villany of the Buccaneers.—The Atrocities of Blackbeard.—Illustrative Anecdotes.—Carousals on Shore.—Alleged Complicity with the Governor.—Hiding-place near Ocracoke Inlet.—Arrangements for his Capture.—Boats sent from two Men-of-war.—Bloody Battle.—The Death of the Pirate.—His Desperate and Demoniac Character.

BLACKBEARD having, as it were, captured the Revenge, raised the black flag of piracy upon both of his vessels. Soon he captured a third vessel, which he manned and armed and added to his piratic squadron. Entering the Bay of Honduras, he took a ship, from Boston, called the Protestant Cæsar, and four sloops. Captain Wyar, of the Protestant Cæsar, as the pirates' balls whistled over his decks, abandoned his ship, and taking to his boats, with all his crew, escaped to the shore. One of the sloops also belonged to Boston. After plundering the ship and sloop of all they wanted, they set both on fire, in revenge, because they belonged to Boston, where some men had been hung for piracy. The other three sloops they plundered and then let go.

They then continued their cruise, for some time, among the West India Islands, capturing vessel after vessel. Thence sailing to the South Carolinian coast, they ran up and down before the harbor of Charleston for a week. Here they took a ship, bound out for London, with several passengers, Captain Robert Clark commander. They also captured three vessels entering the port, one of which had fourteen negroes on board.

Such a strong piratic force appearing before that important harbor, struck the whole province with terror. They were quite unable to resist such an armament. There were eight vessels in the harbor ready for sea. They dared not venture out, and even feared that the pirates would come into the harbor and take them. The trade of the place was thus, for a season, utterly destroyed. It added much to the weight of this calamity that the province had just passed through an expensive and exhaustive war with the Indians.

Teach was in great want of medicines. He therefore detained all the vessels he had taken, with their crews and passengers, and sent Captain Richards, in the Revenge, to Charleston, with the following message to the governor:

"I want a chest of medicines. Send me such a chest, by the bearer. If you do not comply with this my demand immediately, without offering any violence to the persons of my ambassadors, I will cut off the heads of all the prisoners in my hands, and send them to you, and will burn all the ships."

Mr. Marks, one of the prisoners, was sent with Richards and the other pirates to present this demand. While Mr. Marks was making this application to the governor and council, Richards and his piratic gang were insolently riding through the streets, with sabres in their hands and pistols in their belts. The citizens were in a state of the highest indignation ; and yet they dared not speak a word or even look with a frown. The villains returned to their ships with impunity, bearing a chest of medicines valued at two thousand dollars. The lives of so many husbands, sons, and brothers were at stake that the community was eager to conciliate the pirates.

Blackbeard, having received the chest, liberated the vessels and the prisoners. He had taken from the vessels gold and silver coin to the amount of seven thousand dollars, besides provisions and other articles of much value. They then sailed to the coast of North Carolina. Blackbeard's ship they called the Man-of-War. One sloop, as we have mentioned, was commanded by Richards. Blackbeard placed upon another, as commander, a fellow by the name of Hands.   He had also another vessel, which served as a tender.   Thus this piratic squadron was now composed of four vessels.

The amount of plunder, in money and goods, was very great.   Blackbeard formed a plan to secure nearly the whole for himself, and for a few others of his favorites in the gang.   He therefore, under pretence of running his ship into Ocracoke Inlet for repairs, grounded her.   He summoned Hands' sloop to his aid and ran her on shore.

He then went on board the tender sloop, where he had assembled his confederates, forty in number, and had stored all the coin and many of the most valuable goods.   Seventeen of the crew, whom he wished to get rid of, he landed on a small, sandy island three miles from the mainland.   Here they were exposed to perish, without food or water, or any opportunity to escape.   There was neither bird, beast, nor herbs on the island.

The king, as we have mentioned, had issued a proclamation of pardon for all the pirates who would surrender themselves.   This consummate villain, with about twenty of his comrades, sailed to the residence of the governor, and surrendered themselves to his majesty's proclamation, and received a full pardon for all their past offences, while they still retained their ill-gotten wealth.   This was done with no intention of abandoning their mode of life, but only to obtain a respite, and prepare for future operations.

Bonnet was left behind, with the Revenge. He again, with a portion of the men, assumed the command of the ship, of which he had been robbed. But we must leave him for a time until we have followed out the career of Blackbeard.

Charles Eden was then governor of North Carolina. He was either a very corrupt man or a very simple one. The governor gave Blackbeard full possession of the ship he had captured, and which he had named the Queen Anne's Revenge. A court of admiralty was held, and though Teach had never received any commission as a privateersman, and it was a time of peace, and the Queen Anne belonged to English merchants, she was condemned as a prize taken from the Spaniards, and adjudged to belong to Teach.

Blackbeard remained for a few weeks at the capital of the province ; paid his addresses to a beautiful young girl of sixteen, and was married to her by the governor, who had probably received very rich presents from the pirate. His biographer says that this was the fourteenth wife of Teach, twelve of whom were still living. Soon he again went to sea, beneath the pirate's black flag. He directed his course toward the West Indies, capturing two or three English ships by the way, which he plundered, but left the ships and crew unharmed. He then captured two French ships. The cargoes of both he stored in one. The crews of both he placed in the other, and turned them adrift. With his rich prize he returned to North Carolina, and shared the booty with the governor.

Blackbeard and four of his crew went ashore, and took a solemn oath that they found the French ship at sea abandoned, and without a soul on board. It is curious to witness the expedients to which men will resort to appease the qualms of conscience. After removing all the ship's company from their prize the captain and a boat's crew boarded her, and truly found her "without a soul on board." Thus they satisfied themselves that they did not take a false oath. In accordance with this testimony the court adjudged the French vessel to be a lawful prize. The governor had sixty hogsheads of sugar for his share. Mr. Knight, his secretary, collector of the port, had twenty. All the remainder of the booty the pirates divided among themselves.

The French vessel was still on the pirate's hands. He greatly feared that some vessel might come into the river acquainted with her, and that his villany might be discovered. He set her on fire, and burning her to the water's edge, her bottom sunk.

Blackbeard remained for some time cruising along the shores of Pamlico Sound. He was rich, and prodigal of his wealth. Sometimes, in mere wantonness, he would plunder a vessel. Again he would purchase articles, paying for them three or four times their worth.

He often went ashore with his armed followers, and spent the night and sometimes days in boisterous revelry. The planters did not dare to make any remonstrances. He was a brutal wretch, and often, when frenzied with drink, the wives and daughters of the planters were exposed to the most terrible indignities. At times he was very courteous, presenting his entertainers with rum, sugar, and other valuable articles. He frequently assumed a very lordly air, levying heavy contributions, and even bullying the governor, simply to show him what he dared to do.

The traders and planters consulted together to decide what course to pursue in this terrible emergence. It was plain that the governor was either in complicity with the pirate or was overawed by him. It was in vain, therefore, to hope for redress through his interposition. They, therefore, as secretly as possible, sent to the governor of Virginia, soliciting an armed force from the men-of-war then lying before Jamestown, to take and destroy this formidable pirate.

There were two men-of-war in the James River, the Pearl and the Lime. The governor consulted with the two commanders. It was agreed between them that the governor should hire two small sloops, of light draft, which could run easily into the coves and among the shoals of Pamlico Sound. The men-of-war were to place on board these sloops a strong picked crew of thoroughly armed men. They were to take small arms alone, as mounted cannon would require such depths of water as to embarrass their operations. These sloops, rapidly propelled by both sails and oars, could follow the pirate in all his coverts; could overtake him should he attempt to escape by flight, and, by simultaneously boarding the piratic craft, could overpower and cut down the crew.

The expedition was speedily fitted out. At the same time the Virginia governor issued a proclamation, offering a reward of five hundred dollars for the capture, dead or alive, of Captain Teach, commonly called Blackbeard; two hundred dollars for every other commander of a pirate ship; for all inferior officers seventy-five dollars; for every pirate on board such ship forty dollars. This proclamation, a copy of which now lies before me, was dated at Williamsburg, November 24th, 1718, and was signed by the governor, A. Spottswood.

On the 21st of November the two sloops entered the mouth of Ocracoke Inlet, and caught sight of the pirate. The governor of North Carolina, and his secretary, Mr. Knight, hearing of these preparations, and fearing that the capture of the pirate would bring their misdeeds to light, sent him warning of his danger. Knight wrote to him :

" I have sent you four of your men. They are all I can meet with about town. Be upon your guard."

Blackbeard, one of the most reckless and determined of desperadoes, put his vessel in posture for defence. He had with him then a crew of but twenty-five men. Seeing the approach of the sloops, and anticipating a battle with the morning's dawn, he spent the night in drunken carousals. Lieutenant Maynard, in command of the expedition, found the water too shoal and the channel too intricate for him to reach the ship that night. Under cover of the darkness he sent out a boat to mark the way.

The morning was cloudless and calm. There was scarcely a breath of wind ; and not a ripple was to be seen on the mirrored surface of the Sound. There was no escape for the pirate. The gentle breath which swept the waters was fair. The sloops spread their sails, and with lusty arms at the oars bore down upon the pirate. As they approached, Blackbeard stood upon his deck, and with revolting oaths, which we shall omit, interlarding his speech, shouted out:

"You villains, who are you, and what do you want?"

"Our colors show," Lieutenant Maynard replied, "that we are no pirates."

"Send your boat on board," exclaimed Blackbeard, "that I may learn who you are."

"I have no boat to spare," Maynard responded; "but as soon as I can reach you with my sloops, I will come on board myself."

Blackbeard took a tumbler of raw brandy. As he poured the burning fluid down his throat he exclaimed:

"May damnation seize my soul if I give you any quarter, or take any from you."

"I expect no quarter," Maynard responded; "neither do I ask for any."

The gunwale of Maynard's sloop, which took the lead, was scarcely a foot high. The men on the deck were entirely exposed. Blackbeard poured in upon them a broadside of grape-shot. The carnage was awful. Twenty men, by that one discharge, were either killed or wounded. Maynard, apprehensive

of another discharge, ordered all the survivors immediately into the hold, he alone remaining on deck,
at the helm. The men were directed to have their
swords and pistols ready for a rush in boarding, the
moment the command should be given.

As the sloop approached the pirate they threw
in upon her deck a new sort of hand-grenades. They
consisted of common junk bottles, filled with powder,
balls, and slugs, and were exploded by a fuse passing
through the mouth. They would have done great
execution had not the men been concealed in the
hold.

The moment the bows of the sloop touched the
pirate's ship, as the smoke cleared away a little,
Blackbeard, seeing but few on deck, shouted to his
men :

"The villains are all knocked in the head, excepting three or four. Let us jump on board and
cut them down."

The order was instantly obeyed. Fourteen
pirates, with flashing sabres, leaped over the bows
of Maynard's sloop, upon his deck. There were but
twelve men unwounded in the hold. At a given
signal they rushed up, and a battle of utter desperation ensued.

Blackbeard sprang toward Lieutenant Maynard,
who was at the helm. Their pistols were discharged

simultaneously. The pirate received a slight, but not a disabling wound. They rushed upon each other with their swords. In the fierce conflict the blade of Maynard's sword broke in his hand. He stepped back to cock a pistol. Blackbeard was just in the act of cutting him down, when one of Maynard's men struck him from behind, inflicting a terrible gash upon his neck. At the same moment the desperado, who seemed to be almost insensible to wounds, received a shot in his body from the lieutenant's pistol.

The other sloop, called the Ranger, now came up and boarded the pirate. Blackbeard fought like a tiger. At length a pistol-shot pierced some vital part and he fell dead, after having received twenty-five wounds. Eight more of the pirates who had boarded Maynard's sloop were weltering in their blood. The rest, many of them severely wounded, leaped overboard. The drowning wretches cried for quarter. It was granted. They were reserved only that they might be hanged.

Blackbeard's head was cut from his body, and hung at the end of the bowsprit of Maynard's sloop. With this revolting trophy he sailed into Newbern to obtain relief for his wounded men. In examining the papers found on board the pirate's vessel, the correspondence was discovered between Governor Eden

6

and his secretary with the pirate. There were also several merchants in New York who were in friendly communication with him. These papers would doubtless have been destroyed had it not been for the desperate resolve which the pirate had formed.

Blackbeard had but little hope of escaping. He therefore posted one of the most demoniac of the pirates, with a match, in the powder-room. Assuring him that if they were taken they would assuredly be hanged, and that it was far better to die by their own action, in an instant, than to perish upon the scaffold, he instructed him that should the ship be boarded and captured, he was to apply the match and blow them all up together. It chanced that there were two prisoners in the ship's hold. They seized the pirate, and prevented him from executing his design.

It was this same Blackbeard, to whom we have already alluded, who one day, when flushed with drink, said to his boon companions :

"Come, let us make a hell of our own, and see who can stand it longest."

One night, when drinking, in his cabin, with two or three companions, he secretly drew out a small pair of pistols, blew out the candle, and, crossing his hands, discharged them at random into the midst of the company. One of the bullets struck an officer on the knee, and crippled him for life. The other bullet fortunately harmèd no one. Being asked why he did this, he replied:

"If I did not now and then kill some of you, you would forget who I am."

The following entries were found in his log-book, written with his own hand, under different dates:

"Rum all out; our company somewhat sober.

"A damned confusion among us; rogues a-plot-ting.

"Great talk of separation.

"Took a vessel with a great deal of liquor on board; so kept the company hot; damned hot."

It is evident that these godless wretches passed joyless and miserable lives. Experience verifies the declaration of the Bible that "the way of the trans-gressor is hard."

The ship and stores captured by Lieutenant Maynard were in value estimated at but twelve thousand five hundred dollars. Though this wretch-ed pirate had squandered his plunder with great prodigality, it was generally supposed that he had valuable treasure secreted. In the carousal of the night before his capture, one of the men asked if, in case anything should happen to him in the en-gagement, his wife knew where he had buried his money. He replied, "The devil and I alone know where it is. The one of us two who lives the longest will have the whole."

There were sixteen pirates, all of whom were wounded, who were taken prisoners. They were conveyed to Virginia and hanged, excepting two who were pardoned. Governor Eden was so terrified by the discovery which had been made of his complicity with Blackbeard, and so apprehensive that he would be called to account for his conduct, that he fell sick with the fright, and in a few days died. His sixty hogsheads of sugar, and the twenty which had been given to Knight, were seized by Lieutenant Maynard, and confiscated. Thus all these guilty ones were ruined. It is often and truly said, that Satan helps his dupes into difficulty, but never helps them out.

CHAPTER VII.

The Close of Stede Bonnet's Career.

Bonnet's Abandonment by Blackbeard.—Avails Himself of the King's Pardon.—Takes Commission as a Privateer.—Rescues Blackbeard's Pirates.—Piratic Career.—Enters Cape Fear River for Repairs.—Captured by Colonel Rhet.—The Conflict.—Escapes from Prison.—The Pursuit, and Trial and Sentence.

IT will be remembered that Stede Bonnet was deposed by Blackbeard. When Blackbeard abandoned most of his crew, at Ocracoke Inlet, and landed others on a desert island, that he might rob them of their share of the spoil, Bonnet was left behind with the rest. His own sloop, the Revenge, was ashore. He got her off, assumed the command, manned her with pirates, and sailed to Bathtown, where he surrendered himself, taking advantage of the king's proclamation, and received a certificate of pardon.

Just then war broke out between England, France, and Holland, as allies, on the one hand, and Spain upon the other. Bonnet sailed from Bathtown for the Island of St. Thomas, to get a commission to go privateering against the Spaniards. When he was

on his way to the inlet he accidentally learned from
two of the pirates that Blackbeard and his gang
were gone ; and that, carrying away all the money
and effects of value, they had left several men to
perish on a desert island. Bonnet sailed for their
relief. They were nearly starved, and had been a
day and two nights without any food. Bonnet found
the island, and rescued them, adding them to his
crew.

Then, instead of going to St. Thomas for his commission, he directed his course to the coast of Virginia. Meeting a vessel loaded with provisions, he
took from it twelve barrels of pork and four hundred weight of bread. Assuming that he was an
honest man, and not a pirate, he gave in return
eight casks of rice and an old cable. No bargain
was made. He took what he wanted, and gave
what he pleased. Two days after this, Bonnet pursued and captured a sloop of sixty tons. It was an
act of unmitigated piracy. He took from his prize
two hogsheads of rum and two of molasses. The
crew were turned adrift. Eight men were sent to
take charge of the prize. In the night they ran
away, to go pirating on their own account

Bonnet threw off all restraint. Assuming the
name of Captain Thomas, he ranged the seas, plundering every vessel he encountered. A few miles

off from Cape Henry he captured two ships from Virginia, bound to Glasgow. They were comparatively valueless prizes, containing only tobacco. The next day he captured a small sloop. With the strange inconsistency which marked his character, he took from the sloop twenty barrels of pork, which he replaced by two barrels of rice and a hogshead of molasses. From this sloop two men voluntarily joined his company.

The next ship they captured was bound to Glasgow from Virginia. They found nothing on board they wanted but some combs, pins, and needles. For these Bonnet paid a barrel of pork and two barrels of bread. Directing his course toward Philadelphia, he captured a schooner bound to Boston. It proved a barren prize.

Soon after this he took three vessels, two bound from Philadelphia to Bristol, England, and one to Barbadoes. In these Bonnet found nearly a thousand dollars in coin. He robbed them and let them go. The two last days in July he captured two quite rich prizes. They were well supplied with provisions, and had between two and three thousand dollars in money on board. He turned the crews adrift in their boats and kept both the vessels and cargo. His own sloop of war, which he had re-named the Royal James, had become leaky, and needed repairs. He ran into Cape Fear River to find some secluded cove, where, far from observation, he could careen his vessel. One hundred and fifty years ago this stream presented a vast solitude, fringed by the dense and boundless forest.

As Bonnet was entering the river he captured a small vessel, which he ripped to pieces to mend his own. In one of the coves of the broad stream he was detained two months in making repairs. In the mean time a new governor had come to South Carolina. Tidings reached Charleston that a piratic vessel, with two prizes, was concealed up the river. The whole community was alarmed, fearing another visit. The governor and council met to deliberate.

Colonel William Rhet appeared before them and generously offered to fit out two vessels, at his own expense, and attack the pirates. His proposal was accepted, and a commission granted him accordingly. In a few days two sloops were equipped. One, called the Henry, had eight guns and seventy men, and was commanded by Captain John Masters. The other, the Sea Nymph, of eight guns and sixty men, Captain Fayser Hall commanded. Both were under the direction of Colonel Rhet.

On the 14th of September the two vessels sailed. When they reached Sullivan's Island, a small ship from Antigua came in. The captain brought the intelligence that just off the bar he was taken and plundered by a piratic vessel of twelve guns and ninety men, commanded by Charles Vane; that two other vessels had also been captured, one from the coast of Guinea, with between ninety and a hundred negro slaves on board. A pirate, by the name of Yeats, with twenty-five men, had been placed in command of the slaver. Vane had also captured two ships bound from Charleston to London.

Colonel Rhet, upon hearing these tidings, resolved to pursue Vane. It was rumored that the pirates had sailed south. Colonel Rhet, with his two sloops, crossed the bar, on the 15th of September, and directed his course along the southern coast, searching every bay and inlet. Not finding Vane, he turned north, and entered Cape Fear River in pursuit of his first design. In ascending the river both sloops ran aground, which caused considerable delay. Thus the watchful pirates learned that there were two sloops aground in the river. Bonnet sent down three boats, crowded with pirates, to attack them. The crews soon found their mistake, and rowing hastily back to Bonnet, gave him the unwelcome news that two well-armed sloops were ascending the river with the evident design to attack him.

6*

Bonnet made immediate preparations for a battle. He had several prisoners with him. He wrote a letter to the governor, intrusting it to one of these prisoners, Captain Mannering. It was as follows: .

"If the sloops now ascending the river are sent out against me by the governor, I shall get clear off. And I will burn and destroy all ships or vessels going in or coming out of South Carolina."

What effect this letter had upon the governor we know not. But the next morning the tide floated Colonel Rhet's sloops, and he advanced to the attack. The masts of the three piratical vessels were soon plainly seen over a forest-crowned point of land. The sloops pressed forward to attack on each quarter of the pirate, intending to board him. Bonnet, perceiving this, edged in as near the shore as possible. The water was shoal, and the tide being out, soon both sloops ran upon sandbanks. One was very near the Royal James, and could open fire upon her. The other was at more than gunshot distance. The pirates' ship also grounded, and, fortunately for them, careened over with her deck sloping from her foe. Thus the sides of the vessel afforded a rampart, which protected the pirates from shot, and over which they could take deliberate aim at their antagonists.

To add to this calamity, the Henry, in which

Colonel Rhet was, and which had grounded within pistol-shot of the pirate, leaned with her deck inclined toward the pirate. Thus every man was exposed. This gave the pirates an immense advantage, which they were not slow to improve. Neither of them could use their cannon. For five hours the antagonists kept up a brisk fire with their small arms. The pirates spread to the breeze their blood-red flag, and assailed their foes with oaths, taunts, and insults.

"Why don't you come on board?" they shouted, "We are all waiting for you. Come as quick as you can. We will give you the warmest reception you ever had."

Rhet's men replied, "Be patient. We are busy just now. Very soon we will pay you a visit which you will never forget."

The rising tide first floated Colonel Rhet's sloop. Hastily repairing his rigging, which had been much shattered by the fire, he bore down upon the pirate, intending to give a finishing stroke by boarding him. The other sloop would, in a few moments, be afloat to join in the assault. Bonnet saw his case to be hopeless, and sent a boat to Colonel Rhet bearing the white flag of truce. After some time spent in capitulating, Bonnet was compelled to surrender unconditionally.

In the severe battle which had taken place, ten

men had been killed and fourteen wounded on board Rhet's sloop, the Henry. Six of the wounded died of their wounds. A few shot had struck the other sloop, the Sea Nymph, killing two men, and wounding four. The pirates, protected by the position of their vessel, lost seven killed, and five wounded. Two of the latter soon died of their wounds.

Colonel Rhet weighed anchor on the 13th of September, and on the 3d of October entered Charleston with thirty-four pirates as prisoners, and their vessels. The capture excited great rejoicing throughout the whole province. As there was no public prison on the shore, the pirates were all kept, for two days, under a careful guard, in the hold of one of the vessels. The watch-house was in the mean time enlarged and strengthened, and they were transferred to that building, over which a guard of the provincial militia was placed.

Major Bonnet was committed into the custody of the marshal, and imprisoned in a strong room in his house. Two of these miserable men, David Hariot, the sailing-master, and Ignatius Pell, the boatswain, offered to turn state's evidence. They were also taken to the house of the marshal, that they might be separated from the rest of the crew. They were carefully locked up, and two sentinels, every night, patrolled the house with loaded muskets.

Three weeks passed before suitable preparations could be made for the trial. On the night of the 24th of October, Bonnet and his sailing-master made their escape. The boatswain refused to go with them, as he was assured of pardon in consideration of the evidence he bore against his comrades. The flight of the prisoners made a great noise throughout the province. The people were open in their indignant declaration that the governor, and others of the magistracy, had connived at their escape.

The whole community was panic-stricken. It was feared that Bonnet would get up another company of pirates, and take a terrible revenge for the hanging of his comrades. The government was alarmed both by the reproaches and the peril. A proclamation was issued offering a reward of three thousand five hundred dollars for the capture of the fugitive pirate. Several armed boats were sent to skirt the shore, north and south, in pursuit of him.

Bonnet had, in some way, got on board a small sail-boat in the harbor, and put to sea. But a storm arose, and he had no provisions. He was therefore compelled to put back to Sullivan's Island. In some way the governor got an intimation of this. He promptly communicated the intelligence to Colonel Rhet, and gave him a commission to pursue Bonnet.

That night the energetic colonel set out in his sloop, with a number of men for Sullivan's Island. The two pirates had left their boat at the shore and wandered into the woods, where they had concealed themselves. Colonel Rhet tracked them to their covert. They were discovered in a thicket, with a negro and an Indian. As they endeavored to escape they were fired upon. A bullet pierced Hariot's heart, and he fell dead. Both the negro and the Indian were struck down severely wounded. The wretched Bonnet, seeing escape hopeless, and utterly disheartened, surrendered. He was carried back to Charleston in irons.

On the twenty-eighth of October, 1718, a court of vice-admiralty was held, and continued, by several adjournments, until the twelfth of November. Nicholas Trot, chief justice of the province of South Carolina, presided, with other assistant judges. Before this tribunal, Bonnet, and thirty-four of his crew, were arraigned. The indictment enumerated the various acts of piracy which they had committed. All but two pleaded not guilty.

There was but little defence attempted. The crew pleaded that they had been taken off a desert island, and shipped to go to St. Thomas. Being at sea, without provisions, and in a starving condition, they were compelled, to save their lives, to take some food from other vessels. Major Bonnet took the same ground—that they had helped themselves to food which did not·belong to them, but as the only way by which they could save their lives.

But their piratic acts were clearly proved, and that they had shared among themselves their ill-gotten booty. The speech of the lord chief-justice, in pronouncing sentence upon Bonnet, was so admirable in tone, that it deserves, with slight abbreviation, insertion here :

" You, Stede Bonnet, stand convicted of piracy. It is fully proved that you piratically took and rifled no less than thirteen vessels since you sailed from North Carolina, having accepted the king's act of grace, and pretended to leave that wicked course of life.

" You know that the crimes you have committed are contrary to the law of nature, as well as to the law of God, by which you are commanded that you shall not steal. And the apostle·Paul expressly affirms that ' thieves shall not inherit the kingdom of God.'

" To theft you have added the greater sin of murder. How many you have killed, in your piracies, I know not. But this we know, that you killed no less than eighteen persons of those sent, by lawful authority, to put a stop to your rapines.

"However you may fancy that that was killing men fairly in open fight, yet this know, that the power of the sword not being committed into your hands, you were not empowered to use any force, or fight any one. Therefore those persons that fell in the action, in doing their duty to their king and country, were murdered. And their blood now cries out for vengeance against you. For it is the voice of nature, confirmed by the law of God, that 'whosoever sheddeth man's blood, by man shall his blood be shed.'

"And consider that death is not the only punishment due to murderers; for they are threatened to have 'their part in that lake which burneth with fire and brimstone, which is the second death.'

"As your own conscience must convince you of the many and great evils you have committed, by which you have highly offended God, so I suppose I need not tell you that the only way of obtaining pardon and the remission of your sins from God, is by a true and unfeigned repentance, and faith in Christ, by whose death and passion you can alone hope for salvation.

"You, being a gentleman, and having had the advantage of a liberal education, I believe it will be needless for me to explain to you the nature of repentance and faith in Christ. They are so fully mentioned in the Scriptures that you can not but know them.   But, considering the course of your life, I have reason to fear that the principles of religion which had been instilled into you by your education, have been corrupted, if not entirely defaced by the infidelity of this wicked age; and that the time you allowed for study was rather applied to the polite literature than to a serious search after the law and will of God.

" In the Scriptures is found the great mystery of fallen man's redemption.   They would have taught you that sin is the debasing of human nature, and that religion and walking by the laws of God are altogether preferable to the ways of sin and Satan. I hope that the present afflictions, which God has laid upon you, have now convinced you of this.

"And consider how he invites all sinners to come to Him, and He will give them rest; for He has assured us that 'He came to seek and to save that which was lost;' and that 'whosoever cometh to Him, He will in nowise cast out.'   So that now, even at the eleventh hour, if you will sincerely turn to Him, He will receive you.

" But do not mistake the nature of repentance to be only bare sorrow for the evil and punishment which sin has brought upon you.   Your sorrow must arise from the consideration of your having offended a gracious and merciful God. But I need not give you any particular directions as to the nature of repentance. I speak to one whose offences have proceeded, not so much from his not knowing, as from his slighting and neglecting.his duty.

"I only heartily wish that what, in compassion to your soul, I have now said, may have that effect upon you that you may become a true penitent. Having now discharged my duty to you as a Christian, by giving you the best council I can with respect to the salvation of your soul, I must now do my office as a judge. The sentence which this court awards to you is:

"That you, Stede Bonnet, shall go from hence to the place whence you came, and from thence to the place of execution; where you shall be hanged by the neck until you are dead. And may God have mercy upon you."

On Saturday, November 8th, 1718, twenty-two of the pirates were hung upon the same gallows, at White Point, near the provincial city of Charleston. A few days after, Stede Bonnet, the gentleman of wealth, position, and culture, swung from the same gallows.

CHAPTER VIII.

The Portuguese Barthelemy.

Commencement of his Career.—Bold Capture.—Brutality of the Pirates.—Reverses and Captivity.—Barthelemy doomed to Die.—His Escape.—Sufferings in the Forest.—Reaches Gulf Triste.—Hardening Effect of his Misfortunes.—His new Piratic Enterprize.—Wonderful Success.—The Tornado.—Impoverishment and Ruin.

ONE of the most bold and renowned of the buccaneers was a Portuguese, by the name of Barthelemy. He was a man of some property, and followed the great tide of emigration to the West Indies. At Kingston, Jamaica, he heard of the great fortunes which were made by buccaneers preying upon Spanish commerce. Engaging in several expeditions, he became quite rich. Finally he fitted out a small vessel, at his own expense, which he armed with four three-pounders, and a crew of thirty desperate men, armed with muskets, pistols, and sabres. This sloop was fitted out in a British port, to rob the ships of Spain, just as openly as if it were bound upon a fishing excursion.

He commenced his cruise upon the southern

coast of Cuba. But a few days passed ere he caught sight of a large ship, richly laden and well armed, bound from the Spanish colonies in Venezuela to Havana. It had, as he afterward found, a crew of seventy men, with about the same number of passengers and marines, and carried twenty guns.

When Barthelemy's crew saw the size of the ship and the indications of her strong armament, they hesitated to venture upon an attack. All were assembled around the mast to discuss the question. The general voice was discouraging. Barthelemy's speech was short and decisive. He was a man of few words and prompt action.

"We came out," said he, "for prizes. Here is a splendid one. The opportunity must not be lost. Nothing great can be accomplished without risk."

They gave chase. The ship quietly awaited their approach; "as much astonished at the attack," writes Thornbury, "as a swallow would be if it were pursued by a gnat." The pirates made a desperate endeavor to board the ship. We are not informed of the particulars of the fight. The result only is known. After several repulses, and a long and bloody conflict, the pirates raised shouts of victory on the blood-stained deck of their prize. Ten of them were killed; four wounded. All on board the ship but forty were killed. Many of these were severely maimed with bullet wounds and sword-cuts.

The pirates, having searched the pockets of the dead for their loose doubloons, threw the bodies overboard. Those helplessly wounded suffered the same fate. The survivors, after being stripped of everything valuable, were placed in a boat and cut adrift, to fare as they might. The prize proved to be worth between eighty and a hundred thousand dollars. Barthelemy found himself in command of a truly splendid ship, well armed, and well stored with ammunition and provisions. He had also his little sloop as a tender. Though he had a crew of but twenty men, he could at any time double or treble his number in the thronged ports of Kingston or Tortuga. As he was sailing around the western end of the Island of Cuba, he came unexpectedly upon three large ships bound to Havana. The pirate ship was heavily laden and ploughed the waves slowly. The Spanish ships gave chase; captured the buccaneers; stripped them; drove them with sabre-strokes under the hatches, and left them there to meditate upon the reverses of fortune and their own approaching ignominious death by hanging.

The notoriety of Barthelemy, as one of the most terrible of human monsters, had spread far and wide. He concealed his name, and his captors were not aware what a prize they had taken. The ship, containing the crew of pirates, was separated from the rest by a storm. She took refuge at Campeachy, on the western coast of the immense peninsula of Yucatan. Crowds flocked on board to see the pirates in irons. Among them came one who, in former years, had well known Barthelemy. Lifting up his hands in astonishment, he proclaimed in presence of the multitude:

"This is Barthelemy the Portuguese. He is the most wicked rascal in the world. He has done more harm to Spanish commerce than all the other pirates put together."

The glad news spread through the town. There were joyful assemblages in the streets. All hearts were glowing with the desire to take vengeance on the man who had put so many Spaniards to death. The people appealed to the governor to demand the pirate in the name of the king. He was arrested, more heavily ironed, and placed on board another vessel. A gibbet was erected upon which to hang him. The governor did not deem any trial necessary. From his cabin window Barthelemy could see the workmen building the gallows, upon which he was to be hung in chains, there to swing, in sunshine and storm, till the action of the elements should dissolve both skin and bones.

The wretch had a strange power of winning friends. The captain by whom he was captured wished to save him. Some one secretly conveyed to him a file. He soon freed himself from his irons. There were in his cabin two large earthern jars, empty and very buoyant. Carefully he closed the orifices; bound them loosely together by a strong cord; lowered them cautiously into the water, when midnight darkness covered the sea. A sentry was placed at the door of the cabin. He had fallen asleep. Fearful that he might awake and give the alarm, the pirate stealthily approached him with a huge knife in his hand. By a well-directed blow the glittering blade pierced his heart, and the sentinel died without a struggle or a groan.

The pirate noiselessly dropped himself down into the water. Grasping, with one hand, the strong cord attached to the two jars, with the other he slowly paddled himself to the shore. The current floated him to the very spot where the gibbet was erected. There it stood, in its awful gloom, with the hangman's chain dangling from its timbers. Even the iron-hearted Barthelemy shuddered, as at midnight's dismal hour, he contemplated the doom from which he was endeavoring to escape.

He took to the woods. But few of our readers can imagine the entanglements of the tropical forest through which he struggled. Conscious that blood-hounds might be put upon his track, he sought a running stream, and waded along for a great distance in the darkness. He was torn cruelly by overhanging thorns, and bruised as he stumbled over rocks and stones. As the morning dawned he hid himself in a pile of brush, half covered with water.

The windings of the stream were such that he had advanced but a short distance from the town. The tidings of his escape roused the whole population. It was known that he could not have forced his way far through the entanglement of briers and thorns and interlacing vines, in the few hours between midnight and the dawn. The whole forest seemed alive with his pursuers. A thousand slaves were shouting in their barbarian eagerness. Packs of blood-hounds were rushing to and fro, smelling at every track, and making the forest resound with their deep-mouthed bayings. The alarm-bells of the city were rolling forth their loud and solemn peals. Bands of Spanish cavaliers, with indignation in their hearts and oaths upon their lips, passed within sight of the hiding wretch; and he heard their vows of vengeance. Thus passed the wretched day. "The way of the transgressor is indeed hard."

Barthelemy, bleeding, exhausted, starving, and tormented with the bite of insects, endured these long hours of mental and bodily torture, until night again darkened the scene. With the darkness he resumed his terrified flight, he scarcely knew where. His general plan was to reach some distant seaport in disguise, where he hoped to effect his escape as a sailor. Every hour he trembled in danger of being caught ; and his only food was roots and berries, and the raw shell-fish he scraped from the rocks.

He forded streams where he was in imminent danger of being snapped up by the jaws of crocodiles. He waded through swamps, and narrowly escaped being suffocated in the mire. His shoes were torn from his feet, his clothes from his limbs. For fourteen days and nights he endured these tortures. His only guide was the roar of the ocean. He was travelling in a southwesterly direction. It was his constant endeavor to keep the ocean within hearing distance on his right.

There is manifestly no tendency in misery to make men better. The pirate, with all his woes, grew more obdurate and more cruel. " In these fourteen days," writes one of his biographers, " he must have literally tasted death and anticipated the horrors of hell." But this almost demoniac wretchedness led him to no prayers of penitence, and to no promises of amendment. They served only to whet his appetite for revenge.

7

At length he reached a large ocean bay, about one hundred and twenty miles from Campeachy, appropriately called Gulf Triste.   Here, to his immense relief, he found a large ship of buccaneers riding at anchor.   He signalled the ship, and a boat was sent to take him on board.   With feigned glee the wretch told the story of his adventures.   Not a word of penitence was uttered.   There was not the slightest recognition that the punishment he had received was merited.   On the contrary, he said to the pirates:

"I know of a ship at Campeachy, which is richly laden, and but feebly armed.   It can be captured with all ease.   Furnish me with a boat and thirty good men, and in a few days I will bring the ship and all its cargo to you."

His request was granted.   The boat was equipped, and he sailed along the coast, assuming that he was a smuggler, with contraband goods.   In eight days he reached Campeachy.   As the boat entered the harbor, the piratic character of the craft was so concealed that no suspicions were excited.   At midnight the pirates cautiously approached the doomed vessel.   As the crew supposed themselves safe in the harbor, there was but one sentry pacing the deck.   He hailed the boat.   Barthelemy, who spoke Spanish perfectly, stood upon the bows, and replied:

"We are a part of the crew. We have a boat-load of goods from the land for the vessel, upon which no duty has been paid."

At that moment the bows of the boat touched the ship. Barthelemy and his crew leaped on board, drawn cutlass in hand. One plunge of a sabre pierced the heart of the sentinel, and he fell dead. A few others who chanced to be on deck were driven below, and the hatches were closed upon them. Scarcely five minutes elapsed ere the thirty pirates, all veteran sailors, were in perfect command of the ship, and all the officers and crew were firm-ly barricaded, as prisoners, beneath the deck. No noise had been made. No alarm was given to other ships in the harbor. They raised the anchors, spread the sails, and put out to sea.

Thus suddenly the wheel of fortune turned. The trembling fugitive, in danger of the gallows, in rags and starvation, wandering through the wilder-ness, but a few days before, now found himself treading the deck of one of the finest of Spanish ships, well provisioned, well armed, and with a rich cargo stored in her hold. He was the captain and mostly the owner of the majestic craft. His dicta-torial power was recognized by thirty desperate men, ready implicitly to obey his will. The commerce of all seas was apparently within the reach of his piratical grasp.

The imprisoned crew were disposed of as these pirates usually got rid of those who were a trouble to them. They were either crowded into a boat and cut adrift, or landed upon the nearest shore, or thrown into the sea. Familiarity with misery and death rendered the pirates as insensible to human suffering as the fisherman becomes to the struggles of the fish in the bottom of his boat.

Barthelemy, instead of returning with his prize to his comrades in Gulf Triste, spread his sails for Jamaica. He was greatly elated, and boasted loudly of the still greater enterprises which he was about to undertake. With his suddenly found wealth he would create a fleet; he would have crews of five hundred men at his command; his blood-red flag should sweep all seas; he would collect an army and ravage provinces; he would seize some large island, of which he would be the monarch, with his fleets and his armies. Thus the Portuguese pirate dreamed. He did not take God into the account. God had decided otherwise.

It was a beautiful morning, as Barthelemy paced the deck, lost in these ambitious imaginings. The sky was cloudless. A fresh breeze swelled the sails, and delightfully tempered the heat of a tropical sun

A few leagues south of the Island of Cuba is the majestic Isle of Pines. Large as it is, its prominence is lost in the overpowering grandeur of its sister island. The ship was running along its southern coast.

A small cloud was seen in the southwestern horizon. Rapidly it increased in size and blackness. It was a tropical tornado. Already its roar could be heard as it ploughed and lashed the seas. The terrible gale struck the ship and whirled it along as though it had been a bubble. God was there, in his sore displeasure. What could man do? Nothing. The pirates threw themselves upon their knees, and called upon the Virgin and all the saints to come and help them. But neither Virgin nor saint came.

The ship struck the rocks—was dashed to pieces; the silver, the gold, the cargo, everything disappeared before those terrific blasts. Many were drowned. Barthelemy and a few of the crew were swept ashore by the mountain billows. Their clothes were torn from their backs. Their bodies were sorely bruised, and some of their bones broken, by being dashed against the rocks. Exhausted, panting, maimed, and half dead, Barthelemy found himself utterly beggared upon a lonely isle. This was the work of one short half-hour. This was the disposal God made of the pirates' stolen spoil.

A wretched, starving straggler, Barthelemy found his way to Jamaica. Here he enlisted as a common sailor on board a pirate ship, and we hear of him no more. Without doubt, he came to a miserable end ; and his body was probably thrown into the sea as food for sharks.

CHAPTER IX.

Francis Lolonois.

ONE of the most demoniac of those pirates who were ravaging sea and land, calling themselves buccaneers, and assuming that they were conducting a sort of legitimate warfare on their own private account, was a bold wretch by the name of Francis Lolonois. He was a Frenchman. When quite a young man, he, with other adventurers, went to the West Indies, paying for his passage, in accordance with a custom of the times, by being sold as a servant for a certain term.

Having obtained his freedom, he went to the Island of St. Domingo. Here he lived a vagabond life, sometimes hunting, and again engaged as a common sailor in the commerce of the islands. He soon acquired the reputation of being a reckless, desperate fellow, and attracted the attention of the piratic governor of the piratic rendezvous, at the Island of Tortugas. He was intrusted with the command of a small vessel, to prey upon Spanish commerce. His success was extraordinary. He became rich. So terrible were his cruelties, that his fame extended through both of the Indies. Death was the doom of his captives ; often death by torture.

He had all his wealth, gold, jewels, and goods in a great ship, armed with heavy guns. It was wrecked on the coast of Campeachy. The crew barely escaped with their lives. The angry waves dashed to pieces and swallowed up the ill-gotten gains of the pirate. The enraged Spaniards, overjoyed at the wreck, pursued those who had escaped to the dry land, and shot most of them down, mercilessly. Lolonois, disguised as a common sailor, was severely wounded. He smeared himself with blood, and feigned death. Being left on the field unburied, when the Spaniards left, he crept into the woods. It was universally believed that he was dead. The removal of such a wretch from the world was a matter of almost national rejoicing. Bonfires blazed. Cannon were fired. The undevout drank, and swore in their carousal. The devout repaired to the churches, and thanked God that the world was delivered from so cruel a pirate.

Lolonois, slowly recovering from his wounds, disguised in a Spanish habit, entered Campeachy. He made friends with a few slaves, stole a small boat, and, as his piratic biographer has it, "came to Tortugas, the common place of refuge of all sorts of wickedness, and the seminary, as it were, of all manner of pirates and thieves."

His reputation as a successful pirate was such, that he speedily obtained command of another vessel, manned by a crew of twenty-one desperadoes. On the south side of the Island of Cuba, there was a flourishing little village called Cayos. The inhabitants carried on an active trade in tobacco, sugar, and hides. Their harbor had not sufficient depth of water for large vessels. The traffic was in boats. Lolonois decided to sack the place.

It was not far across the island to Havana. Some fishermen informed the inhabitants of the approach of the pirate. In terror they sent to Havana for aid. The governor instantly dispatched a war-ship, of ten guns and seventy-five men, for their relief. The governor, astonished that Lolonois had again come to life, issued written orders, as follows :

"You are not to return until you have utterly

7*

destroyed all those pirates.   Every one is to be immediately hung, excepting Lolonois, their captain. If possible, you are to bring him alive to Havana."

The ship arrived at Cayos before the pirates had made their attack.   They cast anchor just outside the harbor.   The pirates, through their confederates, had been informed of their approach.   They captured two fishing-boats.   In the darkness of the ensuing night, they ran these boats, one on each side of the ship, and with sword and pistol leaped on board. The attack was so sudden, so entirely unprovided for, that the few of the crew who were on deck were speedily struck down or driven below.

Lolonois was in command of the ship, with all his prisoners beneath the hatches.   One by one they were brought up, and their heads cut off.   Not one was spared.   The dismembered bodies were cast into the sea.   The bloody decks were washed.   The pirate, proud of his achievement, and admired by his men, strode to and fro, the proprietor of a strong, well-armed ship, amply provided with everything he could need to aid him in his career of rapine and blood.   He wrote a letter to the governor, and sent it to him by one of his captive fishermen.   It was as follows:

"I shall never, hereafter, give quarter to any Spaniard.   I have great hopes that I shall yet have the pleasure of exercising upon your own person, the punishment I have now inflicted upon those you have sent against me. It is thus that I requite the kindness, which you designed for me and my companions."

The governor was greatly troubled and perplexed by these tidings. In his anger he took a solemn oath that he would never hereafter grant quarter to any buccaneer who should fall into his hands. But the citizens of Havana implored him not to persist in the execution of this oath. They sent a delegation to him to say:

"If this threat is followed out, the pirates will certainly do the same. They have a hundred times more opportunity of revenge than the governor can have. We must get our living by fishery. Hereafter, if this threat is executed, we shall always be at the peril of our lives."

Lolonois cruised for some time among the islands, without success. He then directed his course south toward Maracaibo, an important port in the extreme north of the South American continent. After a run of six or eight hundred miles, he reached the entrance of the vast bay which leads up to the city. Here he captured an outward-bound ship, richly laden with plate and silver from the mines.

What he did with the crew we know not. They vanished. They were probably all thrown into the sea. With ship and cargo he returned to Tortugas, where he was received with public rejoicing. Though now rich enough to live at his ease, his ambition was roused to attain still greater renown. Publicly he proclaimed to all the pirates on the island, that he was about to fit out a fleet sufficient to carry five hundred men. With these he would sail to the Spanish dominions in South America, and sack all the cities, towns, and villages along the coast. He would then capture Maracaibo itself.

All the desperadoes were eager to engage in the service of so brave and successful a leader. His fleet was soon equipped, and his gang engaged. There was a celebrated buccaneer at Tortugas, by the name of Michael Basco. He had become very rich, and filled an important governmental office. The proclamation of Lolonois fired anew his piratic zeal. He had in former years ravaged all those regions by sea and by land. He proposed to Lolonois to become a partner in his enterprise, if he could be placed in command over the land forces. The articles of agreement were soon signed. Eight vessels sailed. The crews amounted to six hundred and seventy-five men. First they directed their course to St. Domingo, and cast anchor in a little harbor called

Bayala. Here they laid in stores for their voyage, and added to their crews quite a number of vagabond Frenchmen.

On the last day of July they again spread their sails. Whether they implored the Divine blessing upon their enterprise we know not. It is not improbable. One of these pirates ran his sword through one of the crew for behaving irreverently in church.

"How can we expect," he said indignantly, "the blessing of the Virgin, if we behave in an unseemly way in her presence?"

Lolonois was admiral of the fleet. He occupied the largest ship, which mounted ten guns. They ran along the northern shore of St. Domingo, and just as they were doubling its most eastern cape, they came in sight of a large, heavily laden Spanish merchantman, bound from Spain to her colonies. But a few leagues beyond them, on the southeast side of St. Domingo, was the Island of Savona. Lolonois ordered the fleet to make a harbor there, and wait for him. He then sailed to capture the Spanish galleon.

Unexpected resistance was encountered. The Spaniards knew that they had no mercy to expect from Lolonois. They fought with desperation, preferring to die in the fierce battle, rather than be massacred by the pirates. The conflict lasted three hours. The ship was captured, and the survivors put to the sword.

Lolonois was delighted on finding the prize much richer than he had anticipated. The ship was one of the strongest and best built of Spanish vessels, and mounted sixteen guns. There were fifty men on board, some doubtless passengers. But they were no match for the reckless pirates, who were veterans in such warfare. The ship, in addition to a very rich cargo, had forty thousand dollars in coin, and ten thousand more in jewels.

Lolonois sent the ship back to Tortugas to be unloaded, and then immediately to rejoin him at Savona, to accompany the expedition. In the mean time another large ship was captured, which was bound to Hispaniola with military supplies and a sum of money to pay the garrison. The ship mounted eight guns. Being entirely surrounded by the hostile fleet, the captain surrendered without resistance.

The passengers and crew were disposed of after the pirates' usual fashion. This important capture contained seven thousand pounds of powder, a large number of muskets and other small arms, and twelve thousand dollars in specie. The governor of Tortugas, a Frenchman, ordered the cargo to be removed as quickly as possible from the ship, and

placing on board fresh provisions and a reënforce-
ment of pirates, to make good the loss of those who
had fallen in battle or by sickness, sent it back to
Savona.

Lolonois made this his flagship, as the largest
and best of the fleet. The city of Maracaibo was
situated on an island, in the lake of the same name,
and at the head of the Bay of Venezuela. The island
was about sixty miles long by thirty-six broad. The
passage to the city was by a narrow channel which
was guarded by a fort. The city contained a mixed
population of about four thousand, and carried on a
thriving trade in hides and tobacco. The dwellings
were delightfully situated, on an eminence running
along the western shore of the lake, and commanding a charming view of land and water scenery.
There was a large stone church in the place, four
capacious monasteries, and a hospital. A deputy
governor, subject to the governor at Caraccas, admin-
istered alike both civil and military affairs.

The inhabitants of the province were rich in
cattle. Immense herds grazed over the luxuriant
pastures, extending nearly one hundred miles around.
The cattle were kept mainly for their hides, which
ever commanded a ready market. Oranges, lemons,
bananas, and other tropical fruits were also very
abundant. The harbor was spacious and secure,

with the very best of timber at hand. There were many fierce Indians in the morasses and thickets around. They were comparatively powerless, though occasionally committing wolfish depredations.

About one hundred and twenty miles beyond Maracaibo, farther up the lake, there was another quite important colonial Spanish town, called Gibraltar. It had a population of about fifteen hundred. These were nearly all engaged in trade, purchasing the products of the country and sending them to other markets. On the plantations around, large quantities of sugar were made. Also immense stores of cacao, from which our word cocoa is derived, were gathered. This was the flat oblong seed of the chocolate-tree, which was one of the most important articles of commerce. They also raised a very superior kind of tobacco, which was in great demand in Europe, called priests' tobacco.

Still farther south, over a high ridge of mountains, there was another settlement called Merida. The summits of these mountains reached the region of intense cold, and were covered with perpetual snow. There were a few narrow passes through this craggy barrier, which could be traversed only by the sure-footed mule.

As soon as Lolonois entered the Gulf of Venezuela, he crept cautiously along its shores, and cast anchor behind a wooded promontory, where he was concealed from all observation. In the early dawn of the next morning he again unfurled his sails, and, with a fair wind, swept rapidly toward the Lake of Maracaibo. Secretly all the men were landed. They marched to attack, on the land side, the fort, about four or five leagues from the city, which guarded the entrance to the harbor. The defences here consisted only of stout wicker baskets, about seven feet high, filled with earth and stones. Within the fort there were sixteen heavy guns.

Notwithstanding all their precautions to attack the fort by surprise, eagle eyes had detected their approach, and had given the alarm. The commandant sent out a party of men to place themselves in ambuscade, on the only route by which the pirates could approach the fort. They were to wait until the pirates had passed that point, then, at a given signal, when the governor attacked them in front, from behind his rampart, they were to fall fiercely upon the rear of the foe.

Lolonois was a demon, with a demon's ability. He discovered the stratagem; crept around the ambuscade; attacked the detachment in its rear, and cut nearly every man to pieces. He then marched upon the fort. The Spaniards were not cowards. For three hours the battle raged, with equal desperation on either side. The reverberation of the artillery explosions alarmed the whole city. The tidings ran through the streets, exaggerated of course :

"The pirates, two thousand strong, are marching upon us."

Their atrocities were well known. The whole community fled, seizing such articles of value as they could—some in boats, some on land. Men, fainting women, and crying babes, they pressed along, in a tumultuous mass, to seek refuge in Gibraltar.

The fort was taken. Nearly all its defenders lay silent in death. The ships, having nothing more to fear, spread their sails and entered the harbor. The pirates demolished the fort, burst all the cannon they could, and spiked the rest. Lolonois practised his accustomed caution. All the adjacent thickets were swept with grape-shot. Under the protection of his guns, the boats, crowded with armed men, approached the shore. One-half landed. The others remained in the boats with guns in their hands, sabres at their sides, and pistols in their belts, to act as reserves.

To their assault there was no response. Not a human being was to be seen. The town was utterly abandoned. They found provisions in great abundance, with large quantities of wine and other intoxicating liquors. These fiend-like men then commenced a scene of feasting, which continued for several days. Their hideous orgies cannot be described. Probably they experienced something of what they called joy, in these revels. But they were only such joys as demons have. Milton describes Satan, exulting over some of his plots, as "grinning horribly a ghastly smile."

At length, satiated with their unrestrained excesses, they turned their attention to the collection of plunder. It will be remembered that it was a hundred and twenty miles to Gibraltar. There were aged men, feeble women, the sick, and newly born babes in the place. It was evident that many of these could not have escaped far, and that they must be concealed in the woods around. Neither could it be doubted that much treasure, which could not be transported to a distance, had been buried.

Gangs of armed men, amounting in all to over two hundred, were sent to explore the woods. They went out every morning, for several days, and returned at night. The first night they brought in twenty thousand dollars in coin, eight mule-loads of goods, and twenty prisoners, men, women, and children. Lolonois put several of these to the rack, to compel them to reveal where other people were concealed, and where other treasures were buried.

The fiend tortured little children, before the eyes of their parents, to extort confession.

Terrible was the condition of the Spaniards in the woods. They were suffering from every kind of exposure. They were devoured by insects. They were starving. They were watching over sick and dying friends. And they were every moment in danger of being captured, and exposed to the most horrible torments, to extort the confession of hidden treasures, when they had no treasure to hide.

The next night another party of prisoners was brought in, with other plunder. Lolonois summoned the captives before him. Drawing his sharp sabre, he, without apparently the slightest emotion, hewed one of them to pieces before the eyes of all the rest. He did this slowly and deliberately, so as to prolong life as much as possible. Then, turning to the rest, he said, with a pirate's oath:

" If you do not reveal to me where you have concealed the rest of your goods, I will serve every one of you in the same manner."

For fifteen days the pirates remained at Maracaibo. They perpetrated cruelties upon their captives so terrible, that we are compelled to spread a veil over them. They then prepared to move on to Gibraltar.

The governor of this province, which was called

Venezuela, or Little Venice, from its many marshes, resided at Merida. He was a veteran soldier, who had gained renown in the wars in Flanders. He was, moreover, somewhat of a braggadocio. The panic-stricken inhabitants of Gibraltar, sent imploring appeals to him for aid. He returned the boastful reply :

"Give yourselves no uneasiness. I will soon be with you, at the head of four hundred experienced soldiers. The pirates shall be utterly exterminated."

He reached Gibraltar with his little army. Rallying the inhabitants, he soon had at his command a force of eight hundred well-armed men. He raised two batteries to command the approaches to the town. Upon one he mounted twenty guns; upon the other eight. He also barricaded the main entrance to the town. To deceive the pirates, he opened a road which led circuitously away into impassable swamps.

As Lolonois approached the town he saw the royal banner of Spain floating over its defences, indicating that he could not take possession of the place without a battle. He called his officers around him, and thus addressed them :

"The difficulties of our enterprise have become very great. The Spaniards have had much time to prepare for their defence. They have an ample supply of ammunition, and have assembled a large number of men. Still, let us be of good courage. We must either defend ourselves like valiant soldiers, or lose our lives with all the riches we have gained. I am your captain. Do as I do. We have fought with fewer men than we have now. We have conquered foes more numerous than can possibly oppose us here. The more they are, the greater our glory, and the greater our riches. But know ye this, that the first man who gives any indication of fear, I will pistol with my own hand."

They landed from their ships, a little after midnight. In all, they numbered three hundred and eighty. Each man had a musket with thirty bullets, cartridges, a cutlass, and two or three loaded pistols in his belt. As they commenced their march, which they knew must lead to the death of some of them, they shook hands with each other in pledge of mutual support.

"Come, my brothers," said Lolonois, "follow me, and be of good courage."

Upon reaching the barricade, where they encountered a heavy fire, they turned aside into the new road which had been opened to insnare them. This battle in the woods, amid swamps and thickets, and intertwining vines and torturing thorns, can not be described. The combatants were sometimes up to their waists in mire. The entanglements of a tropical forest were such that they often could not see or approach each other. Much of the firing was at random. The air was heavy with moisture. The large guns of the batteries hurled balls and grape-shot, crashing through the branches. The sulphurous smoke settled down upon the morass in stifling folds.

The pirates cut down branches of the trees and threw them into the marsh, and thus gradually struggled through, until they reached the firm ground beyond. Here the Spaniards were again ready to receive them, with opposing batteries. Many of the pirates had perished in the swamp. Their situation now seemed desperate. Lolonois was equal to the occasion. He feigned a panic. The pirates fled tumultuously, crying out, "Save himself who can." Their flight was toward the ships.

The Spaniards, deceived by the feigned discomfiture, rushed from behind their intrenchments in eager pursuit, shouting joyfully, "They fly; they fly!" Lolonois and his men, having drawn them some distance from their batteries, turned upon them with the reckless ferocity of tigers. Their bloody work was soon accomplished. A few of the Spaniards escaped in terror to the woods. All the rest were cut down. Gibraltar was at the mercy of the pirates.

Five hundred Spaniards lay dead upon the ground. Many of those who escaped to the woods were wounded, and of these not a few died, for they were destitute of all aid in dressing their wounds. Fearing that so many dead bodies might create contagion, the pirates piled them all in two large boats, and sunk them in the lake. Still many putrefying corpses were left scattered through the woods. The pirates admit that they lost eighty in the conflict. The number was probably greater. Though most of the inhabitants escaped from the town, the victors held about one hundred and fifty prisoners, men, women, and children. They prized these captives because, by torturing them, they hoped to find where money was concealed.

The town was plundered effectually. Every nook and corner they searched. The miserable captives were shut up in the church. Gangs of men were sent out to ravage the plantations around. As provisions became scarce, the prisoners were left without any supply of bread or water. The hearts of the pirates were no more moved by their piteous moans than were the stone blocks with which the church was built. During the four weeks the pirates held Gibraltar, nearly all these captives died of actual starvation.

Their gangs ranged the woods for great distances, bringing in plunder and prisoners. Many women were brought in. Every conceivable measure was resorted to, to get money. The whole region was wantonly turned into a blackened, smouldering desert. Lolonois wished to pursue his mad career over the mountains to Merida. But a pestilential and contagious disease sprang up among his men. God's hand seemed to smite them. All were sick. Skeleton forms staggered through the streets. These men were not ignorant of the crimes they were committing. There were no loving hands to attend them in the languor of sickness, in the agonies of death. In misery, many of these wretches were burned with fever. Moaning and blaspheming they died, and their guilty souls passed to the tribunal of that God who cannot look upon sin but with abhorrence. They had seized their ill-gotten gold, and it had indeed turned to ashes in their grasp.

8

CHAPTER X.

The Plunder ; The Carousal ; and the New Enterprise.

Gibraltar in Ashes.—The Return to Maracaibo.—Division of the
Plunder.—Peculiar Scene.—Reception of the Pirates at Tortuga.
—Fiend-like Carousal.—The Pirates Reduced to Beggary.—Lolonois's New Enterprise.—The " Furious Calm."—Days of Disaster.—Ravaging the Coast.—Capture of San Pedro.

DISEASE was now cutting down the pirates faster
than the bullets or sabres of the Spaniards had done.
The victors, with an abundance of gold and booty,
were starving. The provisions in the place were all
consumed, and no fresh supplies had been brought in.
The woe-stricken wretches were quarrelling among
themselves about the division of the spoil.

Lolonois sent several parties of men into the region around, to search out fugitives from Gibraltar,
and say to them that if, within two days, they
would send in to him fifty-eight thousand dollars,
he would not burn the city ; otherwise he would lay
every building in ashes. He set at liberty several
of his prisoners also, to convey to their friends the
same information. Disappointed in the money he

had found, he still believed that large sums had been secreted by the fugitives.

The two days passed, and the money did not come. Lolonois set fire to the four corners of the town, and in six hours reduced it to ashes. By beat of drum he assembled his sick and starving men, and embarked, with all the riches which were movable. He took several captives with him, male and female. Sailing down the bay, they soon reached Maracaibo. Quite a number of the inhabitants, who had returned tremblingly to their desolated homes, he captured. Beggared as the poor creatures already were, the merciless pirate said to them:

"If you will supply me with five hundred cows, and bring me thirty thousand dollars in coin, I will spare your city. If you do not yield to this demand, I will treat your city as I have served Gibraltar. Not one building shall be left standing."

The cows were driven in. The money was paid. The people, still trembling, and not daring to manifest their joy, saw these Goths and Vandals of modern times, spread their sails, and slowly disappear in the distant horizon. But who can imagine the condition in which the town was left? The people were utterly despoiled. The homes were desolated. Widows and orphans wept and wailed, with life-long penury before them. Not a few of the people, with ruined constitutions, tottered through the streets, slowly recovering from the crushings and the lacerations of the rack. When we read of such crimes perpetrated by man upon his brother, one almost shrinks from owning himself a man. And the weary heart finds little comfort in the thought that the Spaniards deserved it all. These woes came upon them as a righteous retribution. With equal cruelty they had treated the native Cubans, the Mexicans, and the Peruvians.

The fleet sailed for Gonaves on the Island of Hispaniola. There the spoil was to be divided. Each one took a solemn oath, on the Bible, that he had concealed nothing, but that he had thrown everything into the public stock.

The gathering of the pirates for this distribution on the shores of a lovely bay of the Island of St. Domingo, must have presented a very singular spectacle. In the centre of a small verdant lawn, spread upon the grass, were bales of richest silk; cloths of great variety of texture; baskets of gold and silver coin, pistols, sabres, and muskets of the best construction, and costly jewels, and golden cups, vases, and ornaments, of which the churches had been despoiled. Around stood wild groups of heavily armed, half-naked pirates, in ferocity of aspect resembling fiends rather than men. Some countenances were disfigured with sabre gashes; while some hobbled upon crutches. Native Indians had gathered around, their long, black hair streaming in the wind, and their almost naked bodies shining like coin fresh from the mint. Several Spanish captives were there, men and women, looking sadly on at the distribution of the wealth of which their own homes had been plundered. There were also a large number of negro slaves present, with their black limbs and woolly, hatless heads, whom the pirates had brought with them to perform their heavy or menial tasks.

After an exact calculation of the whole spoil in coin, jewels, and goods, the sum total was estimated at only about five hundred thousand dollars. The property was really worth much more. But a very low estimate was placed upon most of the goods. Silver in bullion was valued at eight dollars a pound. The pirates were so ignorant of the real value of jewels, that they were prized at nothing like their real worth. Many of the stores and fabrics were also greatly undervalued.

Still, even at this low estimate, the average was over a thousand dollars for each pirate. Having finished this important business, they set sail for Tortuga, where most of them were, in a few days, to squander all the fruits of their robberies and murders, in the most riotous dissipation. After a four-weeks' voyage they reached the great rendezvous of the buccaneers. The island was crowded with gamblers and abandoned women, and every conceivable haunt of dissipation.

For three weeks Tortuga presented a spectacle of frenzied and maddened carousal, which could not have been surpassed. Men, insane with drink, rushed through the streets, slashing with their sabres in all directions. Casks of rum and wine were placed in the streets, standing on end, with the heads knocked out, and every passer-by was compelled to drink. The women, more loathsome in their wickedness than the men, reeled through the thoroughfares, in the richest silks and satins, and bedecked with glittering jewelry of which a duchess might be proud. There were oaths and brawls and bloody duels. In the delirium of these demoniac orgies gold watches were fried for a costly breakfast, and were served up with boiled pearls and jewels.

Two French vessels chanced just then to enter the port, laden with wine and brandy. This was throwing fresh fuel upon the fiery conflagration of violence, sin, and shame then raging in this miniature city of all the fiends. In the course of three weeks nearly all of these thieves had squandered everything. The riches they had gained by murder and the endurance and the infliction of untold miseries, had all passed into the hands of the gamblers, the liquor dealers, and the abandoned women. John Esquemeling, who witnessed these scenes, of which he wrote an account, says that the governor of the island bought of these. buccaneers a shipload of cocoa, for not one-twentieth part its real value. He sent it to Europe, and realized over five hundred thousand dollars from the profits. Lolonois, though fiercely brave, and with unusual native strength of mind, was a low, degraded, brutal man. He indulged in these bacchanal orgies with the meanest of his crew. No one was guilty of greater excesses. No one sank to greater depths in the mire of loathsome wickedness. Not one short month had passed ere he was reeling through the streets a filthy and ragged beggar. He was also deeply involved in debt.

He could conceive of but one mode of extrication. That was to set out upon another piratic expedition. The ravages of the pirates had been so great that the commerce of those seas was almost annihilated. .Merchant ships abandoned the ocean, unless attended by a very strong convoy. This it was which led the buccaneers to go in fleets, so as to land in sufficient strength to desolate the coasts and to sack towns and cities.

Lolonois's success had given him high reputation as a pirate. There were many on the island ready to furnish him with the means for another adventure. There were hundreds of penniless, starving wretches staggering through the streets, eager to enlist under his banner for any service whatever. Inscrutable is the mystery of God's government. He has allowed miniature hells to exist on earth, and to be crowded with demons in human form. No philosophy, no theology can explain this. The heart, in its anguish, often cries out, " O Lord, how long! how long!" Faith tremblingly and sadly exclaims, " What we know not now we shall know hereafter."

This demoniac man had sense enough to abandon his cups, until his brain was sufficiently clear to organize, even to its details, the plan for a new expedition. The enterprise was communicated to a few men of capital and unscrupulous shrewdness. Money was promptly raised. Six vessels were purchased. There were generally vessels enough in the harbor, from the prizes that were brought in, and from the large number of piratic ships.

Lolonois placarded a proclamation upon the walls, calling for volunteers. More than seven hundred eager applicants thronged his doors. Three hundred of these he took, with himself, on board his largest ship. The rest were placed in five other ships.   None but the leading officers were informed of the destination of the fleet.

They first sailed to a port called Bayaha, on the Island of San Domingo, then, as we have mentioned, called Hispaniola, or Little Spain.   Here they filled their water-casks and supplied themselves with provisions.   Thence they sailed to Matamana, a solitary but commodious harbor on the south side of Cuba.   This region was famous for its rich turtles. Native Cuban fishermen, in large boats, pursued these animals, alike valuable for their flesh and their shells.   The pirates were fond of turtle soup.   Lolonois needed a large number of boats, that he might simultaneously land the crews, from his ships, - upon any doomed city.

These poor men were mercilessly robbed of their boats, into many of which forty sailors could be crowded.   The poor fishermen, having no other means of subsistence, were overwhelmed with grief and dismay.   Lolonois was as heedless of their sorrows as he was of the manifest trouble of the tortoise when deprived of its young.   Again they spread their sails, and had advanced about three hundred miles along the southern coast of Cuba, when they were overtaken by what the Spaniards call a "furious calm."

For four weeks there was not a breath of air.
8*

Day after day the tropical sun rose, pouring down upon their blistered decks his scorching rays. The cabins became as furnaces. There was relief nowhere. The pirates swore, prayed, called upon the Virgin and the saints. All was in vain. Twenty eight days of this terrible imprisonment passed slowly away. In the mean time a strong, but imperceptible and resistless current swept them along into the Gulf of Honduras, which deeply penetrates the eastern coast of Central America. Upon leaving Cuba, the crews had been informed of the enterprise before them. They were to coast along the province of Nicaragua and plunder all its settlements, great and small.

This important Spanish province extended entirely across the Isthmus of Panama, then called Darien, from the Caribbean Sea to the Pacific Ocean. It was bounded on the north by Honduras, and on the south by Costa Rica. By the current, the pirates had been swept nearly five hundred miles west of the point which they wished to make. To return, they must coast, for that distance, along the bleak, almost uninhabited northern shore of Honduras.

The Gulf stream, pouring into the Bay of Honduras, pressed strongly against them. The calm was followed by fresh winds. But these winds were strong and contrary. It was impossible to beat against both wind and current.

Another dreary month thus passed away, as they struggled against adversity. Their provisions were consumed. Their water-casks were empty. Famine compelled them to seek the land. Entering the mouth of a large river, which they called Xagua, and which afforded a harbor for their fleet, they cast anchor. The region was quite densely inhabited by Indians, inoffensive and friendly. They had for some years conducted trade with the Spaniards, which was profitable to both parties. The Indians received, in exchange for cocoa, articles from Europe, to them of priceless value.

There were many picturesque Indian villages, scattered along the banks of the river, beneath cocoa groves, and surrounded by orange plantations and fields of Indian corn. The natives had also learned the value of swine and poultry, and were well supplied with both. When they saw the fleet approaching they were not alarmed, but rejoiced, as they were eager both to sell and to buy. They sprang into their canoes, loading them with vegetables, fruit, and fowls, and with smiling faces paddled out to the ships.

How shall I describe the scenes which ensued? Burke, I think, says, " to speak of atrocious crime in mild language is treason to virtue." These incarnate fiends shot down the poor Indians, men and women, in mere wantonness—for the fun of' it. Boats filled with these armed demons then went ashore. They shot the men, as they could. They took many women captives. They stripped the Indians of everything, swine, poultry, fruit, corn, and then burned their villages.

The renowned French historian, Michelet, though an unbeliever in the Christian religion, says that when writing the account of the atrocities perpetrated by the ancient nobility of France upon the peasantry, he found himself praying to God that there might be some future punishment, where these tyrants, clothed in purple and sumptuously feeding, might receive the due award for their crimes.

The amount of food obtained, furnished but a few days' supply for seven hundred hungry mouths. Lolonois decided to remain there at anchor until the weather should prove more favorable. In the mean time he sent his armed boats up the river and along the shores in both directions for indiscriminate plunder. The whole region was devastated. The terrified Indians fled in all directions, taking with them what they could. Notwithstanding the utmost diligence of the plunderers, they could each day bring in barely enough for the day's supply.

When the pirates had got everything here upon which they could lay their hands, they weighed anchor and worked their way slowly along the coast several leagues, until they reached a harbor called Port Cavallo. This was a trading-post of the Spaniards. They had here two capacious store-houses, to hold the goods which they received from the natives, and the articles brought from Spain to give to them in return. Ships occasionally arrived with fresh supplies, and to transport the purchases to Spain.

There was at that time in the harbor a large Spanish ship, which mounted twenty-four guns and sixteen mortars. But this one ship could make no effectual resistance against the fleet of the pirates. It was immediately seized. Its cargo had been mostly unloaded and carried back into the country, to be exchanged, in barter, with the Indians. They stripped the store-houses, and plundered and destroyed all the adjacent dwellings. They captured many prisoners, and put them to dreadful torture to compel them to confess, often when they had nothing which they could disclose.

Lolonois hacked them to pieces with his sabre; tore out their tongues; dislocated their joints with the rack. He committed upon them, writes Esquemeling, "the most insolent and inhuman cruelties that ever heathens invented, putting them to the cruelest tortures they could imagine or devise. Oftentimes it happened that some of these miserable prisoners, being forced thereunto by the rack, would promise to discover the places where the fugitive Spaniards lay hidden; which, being not able afterward to perform, they were put to more enormous and cruel deaths than they who were killed before."

About twenty miles from Port Cavallo there was, not far from the coast, a small but thriving town called San Pedro. Lolonois took three hundred men and commenced his march to sack the place. He left his lieutenant, Moses Vauclin, in command of the men who were left behind with the ships. A few boats, well armed, were sent along the coast to render such asssistance as might be needful. Before starting he told his troops that he would always march at their head, sharing all their dangers; but that he would cut down the first one who manifested any disposition to retreat or gave the least sign of fear.

There were no broad roads to traverse, but only intricate mule-paths, which could with difficulty be followed through the dense growth of a tropical forest. Two Spanish captives were taken as guides. The inhabitants of San Pedro, informed of their approach, sent out a party of men to intrench themselves in ambush on the way. The narrow road led through gigantic forests with almost impenetrable thickets of brambles and thorns and interlacing vines on either side.

When the pirates had advanced about nine miles, the Spaniards in ambush opened fire upon them. Taking deliberate aim, at the first discharge many of the pirates were killed, and more wounded. The battle which ensued was desperate on both sides. Lolonois, assuming that his guides had led him into the ambush, instantly cut them both down.

The fury of the pirates was irresistible, and the Spaniards were put to flight. They left behind many dead and wounded. The pirates put to death all of the wounded, excepting one or two whom they reserved as guides. These they threatented with instant death if they did not guide them safely to the city. There was but one available path leading there. Intimidated by the awful threats of Lolonois, when he asked them if there were other ambuscades farther on, they said that there were. He then asked them if there were not some other path to the city, by which they could avoid the ambuscades. The guides replied that they did not know of any.

Lolonois was in a great rage. He drew his sabre and cut one of the captives to pieces before the rest. He cut out his heart, seized it, and began to gnaw it, like a ravenous wolf. Then turning to the other captives, he said :

" I swear unto you, by the death of God, that I will serve you all the same way if you do not lead me to the city by another route."

Terror-stricken, the poor creatures endeavored to lead through the thickets. But they could not force their way. Lolonois was compelled to return to the former path. But he swore the most terrible oaths that the Spaniards should pay dearly for causing him so much trouble. The same evening they encountered another ambuscade. Lolonois fell upon his foes with the same fury with which the tiger leaps upon its prey, apparently regardless of his own life, if he can but destroy his victim. In less than an hour the Spaniards were routed, and scarcely one escaped.

The pirates, though victorious, were faint with fatigue, hunger, and thirst. They threw themselves down in the woods that night, and, probably with consciences utterly seared, slept that sound sleep which toil and danger often bring.

The next morning, at break of day, the pirates resumed their march. Ere long, they came upon a third ambuscade. This was much stronger and better planned than either of the others. The pirates had provided themselves with a large number of fire-balls, which they showered down with much effect upon their foes. Lolonois seemed inspired with the fury of a madman. He foamed at the mouth and gnashed his teeth as he shouted:

"No quarter; no quarter! The more we kill here, the less we shall meet in the town."

But few of the Spaniards escaped to San Pedro. Nearly all were killed; for the wounded were immediately dispatched. The pirates had now arrived within sight of the town. There was but one narrow approach, and that the Spaniards had thoroughly barricaded. The thorny shrubs which grew densely around were utter impenetrable. Nothing remained for the pirates but to make an instantaneous attempt to storm the works. Several times they were driven back, but only to renew the conflict with increasing fury. This conflict, of fiend-like ferocity, continued four hours. The white flag of surrender was then unfurled from the town.

After a brief parley, the citizens agreed to yield up the town, without further resistance, if they were allowed two hours to retire with such articles as they could take away with them. Lolonois, who in this last battle had lost forty men, agreed to the terms. The Spaniards, with their wives and children, fled, with such few articles as they could carry in their arms or on the backs of mules.

CHAPTER XI.

The End of Lolonois's Career.

LOLONOIS waited patiently the two hours which
he had agreed to grant the inhabitants to vacate the
place.   He then entered the town, and, in perfidious
disregard of the spirit of his engagement, dispatched
armed bands to pursue the fugitives, and not only
rob them of everything in their possession, but also
to bring them all back as prisoners.

This was done.   But the thieves were much disappointed in the amount of plunder they found.
San Pedro was by no means a wealthy place.   The
inhabitants gained a comfortable but frugal living,
mainly by raising indigo.

The pirates, in their great disappointment, supposed, as usual, that much treasure had been concealed.   They therefore put their captives to the

torture, to force them to point out the places of concealment. Though many died under the terrible infliction, no discoveries were made. The pirates, in revenge, laid the town in ashes. In this fruitless expedition they lost about one hundred men in killed and wounded, endured great suffering, and inflicted inconceivable misery upon their brother man.

About one hundred and fifty miles southwest of San Pedro was the rich old Spanish town of Guatemala, capital of the capacious province of that name. Lolonois, in his frenzied state of mind, was determined to send back to the ship for reënforcements, and then to march upon Guatemala. But his piratic crew refused to accede to so insane a proposal.

For eighteen days these marauders lingered around San Pedro, before they applied the torch. They then, leaving only ruins and misery behind them, returned to the fleet. Those left there had employed their time in robbing the Indians, burning their huts, and inflicting all manner of evil upon their families. Some of these captives on the coast informed them that about sixty miles west, at the mouth of the great river of Gautemala, called Montagua, there was a large Spanish ship, which had recently arrived from Spain.

As soon as Lolonois arrived, several boats filled with pirates, thoroughly armed, were sent to capture the ship. The Indians had informed the inmates of the ship of the presence of the pirates. Anticipating a visit, they had made such preparations as they could to repel them. The ship mounted forty-two guns, was well supplied with small arms, and had a select crew of one hundred and thirty fighting men.

The pirates, after opening fire upon the ship for some time, from one of their vessels with twenty-two heavy guns, sent four boats, each carrying about forty men, to clamber over the bulwarks of the ship, cutlass in hand, at four points. In this assault they were much aided by a dense fog, which, blending with the smoke of the powder, had settled down so heavily as to conceal the approach of the boats.

The crew were sailors. The pirates were veteran soldiers. The conflict was like that between well-trained regulars and raw militia. Very soon the pirates were masters of the ship, and the deck was covered with the dead and the dying. But again these wretched plunderers were disappointed. The vessel had been almost entirely unladen. Its remaining cargo consisted of twenty thousand reams of paper and one hundred tons of iron bars. Neither of these were of any use to the pirates. The ship, however, with its great guns, its small arms, and its abundance of ammunition, was deemed a great acquisition. But God so ordered it that even this capture proved a calamity rather than an aid to the enterprises of Lolonois.

The desperate leader of this piratic gang called a general council, and insisted upon the march across the country to Guatemala. It was a stormy session. The general discontent was expressed in curses and oaths, and bitter recriminations. . Nearly one-fourth of their number had perished. They had endured almost intolerable sufferings. As yet they had accomplished nothing in the way of enriching themselves. And now they were urged to embark on a desperate enterprise, where they certainly would be exposed to the greatest hardships, and where all would probably perish.

These men had embarked from Tortuga, with the expectation that dollars and doubloons would be gathered by shovelfuls. They were now poor, hungry, mutinous, angry with each other, and the prospect before them was discouraging in the extreme. All thoughts of ravaging Nicaragua, in their present state of despondency and with the great diminution of their numbers, were relinquished.

Moses Vauclin had charge of the splendid ship recently captured. His ship was a swift sailer. With one or two officers conspiring with him, and his crew of nearly one hundred and fifty men gained over, they decided to run away and cruise on their own account. In the night they silently raised their anchors, took advantage of a fresh breeze, and, before the morning's dawn, disappeared beyond the horizon. When Lolonois awoke and found that he was thus deserted, the madman paced his deck in a frenzy of impotent rage.

The fugitives could not endure the idea of returning penniless to Tortuga, where they would thus become the laughing-stock of the whole community. The wind favored them. They ran along the coast of Honduras and Nicaragua to the south, until they reached the province of Costa Rica. In their desperation, being resolved to accomplish something, they landed and attacked and sacked the poor little town of Veruguas, killing many of the inhabitants. The furniture in the huts of these poor people was of no value to them. They gained only the pitiful sum of about forty dollars' worth of gold, which the slaves had washed out from the mud of the rivers.

This region was low and unhealthy. The Spanish grandees, who owned the mines and cultivated them by the compulsory labor of slaves, had their residences in the more healthy region of Nata, at the distance of several leagues. The Spaniards began to gather in large numbers to repel the invaders. The pirates, alarmed, fled to their ship, and returned to Tortuga. Here they disbanded, and we learn no more of the fate of this portion of Lolonois's army. Each one, doubtless, found his way, through crime and misery, to death and to the judgment-seat of Christ.

Lolonois was left at Port Cavallo, with but about two hundred men. He was almost destitute of food; most of his ammunition was consumed; many were sick from the insalubrity of the climate, and all were dissatisfied, clamorous, and angry.

Lolonois remained for some time in the Bay of Honduras. Esquemeling writes: " His ship was too great to get out at the time of the reflux of those seas, which the smaller vessels could more easily do."

Every day he sent his boats ashore for food. The fruit of the region was soon all consumed, and they fed on the flesh of parrots and monkeys. Slowly working their way along the coast by the night breeze, they found the days generally calm. Casting anchor in the morning, they sought provisions in fishing and hunting. At length they rounded the extreme eastern point of Honduras, at Cape Gracios à Dios. Just beyond, a group of islands called the Pearl Islands, hove in sight.

The indomitable Lolonois was still determined to ravage a portion of the rich province of Nicaragua.

It was his plan to anchor his vessels at the mouth of the river St. John, by which the great inland sea called Lake Nicaragua empties its waters into the ocean, and then to ascend the majestic stream in his armed boats. While sailing among the islands in an almost unknown sea, he ran his ship upon a sandbank. All his efforts to float the ship again were in vain. With infinite labor he took out the heavy guns and the iron ; but the ship had sunk too deep in the sand to be moved.

Finding his ship thus hopelessly wrecked, he decided to break her to pieces, and with her planks and nails to construct a large and strong boat with which he could ascend the river. The crew all landed upon an island, built themselves huts in the Indian fashion, and, with a reckless disregard of misfortune, commenced building their boat. Expecting that it might be necessary to spend some time there, they dug gardens and planted peas and other vegetables.

The island upon which they were was large, and was inhabited by a very fierce tribe of Indians. But their clubs and lances armed with crocodiles' teeth were but impotent weapons, when met by the muskets, the pistols, and the sabres of the pirates. The Indians had doubtless heard of the atrocities committed by these rovers over seas and land, for they fled precipitally at their approach, and taking to their canoes, actually abandoned the island.

The vegetables which the pirates sowed grew rapidly. It was six months before their large boat, or rather small vessel, was completed. In the mean time they raised quite large crops of beans, wheat, potatoes, and bananas. It is strange that this experience did not teach them that they could much more easily and happily gain a living by honest than by dishonest means. But still they clung to the misery of piracy, with its crime, its cruelty, and its wild revelry.

When the vessel was finished, Lolonois took one-half of his company, or about one hundred men, in this vessel and a ship which remained to him, and sailed for the mouth of St. John's River. The other half were left behind. As nothing was said about the other smaller vessels of the fleet, it is probable that they all had been lost in the various casualties of their voyage, or had escaped with Vauclin. It was known that the Indians on the river had very large boats, formed by hollowing out the trunk of a gigantic tree. These boats, ingeniously made, and the result of almost incredible labor, would accommodate forty or fifty warriors. It was Lolonois's intention to rob the Indians of some of their boats, send them back to the island for the pirates who were left behind, and then, with his whole party, to ascend the river in an invincible fleet.

Lolonois set sail, and in a short time reached the mouth of the St. John's River. But the Indians, who had fled from the island, had spread the news, all along the coast, of the arrival of the terrible pirates. Spaniards and Indians were thus influenced to combine to meet them wherever they might land. Their progress in building their vessel had been carefully watched by spies, who effectually concealed themselves from sight.

As Lolonois and his party entered the river they expected to take the inhabitants by surprise, and had not the slightest idea of being surprised themselves. But their vessel had been watched as it approached. There was a pleasant sheltered cove surrounded by the luxuriant and magnificent growth of the tropics. It could not be doubted that this spot would be selected for their landing-place. Nature had decked it with the charms of Eden. Here a well-armed band of Spaniards and Indians posted themselves in ambuscade. Palm-trees and cocoanut-trees rose gracefully around them. Golden oranges and lemons hung profusely from orchards which God had planted and cultivated. Birds of every variety of brilliant plumage flitted from bough to bough. All the sights and sounds of nature seemed to say that God had made this for a happy world; that his children might live here in fraternal love, surrounded by abundance.

The pirates cast anchor in the lovely cove, where the glittering sand could be seen fathoms deep, beneath the water of crystal clearness. They had several small boats. All were impatient to reach the land. Scarcely had their boats touched the beach, and the men were clustered together in landing, when the Eden-like scene of peace and loveliness, was changed into an earth-like scene of noise and tumult and smoke and groans and blood.

There was a sudden discharge of musketry from the surrounding thickets within half gun-shot. The Spaniards had armed the Indians and taught them to take unerring aim. Both Spaniards and savages united in the most hideous yells to appal the pirates with an idea of their superior numbers. Rapidly the unseen foe continued the discharge of the murderous bullets. Scarcely a minute elapsed ere many were dead, weltering in their blood. Others were severely wounded. And still the pitiless storm of leaden hail swept through the group, crashing bones and tearing nerves, and still the yells of the invisible assailants resounded through the forest. There was not a breath of air. The sulphurous smoke settled down, half concealing the awful spectacle of blood and death.

Even the demoniac pirates were so panic-stricken that they dared not by a charge rush into the very jaws of destruction. Every instant their comrades were dropping. There was no time for thought. Those not yet struck leaped into the boats and pushed from the shore, leaving the dying and the dead in the water and upon the sand. Still the pelting storm pursued them till they were beyond gun-shot reach.

Lolonois, the greatest villain of them all, escaped unharmed. Did God preserve him that he might drain to the dregs the cup of mental and bodily misery which he had so often presented to the lips of others? In view of what he had yet to endure, he might indeed have deemed it one of the richest of mercies had a bullet pierced heart or brain, and laid him instantly with the dead.

The wretch had sufficient intelligence to perceive that he was ruined. There was no longer any hope of ravaging Nicaragua. His provisions were exhausted. He had no doubt that the whole coast was armed against them. As by lightning-bolts he had lost nearly one-half of his crews. Desponding, starving, he divided his company into two bands, to sail where they could, to save themselves from perishing by hunger.

Lolonois, with thirty or forty men, ran along the

THE END OF SOLONIS.

coast toward South America, till they reached the region of Carthagena. They were few and feeble, and feared to land. The atrocities committed by the pirates were everywhere known. Upon every league of the coast either the Spaniards or the Indians were watching for their approach, ready to give the general alarm, and to summon all who could be rallied to repel them.

Their water-casks were empty. They must obtain fresh water or perish of thirst. Having passed the Gulf of Darien, he ventured to land, taking his whole force with him. It so chanced, or Providence so ordered it, that he landed on the territory of one of the fiercest tribes of Indians known in all that region. They were called Bravos. The Spaniards had never been able to subdue them. These fierce and cunning savages surrounded the pirates and shot down or captured the whole band. Still not a bullet struck Lolonois. He was reserved for another doom. Most of the captured pirates were burned alive. But the savages thought that too merciful a death for the leader of the band.

They bound him to a tree. Hour after hour, according to their custom, they tortured him, being careful to prolong his sufferings by not piercing any vital point. Every device of savage ingenuity was resorted to, which might extort agony from his quivering nerves.   There was no one to pity.   Even humanity says he merited it all.   At last the savages, howling in frenzied merriment around him, and raising new shouts whenever they could force from him new shrieks of agony, weary with the demoniac pastime, hewed off one of his arms and threw it into the fire.   They then hewed off the other and committed it to the flames.   The same was done with his legs.   Then his head was cut off, and with his memberless body was consumed to ashes.   Such was the earthly life, and such the earthly death of Francis Lolonois.   We say the *earthly* life.   There is another life.   There is a second death.   Lolonois still lives in the spirit-land.   What is his character there?

The pirates who remained upon the island, weary of waiting for the boats, were quite in despair.   But one morning their eyes were cheered by the sight of a very large ship passing near by.   Their signals were seen and the ship hove to.   It proved to be a pirate bound for the sack of Carthagena.   The captain was delighted to add a hundred desperate fellows to his gang.   The pirates, who had now been ten months upon the island, and were in a state of great despondency, destitution, and suffering, were as glad as such wicked men could be in this escape from their miseries, and this new opportunity to renew their ravages.

There were several Carthagenas in the various provinces of the New World. The one they were to attack was in Honduras, on the river Segoria, which empties into Cape Gracios à Dios. Their plan was to cast anchor in the mouth of the river, and ascend the stream in boats. The piratic captain was greatly elated, for he had now at his command between five and six hundred men.

They reached the mouth of the river in safety. A few men were left in charge of the ship. Over five hundred were crowded into the boats. There was no space for storing provisions; neither was it thought necessary. It was supposed that an ample supply of food would be found in the villages on the river banks. But the Indians transmitted intelligence with almost the rapidity of telegraphic dispatches. From village to village the tidings ran.

The Indians, conscious of their inability to contend with the well-armed pirates, fled. They took with them all the food they could. The rest they destroyed. The invaders found themselves reduced almost to starvation. They ate roots and herbs, and even the leaves of the trees. A blazing tropical sun poured its rays down upon their crowded open boats, blistering their skin with the intense heat. Sickness came, with languor, pain, wretchedness. Their own crimes were chastising them with scorpion lashes.

There was but misery in those boats, with universal discontent and oaths and fightings. In their despair they landed, five hundred maddened, starving men, hating themselves and hating each other. They hoped that at a little distance back from the river they might find some villages which had not been abandoned. In this they were disappointed. The natives watched them closely, and fled before them.

They commenced a retreat back to the ship. Many died. Many fell by the wayside and were captured by the savages. The Indians pursued them, watching every opportunity to strike a blow. They were too weak to resist. They could scarcely wield a paddle or lift a musket. Their starvation and misery was so great that they resolved to kill and devour the first Indian they could meet. But this kind of game kept beyond the reach of their balls. They ate their shoes, their leather belts, even the sheaths of their swords.

At length a skeleton band reached the ship. There was but little food there. Still they spread their sails, and disappeared. We hear of them no more.

CHAPTER XII.

The Female Pirate, Mary Read.

IN writing the account of Captain Kidd and
other conspicuous pirates of his day, we have had
occasion to refer to many ancient documents. In
their examination we have come across numerous
incidents, extraordinary in their character. Among
these are the well-accredited careers of two female
pirates, Mary Read and Ann Bonny. Their lives
illustrate the common remark that fact is often
stranger than fiction. We are mainly indebted, for
the wild and wondrous story of their adventures,
to the narrative of Captain Charles Johnson. The
second edition of his valuable history of the pirates
now lies before me. It was published in London, in
the year 1724. In the preface to this work the writer
says:

9*

" As to the lives of our two female pirates, we must confess they may appear a little extravagant, yet they are nevertheless true. But as they were publicly tried for their piracies, there are living witnesses enough to justify what we have laid down concerning them. It is certain that we have produced some particulars which were not publicly known. The reason is we were more inquisitive into the circumstances of their past lives than other people who had no other design than that of gratifying their own private curiosity. If there are some incidents and turns in their stories, which may give them a little the air of a novel, they are not invented or contrived for that purpose. It is a kind of reading this author is but little acquainted with. But as he himself was exceedingly diverted with them, when they were related to him, he thought they might have the same effect on the reader."

A young girl in one of the seaports in England, about one hundred and seventy-five years ago, married a sailor. Not many months after their marriage the sailor left home for a distant voyage, and never returned. She never knew whether he deserted her, or whether he died far away. When he sailed she was expecting soon to become a mother. She resided with her husband's relatives. In due time the child was born, and proved to be a boy. .

The mother was a young, light, trifling girl, of fair reputation, and not very careful habits, who ere long found that she was about to become a mother again. As the months advanced, in order to conceal her shame, she took leave of her husband's relatives, informing them that she was going to visit her own friends at some distance in the country. Her little boy, who accompanied her, was then not a year old.

Soon after her departure her son died; and she, ere long, gave birth to another child, who proved to be a girl. The mother remained away four years. In the mean time she had very little communication with her former relatives; and they had no knowledge of the death of her son, or of the birth of her daughter. Her husband's mother was still living. She was in comfortable circumstances, though aged and infirm, with impaired vision. The mother of the little girl thought that if she could pass her child upon the aged mother of her husband, as his son, whom she had seen and loved, the child would be liberally provided for. But the changing of a girl into a boy seemed to be an insuperable difficulty. She, however, dressed the child up as a boy, and presented it to her mother-in-law as her husband's son. No one suspected the deception. The good old woman embraced it cordially, and was anxious to adopt it as her own, promising amply to provide for it.

But the cunning mother declared that it would break her heart to part with the child, that she could not be separated from it. It was, however, agreed that the child should reside with the mother, while the supposed grandmother should allow a crown a week for its maintainance. The child was thus brought up as a boy. The mother watched over her with the utmost vigilance, instructing her to guard the secret of her sex with the greatest possible care.

At length the grandmother died: the little property vanished, and the mother and child were in a situation of much destitution. The child was now thirteen years of age, bright, well formed, and good looking, with a thoroughly boyish character. There was a French lady, in the neighborhood, who took the child into her service, as page and footboy. The feminine nature was soon entirely swallowed up in manly yearnings and desires.

She was bold and strong, and developed a roving disposition and a love for wild adventures. We are not informed of her masculine name. Her feminine name was Mary. For convenience' sake we will call her Frank, during the period of her disguise. Frank enlisted on board a man-of-war, and served in the capacity of a sailor, energetically and successfully, for several months. No one was more nimble in running up the shrouds, or in taking in reefs when the majestic fabric was tossed like a bubble upon the gigantic waves.

Soon weary of this employment, Frank, apparently a graceful, well-built boy of nineteen, enlisted in the army. Shouldering a musket, and very rapidly becoming a proficient in military drill, she fell into the line and accompanied a regiment of foot to Flanders. She was in several severe battles. It is said that in time of action, no one of the regiment conducted with more reckless bravery. She seemed to lose all consciousness of danger, and, if we may so express it, in a state of frenzy which rendered her calm by its very intensity, was as regardless of shells, cannon-balls, and bullets, as though they had been snowflakes.

She would certainly have been promoted could merit have secured that honor. But in mercenary England, at that time, no commission could be obtained but such as was purchased with gold. Ever consumed by restless desires, Frank, ere long, succeeded in exchanging the infantry service for a situation in a regiment of horse. Here Frank's lithe and graceful figure showed to great advantage. There was not in the company a bolder rider, a more dexterous manager of the war-horse than she.

Even the steed she strode seemed conscious that he bore a more than ordinarily precious burden. There was something in the gentle tones of her voice, and in her caressings, which the proud horse seemed to recognize, ever welcoming her approach with his neighings. The officers greatly admired Frank, and felt a strange kind of interest in the unboastful yet chivalric heroism he displayed in several bloody engagements.

The old Latin maxim hath it, " Amor omnia vincit," *Love conquers all things*. It so happened that there was in the ranks a comrade, ever riding by the side of Frank, who was a very handsome young Fleming, about twenty-three years of age. He was a gentle, lovable fellow, and equally brave as his gentle, lovable comrade, for whom he formed a very strong friendship. He slept in the same tent, and by the side of Frank. They were ever together, helping each other.

The girl nature of Frank could not resist all this. She fell desperately in love with the fair-faced, flaxen-haired Flemish boy. Whenever the young Fleming was ordered out upon any party, Frank insisted upon accompanying him ; and the more desperate the adventure, the more resolute were her importunities to share the peril with him. It was observed that frequently Frank would rush into the greatest danger, simply that she might be near her friend, even when she could render him no assistance.

This extraordinary devotion of Frank to her comrade the Fleming, attracted the attention of the whole company. As no one suspected, in the slightest degree, her disguise, it was supposed that there must be a vein of insanity in the nature of the quiet, retiring, handsome soldier boy.

Mary had a very fair complexion. One morning, in her tent, she pretended to be asleep, and allowed her drapery so to fall as partially to expose her fair and beautiful bosom. The Fleming gazed upon the spectacle bewildered equally with astonishment and delight. Her sex was revealed. The young Fleming, accustomed to the license of the camp, kept the secret; but was surprised to find that he could not approach the fair sharer of his tent with the slightest movement of indelicacy.

Mary was instinctively proud; and for years she had so resolutely triumphed over so many temptations, that she could not be led to degrade herself. She felt proud in the consciousness that, thus far, there was not a single blot upon her fair fame. She was more than ready to be wooed and won as a wife.

But no lady in the parlor of home could be more modest and reserved in receiving the addresses of a lover, than was Mary in her intercourse with the lover who shared her tent. Her good sense taught her that if she would secure and maintain his love, she must, by indubitable proof, win his highest confidence and respect.

Strange as this story may appear to the reader, there seems to be no reason to doubt its accuracy. The young Fleming urged her to become his wife. To this proposal she did not long hesitate to accede. They plighted their mutual faith. The campaign soon ended. The regiment went into winter quarters. The two lovers united their purses, and purchased a woman's wardrobe as the bridal outfit for Frank. She assumed her new garb, and announced her sex to her amazed fellow-soldiers.

These strange tidings created great excitement in the camp. They were publicly married. A great crowd attended the espousals. Many of the officers assisted in the ceremony, and the bride received many presents. There was a general contribution among all her comrades to raise a sum to assist her in commencing housekeeping. Frank had been a universal favorite, and had secured the esteem of all.

Being thus comfortably established, they both had a desire to quit the service. The circumstances were so romantic and peculiar that they found no difficulty in obtaining their discharge. They then established themselves in Flanders, in a restaurant or eating-house. Their little inn, kept with British neatness, was near the Castle of Breda, and was known far and wide by the name of its sign, "The Three Horse-Shoes." They had a large run of custom, and were particularly patronized by the officers of the army.

They were very happy. But prosperity, in this world, does not long shine upon any one. Peace came. The army was dispersed. There were no longer any guests at "The Three Horse-Shoes;" and Mary's husband was taken sick, and died. She was left childless and without any means of support. She had been trained to the pursuits of manhood. She was a young widow, but little more than twenty years of age. As a woman, she knew not in what direction to turn to obtain a living. Only for a few months had she assumed the character of a woman, and worn the garb of a woman. All the rest of her years she had worn the dress and followed the pursuits of a man. As a man, there were many opportunities opening before her, and all congenial ones, for obtaining a support.

Again she assumed her masculine attire, sold out all her effects, and with gold enough in her purse to meet her immediate wants, set out for Holland, where, a perfect stranger, she entered again upon her masculine career, without any fear of detection. Quartered upon one of the frontier towns of Holland there was an English regiment of foot. It was a time of peace, and the soldiers were living in indolence, with nothing to do. It was easy, under these circumstances, to join the regiment, and to purchase a release, at any time when one might wish to do so.

Again Frank enlisted. After a few months, weary of the monotonous life, she obtained a discharge, and shipped herself, as a common sailor, on board a vessel bound for the West Indies. It was a Dutch vessel. Frank was the only English person on board. On the voyage, an English pirate hove in sight and ran down upon the merchant-ship. The pirate was so well armed, and such a throng of desperate men crowded its decks, that resistance would have been but folly. The ship was captured without a struggle.

The pirate, after plundering the ship of all its treasures, impressed the English Frank as an addition to its own crew : and then turned the despoiled ship adrift, inflicting no personal injury upon the officers or sailors. As we have before mentioned, these buccaneers did not regard themselves, at that time, neither were they regarded by others, as ordinary pirates would now be judged. They were acting in a certain sense under the royal commission. They were authorized to plunder all *Spanish* ships. And if they occasionally made a mistake, and did not read the flag aright, it was an irregularity not entirely unpardonable.

This piratic ship continued its cruise of plundering for several months. Frank had been impressed on board, and could not escape had she wished to do. Probably her moral sense was not sufficiently instructed to lead her to make any remonstrances, which would, of course, have been entirely unavailing, or to feel any special qualms of conscience. Accustomed as she ever had been to the masculine dress, and to all the habits of the sailor and the soldier, she did not feel the least embarrassment in her new situation. No one moved about the decks or clambered the shrouds with more free motion than Frank.

Just about this time the royal proclamation, to which we have referred, came out, offering pardon to all pirates who would surrender themselves, excepting Kidd and Avery. The crew of this ship of buccaneers decided to take advantage of this proclamation.

The West-Indian group, called the Bahamas, consists of several hundred islands of various magnitudes. One of these, San Salvador, was the first land, in the New World, which was discovered by Columbus. The most important of the group, from its excellent harbor, and its situation in reference to Florida, is New Providence. The island was originally settled by the English in 1629. It was captured by the Spaniards, and the English were expelled, in the year 1641. The merciless Spaniards murdered the governor, and committed many other great outrages. Again, in the year 1666, the thunders of British broadsides echoed along its shores, and the banners of England were again unfurled over its mountains and fertile vales. Forty-seven years passed away, over this war-cursed globe, when, in 1703, a united fleet of French and Spanish ships expelled the English, and, neglecting to take military possession of the island, it became a rendezvous for pirates, where scenes of revelry, sensuality, and crime were perpetrated which no pen can describe.

Thus for eighty years Heaven looked down upon its enormities. It was then again formally ceded to the English, and has since remained in their possession. At the time of which we are writing, England held the island, and a British governor was in command there. The buccaneers, with their purses well filled with gold, the result of their cruises as freepooters, ran into the harbor of New Providence. They made their surrender to the governor, and received the royal pardon.

Frank had been but a short time among them. Her purse was not a heavy one. It is not known that she added anything to it during her short and compulsory cruise on board the buccaneer. Her money was soon expended. The British governor at New Providence was at that very time fitting out several armed vessels to cruise against the Spaniards, as privateersmen. He was eager to enlist any of the bold buccaneers who could be lured to enter that service. Nothing could be more congenial to the wishes of these desperate men. Frank, being out of employment, enlisted as privateersman, on board of one of these Government ships.

CHAPTER XIII.

Anne Bonny, the Female Pirate.

THERE was upon the island of New Providence,
at that time, a very consummate villain by the name
of Rackam. He had been captain of a pirate ship,
and shared his cabin with his wife, a very depraved
woman, who was disguised in boy's clothes. She
apparently discharged the duties of a cabin-boy.
This Captain Rackam had taken advantage of the
king's proclamation, had surrendered himself as a
pirate, and had received a pardon.

Eagerly he enlisted, with his wife in man's garb,
as a messmate, in one of the governor's privateers.
No one on board the ship was aware of the sex of
his companion. She was truly his wife, and her real
name was Anne Bonny. She had been a rude, ungovernable girl, and her parents were so displeased
that she should have married such a worthless

wretch as Rackam was known to be, that they would no longer recognize her. Having nothing to live upon, she assumed a sailor's dress, and they both shipped for New Providence. He doubtless intended there to resume the career of a pirate.

Rackam and Anne Bonny enlisted on board the same ship. Here then there were two women in male attire, neither of whom had any suspicion of the real sex of the other. No one could associate with such companions as those of Mary Read, or encounter the influences to which she was constantly exposed, without becoming in some degree corrupted.

The privateersman had been out but a few days when Rackam, who had many of his old confederates on board, formed a conspiracy, rose upon the officers, set them adrift, seized the ship, and turned to his old trade. Mary Read, in the character of Frank, was, as we have mentioned, a very handsome young fellow. The captain's cabin-boy, Anne Bonney, fell desperately in love with Frank, and revealed to *him*, as she supposed, her sex. She approached Frank with all the seductions and allurements with which Potiphar's wife solicited Joseph. Thus importuned, Frank confided to her that she was also a woman in disguise. This led to increased intimacy between the two young sailor women.

Captain Rackam became intensely jealous of·his wife, in consequence of her familiarity with Frank. He threatened Anne that he would certainly cut Frank's throat. Anne, well aware of the desperate character of the pirate, felt constrained, that she might save Mary's life, to let the captain into the secret also. He did not divulge it, knowing that she might be exposed to very cruel treatment from the unprincipled wretches who thronged his decks.

But again the all-devouring passion took possession of the bosom of Frank. Many vessels were captured. After being plundered they were generally turned adrift again, with their crews. If the pirates, however, found on board these ships any one who could be of use to them, he was detained on board their ship. It so chanced that one day they took a ship where there was a young English artist. Rackam, thinking that the artist might be of service to him, in sketching scenes and drawing charts, detained him as a captive. He was a genteel young fellow, handsome, of fascinating manners, very skilful with his pencil, and possessed of very attractive conversational powers. Frank and the young artist were instinctively drawn toward each other.

And when Frank told her companion that she loathed the life of a pirate, that she was one of the crew by compulsion, and that she should embrace

the first possible opportunity to escape, a new bond
of union was formed between them. They became
messmates, and were always together. He never
had a doubt that the masculine pronoun, *he*, belonged to his bronzed but smooth-cheeked and soft-
voiced companion.

Even on board a pirate ship there are many
opportunities for seclusion. In the dark and tempestuous night, when the wine-heated officers were
carousing in the cabin, and the crew were rioting in
the forecastle, Frank and the artist, wrapped in
those thick sailor-jackets which defy both wind and
rain, would seek some retired position upon the
deck, beneath the stormy sky, and beguile the
weary hours in relating to each other the story of
the past, and in planning measures for escape.
Frank was the younger of the two, and in these
hours of midnight communings, loved to recline
with her head in the lap of her unsuspecting comrade.

The inevitable result ensued. The whole passionate nature of the woman, still almost in her
girlhood, became aglow with love of the young
artist. In one of these midnight communings she
revealed to her astonished friend her sex. His
friendship was speedily converted into impassioned
love. He had ever, under her assumed character,

had occasion to respect her. He could not recall a single action of immodesty or impropriety. Alone in the darkness of the night, upon the solitary deck, with the stars alone looking down upon them, they went through the ceremony of what they both deemed a secret *marriage*.

Mary Read ever averred that she regarded those nuptials as sacred as if the rite had been performed in the church, by the robed priest, and in the presence of any number of witnesses. She was never accused of being unfaithful to her marriage vows, or of ever having been even indiscreet in her conduct.

Still the months passed away. The ship continued its piratic cruise. Frank, though secretly the wife of the artist, had excited no suspicion of her disguise. In her sailor's garb she still performed every duty imposed upon others of the crew. There were several bloody actions fought. In these engagements both she and Anne Bonny were called upon, like the rest, to work at the guns.

It was one of the laws of the ship, that if any quarrel arose between any two of the crew, there should be no contention on board the ship, but that when they next approached an island, they should, with their friends, land in a boat, and settle the quarrel in a duel on the shore. The artist was so grossly insulted by one of the pirates, that he either challenged him, or accepted a challenge from him to fight a duel. Frank would not have had her husband, on any account, refuse the hostile meeting. Public sentiment was such among the pirates, that had he done this, there would have been no end to the insults and abuse he would have received as a coward.

Frank was in a state of great agitation and anxiety for the fate of her lover. She was an admirable swordsman, and no one of the piratic crew was a truer shot with the pistol. Her love was so passionate that she felt that she could not live without that husband, whose union with her was so enhanced by the attractions which secrecy and romance give. She was far more ready to peril her own life than to have his endangered.

She therefore deliberately provoked such a quarrel with the pirate who was soon to have a hostile meeting with her husband, as to compel him to an immediate and angry challenge. Adroitly she succeeded in having the time appointed for their meeting two hours before the duel was to be fought with her husband. In her intensely excited frame of mind she resolved to make sure work of it.

They were to meet at but a few paces distance, discharge their pistols at each other, and then, with drawn swords, advance and fight until one or the other was effectually disabled or killed. The pistols were discharged. Neither of them was seriously wounded. They then crossed swords. There was a fierce clashing of the weapons for a few minutes; and then the agile Frank passed her sword through the body of her adversary, and he fell before her a bloody corpse.

Such rencontres were too common with that ship's crew, and Frank had been too conversant all her days with such scenes of blood to have it produce any serious impression upon her mind. With much composure she wiped her crimsoned sword and returned to the ship, exulting in the thought that she had saved her husband's life. The attachment between Frank and her lover before this seems to have been very strong. But this event bound them more firmly together than ever before.

Almost invariably, even in this world, retribution follows crime. After many successful captures, and much rioting and revelry with this godless crew, the hour of vengeance came. One day a swift-sailing English frigate, of powerful armament, caught sight of the pirate and gave chase. The vessel was overtaken and captured, and all her crew, in irons, were carried to England for trial. There was no disposition to deal tenderly with these wretches, whose crimes could scarcely be numbered. The trial was

expeditious and the execution prompt. The young artist easily proved that he was a prisoner on board the ship, and had never taken any part in their piratic exploits. He was promptly released. Frank was one of the pirates. Her assertion that she was reluctantly so, was of no avail. She had been of their recognized number; she had been identified with them in all the employments of a sailor; she had taken an active part in their battles.

One of the witnesses, who had been taken a prisoner by Rackam, and detained for some time on board the pirates' craft, gave the following testimony against Frank, or rather against Mary Read; for during the trial her sex had been divulged, and the embarrassing fact had been discovered that, ere long, she was to become a mother. The testimony was as follows:

"I was taken prisoner by Rackam, and was detained for some time on board the pirate ship. One day I accidentally fell into discourse with the prisoner at the bar. She was dressed like the ordinary seamen, and I did not suppose her to be anything different. Taking her for a young man, I asked her what pleasure she could find in such enterprises, where her life was continually in danger by fire or sword; and not only so, but she must be sure of dying an ignominous death if she should be taken alive?

"She replied, that as to hanging, she deemed it no great hardship; for were it not for that, every cowardly fellow would turn pirate, and so infest the seas that men of courage must starve. She said that were it put to the choice of the pirates, they would not have the punishment less than death; for it was only the fear of death which kept many dastardly rogues honest. Many of those, she said, who are now cheating the widows and orphans, and oppressing their poor neighbors who have no money to obtain justice, would then rob at sea. Thus the ocean would be crowded with rogues like the land. No merchant would venture out. Trade in a little time would not be worth following. It is the fear of hanging alone which restrains thousands from piracy."

When we consider the impossibility of making an exact report of conversation, and when we consider the situation of Frank among the pirates, and that her life would instantly have been forfeited if they had suspected her of unfaithfulness, we can imagine that essentially these remarks might have been made, without indicating any special moral delinquency. Frank did not deny having made them.

Several of the crew, however, brought forward

much more damaging testimony. When, to the astonishment of all, the sex both of Mary Read and Anne Bonny was made known to the court, the pirates seemed very desirous that their fate should be inseparably connected with their own. The testimony against Anne Bonny was very strong. She had accompanied her infamous husband in most of his adventures, and had rendered herself very conspicuous by her courage and her energetic action.

When the frigate took the pirate there was a short conflict. But the great guns of the frigate swept the pirate's deck with such a storm of grapeshot, that every one rushed into the hold, excepting Mary Read and Anne Bonny. Mary Read, it was said, called upon those under the deck to come up and fight like men. As they refused, in her rage she fired her pistol down among them, killing one and wounding others. This latter charge, which went far to condemn her, she utterly denied. Such bravado was not at all in accordance with her general character. But it was just the conduct to be expected of Anne Bonny. She was a desperado, as robust in person as she was masculine in character. Rumor said that before she entered upon her piratic career she stabbed a servant-maid with a carving-knife, and so severely beat a young fellow whom she disliked that he narrowly escaped with his life.

They were both pronounced guilty of piracy, and condemned to be hung. As it was not deemed right that Mary Read's child should forfeit its life in consequence of its mother's sins, Mary was allowed a reprieve, until after the birth of her child. Being remanded to her gloomy and solitary cell in Newgate prison, she awaited, with anguish, her approaching maternity, to be immediately followed by an ignominious death upon the scaffold. The horror of her situation threw her into a fever, of which she fortunately died. Thus she escaped the scaffold; and she and her unborn babe slept in the grave together.

Rackam was hanged just before the time appointed for the execution of his wife. The morning on which he was led to the scaffold, he was first conducted to the cell of Anne Bonny. Her characteristic speech to him was:

"I am sorry to see you here; but if you had fought like a man, you need not have been hanged like a dog."

In an hour from that time he was struggling in death's agonies. Anne was reprieved from time to time, and finally escaped execution. What at last became of her no one knows.

CHAPTER XIV.

Sir Henry Morgan.

His Origin.—Goes to the West Indies.—Joins the Buccaneers.—
Meets Mansvelt the Pirate.—Conquest of St. Catharine.—Pi-
ratic Colony there.—Ravaging the Coast of Costa Rica.—Sym-
pathy of the Governor of Jamaica.—Death of Mansvelt.—Expedi-
tion of Don John.—The Island Recaptured by the Spaniards.—
Plans of Morgan.—His Fleet.—The Sack of Puerto Principe.—
Horrible Atrocities.—Retreat of the Pirates.—The Duel.—They
Sail for Puerto Velo.—Conquest of the City.—Heroism of the
Governor.

THOUGH the name of Sir Henry Morgan has not
attained equal notoriety with that of Captain William Kidd, his achievements were far more wonderful
and infamous.   He was born of a good and wealthy
family in Wales.   Early developing a roaming disposition, he left his home for the seacoast, and
there took passage for Barbadoes.   In those days
any man could obtain a passage to the colonies, by
agreeing to pay the fare in service on the other side.
Labor was in great demand.   Upon the arrival of
the ship the planters would hasten on board and
pay the passage money, which the emigrant was to
repay by certain stipulated months of labor.

10*

In this way Henry Morgan reached Barbadoes. Here his labor was sold to pay his passage, and he faithfully served out his term. He had come from a virtuous home, but rapidly the reckless boy yielded to the influences which surrounded him, until he became the worst of the bad. From Barbadoes he wandered over to Jamaica, seeking his fortune. Though there was then peace between England and Spain, the British Government was encouraging private piratical excursions against the commerce of Spain. As we have had frequent occasion to mention, these buccaneers had nothing to fear from the English courts so long as they confined themselves to robbing the Spanish ships.

At Jamaica, Morgan found two vessels openly fitting out for these buccaneering expeditions. He shipped on board one of them, and made two or three very successful voyages. Some men seem born to command. Such do not long remain in a subordinate position. Morgan was a man of the imperial mould. As he now had considerable money at his disposal, he proposed, to some of his comrades, that they should join stocks, purchase a vessel, and cruise on their own account. This was promptly done, and Morgan was unanimously chosen commander.

Morgan was already a desperado. With a numerous crew and a well-armed vessel he set out to cruise along that portion of the Mexican coast called Campeachy. After an absence of a few months, he returned triumphantly to Jamaica, his ship laden with the spoil of many captures. This pirate took refuge beneath the flag of England and under the guns of her fort. At that time the British Government was the most atrocious pirate earth had ever known ; for while at peace with Spain, the Government encouraged all private piratical expeditions against her commerce.

In the streets of Jamaica, Morgan met a notorious pirate by the name of Mansvelt. The renown of this sea-robber had spread far and wide. He was then equipping a very considerable fleet, intending to man it with a sufficiency of troops to enable him to land upon the territory of the Spaniards and to plunder their cities. Mansvelt, seeing Morgan return with so many prizes, formed a high opinion of his skill and courage, and appointed him vice-admiral of his squadron.

A fleet of fifteen ships was soon ready for sea, with a crew of five hundred pirates. About a thousand miles southwest of Jamaica, in Central America, was the Spanish province of Costa Rica, reaching across the narrow Isthmus of Panama from sea to sea. A few leagues from the shore, and but about one hundred miles north of the river Chagres, was the Island of St. Catharine, where the Spaniards had a small garrison. The pirates landed, captured the island, took the Spanish soldiers prisoners, and garrisoned the fort with a hundred of their own men. They left a numerous band of slaves, taken from the Spaniards, to cultivate the soil for their new masters. A Frenchman, by the name of Le Sieur Simon, was placed in command. He was directed to put the island in the best posture for defence, and to set all the slaves at work to raise provisions on the fertile plantations. He was thus expected to revictual the fleet upon its return. It was evidently the intention of Mansvelt to establish there a colony of buccaneers, with fleet and army, of which colony he was to be the king. He had no fears of being interrupted in his operations by the British Government.

Mansvelt again spread his sails, and, accompanied by his energetic vice-admiral Morgan, cruised along the eastern coast of Costa Rica. At various points he sent boats, armed with pirates, ashore to rob the villages. The Spanish governor of the adjacent province of Panama, on the south, hearing of these depredations, gathered all the forces at his disposal, and rousing the whole country, advanced to expel the pirates. Mansvelt retreated, and returned with his fleet to St. Catharine. Here he found that his agent had been very efficient, and that an ample supply of provisions was ready for his ships.

This most infamous of pirates returned to the Island of Jamaica, held an interview with the governor, informed him frankly of his plans, and solicited the loan of a portion of his garrison to enable him to hold the island against any attempt of the Spaniards to regain it. The governor received the pirate courteously, expressed the fear that the King of England might not exactly approve of such undisguised hostility, when there was peace between the two countries, and stating also that his garrison was then so feeble that he could not with safety diminish its strength.

Mansvelt then repaired, with one of his ships, to the celebrated rendezvous of the buccaneers at Tortuga. While endeavoring to raise recruits among the desperadoes assembled there, he was taken sick, and passed away, to answer for his guilty life at the tribunal of God.

In the mean time, on the 14th of July, 1665, Don John, the governor of Panama, commenced organizing an expedition to regain the island. He sent a ship, under Captain Joseph Ximines, thoroughly equipped, and manned by three hundred and eighty-two soldiers. The ship touched at Carthagena, with a letter to the commandant of the Spanish settlement there. He promptly added to the expedition three small armed vessels, with one hundred and twenty-six men. On the 2d of August this little fleet came in sight of the western end of the Island of St. Catharine. The wind was contrary. It was not until the 12th they entered the harbor and cast anchor before the pirates' strong fort.

There was an interchange of a few shots between the stone castle and the fleet, which effected but little injury on either side. Ximines sent one of his officers on shore bearing a flag of truce, with the following summons:

"In the name of the King of Spain, I demand the surrender of this island. It was taken in the midst of peace between England and Spain. If the surrender is refused, and I am forced to take the works by storm, I shall certainly put all the garrison to the sword."

The piratic commander returned the answer: "This island once belonged to the King of England. It rightly belongs to him now. We will sooner die than surrender."

During the night of Friday, the 13th, three slaves swam off to the ships, and informed the command-ant that there were but seventy-two soldiers in the fort ; and that they were in great consternation in view of the force brought against them. Saturday was devoted to preparations for landing in the boats and storming the works.

The morning of the Sabbath dawned beautifully over the Eden-like luxuriance of the tropical isle.

The vessels brought their broadsides to bear upon the fort, and, under cover of their fire, three strong parties were landed in the boats. Captain Leyva led sixty men to attack the principal gate. Captain Galeno, at the head of ninety men, took a circuitous route through the forest to attack the castle in the rear. The commander-in-chief, Ximines, with a still stronger force, assailed one of the sides. The conflict was short, but not very bloody. Six of the pirates were killed, and a pretty large number wounded. The Spaniards lost but one man killed, and four wounded.

The pirates endeavored to escape into the woods, but were cut off and all captured. There were found, in the fort, eight hundred pounds of powder, two hundred and fifty pounds of bullets, and also a large supply of provisions and other material of war. Two Spaniards were taken who had enlisted with the buccaneers, to rob the commerce of Spain. They were immediately led out and shot.

The fort proved to be very strong, and an excellent piece of workmanship. It was built of stone, quadrangular in form, with walls eighty-eight feet high. While these scenes were transpiring, Captain Morgan, unconscious of them, was at Jamaica. Hearing of the death of Mansvelt, he, without opposition, assumed the admiralship. He was straining every nerve to retain possession of St. Catharine, and so to strengthen the works as to make the island a safe and convenient store-house for the vast plunder of the buccaneers.

As the governor of Jamaica declined adding to the piratic force, in St. Catharine, at the expense of his own garrison, Morgan wrote to leading merchants in Virginia and New England, urging them, by the promise of the most liberal pay, to send him provisions, ammunition, and other necessary articles. When the tidings reached him that the Spaniards had regained the island, he lost no time in unavailing regrets, but immediately turned, with demoniac energy, to other enterprises.

With great vigor he commenced organizing a new fleet. His agents proudly strode through every English port, openly purchasing vessels and ammunition, and mounting the guns. All the vessels were ordered to rendezvous, within a given time, at a solitary harbor on the south side of the Island of Cuba.

This magnificent island is eight hundred miles in length, and from twenty-five to one hundred and thirty in breadth. The principal towns of Cuba, at that time, were Havana on the north and Santiago on the south. Havana was fortified by three strong forts. There were many other small and flourishing settlements scattered along the extended coast. There were ten thousand families in Havana, and its commerce was immense.

Captain Morgan had, in the course of two months, assembled in his retired harbor a fleet of twelve vessels, large and small, with over eight hundred fighting men. He called a council of his officers to decide as to the enterprise upon which they should embark. Several urged a midnight attack upon Havana. They said that there was immense wealth in the city, that it might be attacked by surprise, as no one suspected danger; and that the city could be plundered before the inhabitants would have any time to organize for defence.

Others affirmed that they were not strong enough for so great an achievement; that they needed at least fifteen hundred men to attempt the capture of a city of fifty thousand inhabitants. After much discussion it was decided to attack a flourishing inland town of Cuba, called Puerto Principe. It was situated a few leagues from the southern shore, and was utterly unprepared for such an attack as the pirates could bring against it. One of the pirates was familiar with the place and with all of its approaches. He said that the town had never been sacked, and consequently was very rich.

The whole fleet speedily set sail, and ran along the southern shore of Cuba toward the doomed town. The nearest available landing - place, for Principe, was at a bay called St. Mary's. Here, in the night, a Spanish prisoner, on board one of the ships, secretly let himself down into the dark water, and, at the imminent danger of being devoured by sharks, swam ashore. He hastened through the mule-paths of the forest to Principe, with the tidings of the terrible danger impending over the town.

The inhabitants were thrown into an awful state of consternation. They knew full well that they had as much to dread from the pirates as from so many fiends from the bottomless pit. Men, women, and children were running in all directions to convey away and hide their treasures.

All these Spanish towns had a governor appointed over them by the king. The governor summoned all the able-bodied men he could, and armed the slaves, and placed his little force in ambush along the route which he supposed that the pirates must of necessity traverse. He had also the immense trees of the dense tropical forest felled across the path, and other obstructions thrown in the way, to retard their march. But Morgan, as he approached these impediments, cut a new road with great difficulty through the woods, and thus escaped falling into the ambuscades.

Morgan had left but a small guard to keep the fleet. Nearly eight hundred men were on the march with him. The pirates advanced in three divisions, with beating of drums, flying banners, and an ostentatious display of military array. The town was in the centre of a smooth plain. The governor had retreated from his ambush, and, as the pirates approached, stood before the town at the head of a troop of horsemen. Morgan formed his men in a semicircle, and marched down upon them.

Both parties fought with desperation. The greatly outnumbering pirates soon shot down the governor, and so many of his soldiers, that the remainder attempted to escape to the woods. They were hotly pursued, and most of them were killed. The battle, with the skirmishing, lasted nearly four hours.

The pirates, having encountered but little loss, entered the town. Still, as they marched through the narrow streets which were ever found in these old Spanish towns, many of the inhabitants continued a brave resistance. They fired upon the pirates from the windows of their stone houses, and hurled down heavy articles of furniture upon their heads from the roofs. Morgan had it loudly proclaimed that if they continued this resistance he would lay the whole town in ashes, and put every man, woman, and child to the sword.

The Spaniards, hoping that by submission they might save their own lives and their houses from conflagration, threw down their arms and raised the white flag. There were several large stone churches in the place. The demoniac pirates drove the whole population, men, women, and children, into these churches, and imprisoned them there. They then commenced their system of plunder and wanton destruction. Every house and by-place, and the region all around, were searched. The night was rendered hideous by their drunken orgies. There was scarcely a conceivable crime of which these wretches were not guilty. They were fiends of the foulest dye, with no pity. Their outrages cannot be described. Even the imagination of most readers cannot conceive of the crimes they perpetrated.

They either forgot the captives they had crowded into the churches or intentionally left them to starve. No provision whatever was made for their wants, and they were not furnished with any food. The piteous moans of women and children touched not their hearts. Large numbers perished in the lingering agonies of starvation.

Disappointed in the amount of treasure they found, they began to put their prisoners to the torture, men, young girls, and even little children, to extort from them the confession of where riches were secreted. While perpetrating atrocities which cannot be named, a man was captured who had letters from the governor of Santiago to some of the leading inhabitants. In these documents the governor wrote:

"Do not be in too much haste to ransom your town or persons from the pirates. Put them off as long as you can, with excuses and delays. In a short time I will certainly come to your aid."

This alarmed Morgan. He feared that the governor of Santiago might rally a sufficient force perhaps to seize his ships, perhaps to cut off his retreat. He ordered his men immediately to march, as rapidly as possible, to their fleet, with all the plunder they had gathered. He also made renewed efforts, by all the energies of torture, to wrest from the wretched inhabitants the treasure which he supposed they had hidden. Those who had nothing to reveal, had their nerves lacerated and their bones crushed to force a confession of that which did not exist. He compelled his captives to drive all the cattle to the bay, kill them and salt them, and convey the barrels to his ships.

A quarrel arose between two of the pirates. One challenged the other to a duel. The party consequently went ashore in the boats. As they drew near the appointed spot, one of the two, treacherously approaching the other from behind, ran him through the back with his sword, and he fell dead. Morgan, who had just committed crimes which should cause the foul fiend himself to blush, said that it was not *just* and *honorable* to kill a comrade thus treacherously. He therefore, with the assent of the whole demoniac gang, put the offender in irons and hung him.

The fleet speedily set sail for a distant island, where they were to divide their ill-gotten plunder. Here they were greatly disappointed in the amount which they had taken. It was all estimated at but fifty thousand dollars. This was a small sum to be divided among so many greedy claimants. This being known, it excited a general commotion. Many of the pirates owed debts in Jamaica, which they were anxious *honorably* to pay.

Some of the gang were so dissatisfied that they left, with a part of the vessels, to cruise on their own account. Morgan soon inspired those who remained with his own indomitable energy. In a few days he gathered a fleet of nine sail, manned by four hundred and seventy-five pirates. Morgan told them that he had formed a plan which would enrich them all. It was, however, necessary to keep it a profound secret. If any one should turn traitor and reveal it, the plan might be frustrated. They must therefore, for the present, trust in him and implicitly follow his directions. He had already inspired them with such confidence in his sagacity, zeal, and courage, that, without a murmur, they yielded to these demands.

The whole fleet set sail for the continent, and, in a few days, arrived off the coast of Costa Rica. Then Morgan assembled the captains of all the vessels in his cabin, and informed them of his plan, which they were to communicate to their several crews.

" I intend," said Morgan, " to attack and plunder the city of Puerto Velo. I am resolved to sack the whole city. Not a single corner shall escape my vigilance. Large as the city is, the enterprise cannot fail to succeed. We shall strike the people entirely by surprise ; for I have kept my plan an entire secret, and they cannot possibly know of our coming."

Some of the captains were alarmed in view of so bold an undertaking. They said :

"Puerto Velo is the largest Spanish city in the New World excepting Havana and Carthagena. It contains a population of between two and three thousand, and has a garrison of three hundred soldiers. It has two forts, which are deemed impregnable. These forts guard the entry to the harbor, so that no ship or boat can pass without permission. We have not a sufficient number of men to assault so strong a place."

Morgan replied: "If we are few in numbers, we are bold in heart. The fewer we are the greater will be each man's share of the plunder."

This last consideration had great weight with the pirates. The number engaged in the sack of Puerto Principe was so great, that each one murmured at the meagre share he received. Morgan was very familiar with all this region, and was thoroughly acquainted with the avenues to the city. In the dusk of the evening he ran his little fleet into a solitary harbor, called Naos, about thirty miles from Puerto Velo. There was a river, flowing into the harbor from the west, threading a dense, tangled, almost uninhabited wilderness. Leaving their ships at anchor, under guard of a few men, the pirates, "armed to the teeth," in crowded boats and canoes, ascended the river until, at midnight, they reached a point but a few miles distant from the city. They then landed and rapidly marched through a solitary Indian trail, overshadowed by the gloom of a dense tropical forest, until they came within sight of the lights gleaming from the battlements of the forts.

On the main avenue to the city, not far from the gate, they came upon a solitary sentry, pacing his beat. Four men crept cautiously forward in the darkness, seized him, gagged him, and brought him a prisoner to Morgan. The pirate questioned his captive minutely, respecting the troops in the city, and the means for defence. The trembling man was threatened with death by the most horrible tortures, should it be found that he had in the slightest degree deceived them. Having gained this important information, they advanced upon the city.

The march of a mile brought them to the main fort, or Castle, as it was called. The morning had not yet dawned. In the darkness they surrounded it so completely that no one could either go in or out. Morgan then sent the sentinel, whom he had captured, into the fort, with a demand for its immediate surrender.

" If you yield at once," said the message of the pirate, " your lives shall be spared. But if there be the least resistance, or any delay, I will cut to pieces every individual within the fort. Not one shall escape."

11

The commandant of the castle heeded not the threat, but opened fire upon his foes. The report of his guns roused the city. The governor, as speedily as possible, rallied all his forces and made such preparation as he could for defence. The slumbering garrison, attacked so utterly by surprise, were speedily overpowered. The pirates, breaking down the gates, rushed in, and soon gained possession of the works. The castle was but feebly prepared to repel an asault from the land side.

Morgan wished to strike a blow which should appal the whole city. The magazine was abundantly stored with powder. There was a room by its side, into which Morgan drove all his prisoners. Barring them in, he laid a slow match, applied the torch, and with his gang retired. There were a few moments of appalling silence. Then came a roar as of ten thousand thunders. The very earth shook beneath the terrific convulsion. There seemed to be a volcanic eruption of forked flame, rocks, earth, guns, and mangled limbs, and the castle disappeared. Every one of its inmates perished beneath its ruins.

The consternation in the city was terrible. There were runnings to and fro, cries of anguish from mothers and maidens, while some were seeking to conceal their treasures by throwing them into the wells or hastily burying them in the cellars and the fields. In the frenzy of the hour the governor found his attempts to rally the citizens utterly in vain. With a few soldiers he threw himself into the second and only remaining castle. The little band here assembled, knowing that no mercy could be expected from the pirates, resolved to make as many of them bite the dust as possible, before they themselves should fall. They therefore opened an incessant and well-directed fire upon their assailants.

Near by there was a cloister, where there were priests and nuns. The Spaniards regarded these religious orders with superstitious reverence. Morgan seized them all as prisoners. He ordered his carpenters immediately to make a number of scaling-ladders, so broad that four men could ascend them abreast. He then compelled the ecclesiastics and the nuns to carry the ladders and place them upon the walls of the fort. The armed soldiers followed closely behind, shielded by their bodies.

The governor believed that the life of every Spaniard would be sacrificed should they be taken. And he thought it better for both priests and nuns that they should die outright than that they should be left in the hands of the pirates. He therefore opened a vigorous fire upon the approaching assailants, notwithstanding the rampart of living bodies they had so infamously placed before them. The unhappy inhabitants of the cloister cried out piteously to the governor, imploring him to surrender the castle and thus spare their lives.

But the governor steeled his heart against their appeal. He fought with desperation. Many of the priests and nuns were shot down. But the pirates, in overpowering numbers, rushed on. They reached the top of the wall. They threw down fire-balls and hand-grenades upon the despairing defenders. When many had perished they leaped down, sword in hand, amidst smoke and flame, and mercilessly slaughtered all the survivors.

The heroic governor fought to the last. His wife and children, weeping bitterly and upon their knees, entreated him to yield, hoping that thus his life might be spared.

"No!" he exclaimed, "never. I had rather die like a soldier than be hanged like a coward."

Covered with wounds, he was at length cut down, and his gory, mangled body was left uncared for. The castle was taken. The soldiers were destroyed. The city was at the mercy of the captors. All the surviving inhabitants of the town, who had not escaped into the woods, were driven into the castle. Then the pirates commenced a scene of carousal which pandemonium could not outrival.

The nuns and all the mothers and maidens were at their mercy. A veil must be cast over their horrid deeds. When satiated with drunkenness, and every conceivable excess, they commenced plundering the city.

CHAPTER XV.

The Capture of Puerto Velo, and its Results.

The Torture.—Sickness and Misery.—Measures of the Governor of
Panama.—The Ambuscade.—Awful Defeat of the Spaniards.—
Ferocity of the Pirates.—Strange Correspondence.—Exchange of
Courtesies.—Return to Cuba, and Division of the Spoil.—Wild
Orgies at Jamaica.—Complicity of the British Government with
the Pirates.—The New Enterprise.—Arrival of the Oxford.—De-
struction of the Cerf Volant.—Rendezvous at Samona.

THE wretched citizens of the captured city of
Puerto Velo were exposed to every species of torture to force from them the discovery of where their
riches were concealed. Many of them had no
knowledge they could give of any hidden treasure.
Day after day the most horrid scenes of cruelty
were enacted. Multitudes of men and women died
under the torture. For fifteen days ·the pirates
remained amidst the ruins they had created.

But in this world blows are seldom given without
others being received in return. Sickness came,
with languor, pain, and groans of agony. The death-
bed is cheerless enough even when surrounded with
all the attentions of sympathy and love and tender

care.   To these wretched men, in their homelessness and their terrible guilt, death must indeed have come as the king of terrors.   A painful, pestilential disease seized them.   Surrounded by the oaths and the clamor of demoniac men they passed to the seat of final judgment.

In consequence of the unhealthiness of the climate at Puerto Velo, many of the merchants, who had their warehouses at that port, resided in the far more attractive city of Panama, but a few leagues distant, on the Pacific coast.   The governor of the province also resided at Panama.   Morgan sent two prisoners to the city to say to the residents there that unless one hundred thousand dollars were sent to him he would lay Puerto Velo in ashes.

But the governor had already heard of the arrival of the pirates.   He had collected an armed force, and was on the march to cut off their retreat.   In the mean time the vessels were brought up into the harbor and were laden with the plunder.   The ramparts were repaired, the guns remounted, and all things put in readiness to repel an attack.   Every day many were put to the torture.   Some died under the terrible infliction.   Many were maimed for life.

Hearing that the governor was on the march to attack them, Morgan placed himself at the head of a hundred of his most determined men, and marched forward to meet the foe. Every man was armed, in pirate fashion, with a musket, several pistols in his belt, and a keen-edged sabre. At a few leagues from the city they came to a narrow defile, along whose circuitous path but two could march abreast. The tangled thicket was on each side, with gigantic trees, and huge rocks buried in the luxuriant verdure of the tropics. Here a whole army might lie in impenetrable concealment.

And here Morgan, with great skill, placed his troops. Every man took a position where he could have perfect command of some portion of the track. With his hatchet he cut a loop-hole through the dense growth of shrubs and interlacing vines. Thus, while quite invisible, he could take deliberate aim. They were to wait in perfect silence until the winding defile was filled with unsuspecting troops. Then, at a signal from Morgan, every man was to fire. And every man was to take such aim as to be sure that his bullet would strike down his victim.

The Spaniards, four or five hundred in number, soon appeared in rapid march. Anticipating a bloody struggle with the pirates behind their ramparts, they had no thought that they would leave such vantage-ground to march forth to the encounter. Their only fear was that the pirates might rush to their ships and thus escape. Hurrying heedlessly along, they had filled the labyrinthine trail, when the deadly signal was given. One hundred muskets were instantaneously exploded. One hundred bullets were sent on their fatal mission. One hundred Spaniards were either struck down in instantaneous death or wounded.

There was no time for thought ; no time to rally. The case was clear. The defeat was entire and remediless. Rapidly the pirates reloaded and kept up a continuous fire. The Spaniards discharged their muskets at random, hitting no one. Pell-mell, in awful confusion, they turned, and struggling against their own numbers, rushed, as best they could, from the defile. The narrow path was strewed with the dying and the dead. With a shattered and bleeding remnant the governor returned to Panama for reënforcements.

Morgan and his men, wishing that their deeds should strike terror all around, emerged from their covert, dispatched the wounded with pistol-shots or sabre-thrusts, searched the pockets of the dead, and, leaving their bodies unburied, returned in triumph to their comrades.

In triumph! But what a triumph! They had now been fifteen days in Puerto Velo. Famine and disease were assailing them with more cruel attacks than sabre or pistol can inflict. Recklessly they had wasted their provisions. They could not eat their gold or their silver, or the spoil which they had stored away in the holds of their ships. They had already consumed the mules and the horses. Their blood, inflamed by debaucheries and almost boiling beneath a meridian sun, produced the most loathsome and painful disorders. The slightest wound would fester and cause death. No wonder they were reckless. Better far to die than to live in such misery. This was the triumph to which the pirate Morgan returned.

The Spanish prisoners suffered still more than their captors. Crowded together in apartments whose awful impurity tainted the air; deprived of every comfort; witnessing intense sufferings which they could not alleviate, but which they were compelled to share ; despondent, starving, dying, there was for them no relief but such as death gives.

The Spanish governor, who had shown such utter want of military ability in marching into the ambuscade, was as self-conceited and boastful as he was incompetent. Notwithstanding his ignominious repulse, he sent to Morgan the following message :

" If you do not immediately withdraw, with your ships, from Porto Velo, I will march upon you with a resistless force. You shall receive no quarter. Every man shall be put to death."

Morgan sent back the reply, " If you do not immediately send me one hundred and eighty thousand dollars in gold, I will lay every building in Puerto Velo in ashes; I will blow up the forts; and I will put every captive I have to the sword, man, woman, and child."

The pride of the governor would not allow him to purchase the retreat of the pirates. He sent to Carthagena imploring that some ships might be sent from there to block up the pirates in the river. But they had no sufficient force to make the attempt. The citizens were very anxious to have the money sent. But the governor kept them in suspense in hopes of gaining time.

" He was deaf and obdurate to all the entreaties of the citizens, who sent to inform him that the pirates were not men, but devils, and that they fought with such fury that the Spanish officers had stabbed themselves in very despair, at seeing a supposed impregnable fortress taken by a handful of people, when it should have held out against twice that number." *

The governor was astonished at their exploits. Four hundred men had captured a city which he said any general in Europe would have found it

* The Monarchs of the Main, by George W. Thornbury, Esq., vol. ii. p. 35.

necessary to blockade in due form. It is indicative of the almost inconceivable state of public opinion in those times, that the governor of Panama, Don Juan Perez de Guzman, who had acquired considerable renown for his bravery in the wars in Flanders, should have sent a courteous message to Morgan, expressive of his astonishment and admiration in view of his heroic achievement, and begging Morgan to send him a pattern of the arms with which he had gained so wonderful a victory. The scornful pirate sent a common musket and a handful of bullets to the governor, with the following sarcastic message :

"I beg your excellency to accept these as a small pattern of the arms with which I have taken Puerto Velo. Your excellency need not trouble yourself to return them. In the course of a twelvemonth I will visit Panama in person, and will fetch them away myself."

The governor replied : "I return the weapons you sent me, and thank you for the loan of them. It is a pity that a man of so much courage is not in the service of a great and good prince. I hope that Captain Morgan will not trouble himself to come and see me at Panama. Should he do so, he surely will not fare so well as he has at Puerto Velo."

It is very difficult to credit the statement made

by Thornbury that "the envoy, having delivered this message, so chivalrous in its tone, presented Morgan with a beautiful gold ring, set with a costly emerald, as a remembrance of his master Don Guzman, who had already supplied the English chief with fresh provisions." *

Puerto Velo was left to its fate. The pirates left scarcely anything behind but the tiles and the paving-stones. Many of the best guns Morgan carried off. Of the rest, all which he could not burst he spiked. He then set sail. Behind him were smouldering ruins, pestilence, poverty, misery, and death.

Eight days' sail brought the fleet to Cuba. Upon that vast and sparsely inhabited island there were many solitary harbors and coves where the silence of the wilderness reigned. Into one of these lonely spots Morgan ran his fleet. Here he divided the spoil. It was indeed a beggarly pittance which they had obtained as the fruit of so much toil, suffering, and crime. In coin or bullion they counted but two hundred and sixty thousand dollars. There was a large amount of silks and other merchandise, which was not deemed of much value.

The division was amicably made, and they spread their sails to return to Jamaica, there to squander,

* Monarchs of the Main, vol. i. p. 38.

in a few days of insane excess, all that they had
gained through weary months of danger, toil, suffering, and crime. The entrance of a richly laden
piratic fleet into the harbor of Kingston was an
occasion of public rejoicing. The gamblers, the
courtezans, the rumsellers were all overjoyed.
Even the children expected to see the strange vis-
itors scatter their doubloons through the streets to
be scrambled for.

We are told that every door was open to
them, and that, for a whole week, all loudly praised
their generosity and their courage. At the end of a
month they had squandered all, and every door was
shut in their faces. Morgan was a drunkard as well
as a robber. He spent his gains as infamously and
as speedily as did the rest. Shrewder men than
he emptied his purse at the gambling-table. The
Delilahs of Jamaica speedily transferred his jewels
to their necks. But one short month had passed
away when Morgan and all his crew, utterly impoverished, were eager for another expedition.

Undismayed by the past, this bold adventurer
planned an enterprise of such magnitude that he
boasted that, at its close, both he and his men might
be able to retire, if they wished, with a sufficiency
for the rest of their days.

A rendezvous was appointed at De la Vaca or

Cow Island, on the south side of the Island of Hispaniola. This would be easily accessible by the pirates, both French and English, ever swaggering through the streets of Tortuga. Again the desperadoes rushed to his banner. They came in boats and in small vessels and by land. Men enough were found to furnish the adventurer with funds.

A large English ship, which mounted thirty-six guns, entered the harbor of Kingston, Jamaica, from New England. This ship, the Oxford, carried a crew of three hundred men. It was on a buccaneering cruise against Spanish commerce. Oexemelin says that the ship actually belonged to the King of England, Charles II. He had fitted it out at his own expense, and the captain was employed in his service. What authority he had for this astonishing assertion we know not. But it is certain that the governor at Jamaica felt at liberty to send this ship to join Morgan's expedition. And when we subsequently find Charles II. conferring the honor of knighthood on this desperate marauder, and appointing him governor of Jamaica, the report receives much confirmation.

The harbor at Isle de la Vaca was a fine one. A large French ship, the Cerf Volant, on a trading excursion, entered the port. The ship was well armed, mounting twenty-four iron guns and twelve guns of brass. The captain and crew, disappointed in the results of trade, were disposed to try their luck as buccaneers. Morgan, anxious to secure so powerful a ship, urged them to join his expedition. But the French officers would not accede to his terms.

The Frenchman was about to weigh anchor and return to Tortuga. Several of his crew, who were English sailors, had deserted him, and had been received on board Morgan's ships. Through them Morgan learned that the captain of the Cerf Volant, being out of provisions, had stopped an English vessel, taken from her sundry articles of food, for which he had paid, not in coin, for he had none on hand, but in bills of exchange cashable at Jamaica.

Morgan, who was seeking for some pretext under which he might seize the French ship, decided to consider this an act of piracy. He invited the officers of the Volant to dine with him, on board the splendid ship which the governor of Jamaica had sent him. Unsuspicious of treachery; the captain and his officers all came. While in the cabin, drinking their wine, Morgan rose and denounced them as pirates who had robbed an English vessel, and declared them to be his prisoners. At the same moment a band of armed men came in and put them in irons. They could make no resistance. He then took possession of the ship.

Soon after this he called a council of his officers to decide upon their first expedition. They met in the cabin of the Volant. Several of the French who had refused to join Morgan were prisoners in the hold. After much deliberation they decided first to repair to the Island of Savona, a few leagues south-east of San Domingo. A flotilla of merchant-ships, under convoy, was daily looked for from Spain. It was to be expected that, during this long voyage, some vessels would get separated from the rest. These stragglers they hoped to cut off.

Having settled this question, the desperadoes commenced drinking and carousing. A scene of uproar ensued with the intermingling of drunken songs and unintelligible blasphemies. While the officers were thus carousing in the cabin, the sailors, four hundred in number, were engaged in equally wild orgies in their quarters of the ship. As the toasts were drained, broadsides were discharged, by men reeling in drunkenness around their smoking guns. Some were cursing, some fighting, some sleeping in deathly stupor.

The magazine, amply stored with powder, was near the bows of the boat. Powder was carelessly scattered over the decks. Suddenly there was a terrific explosion. The whole ship seemed lifted into the air, as by some volcanic power. Dense volumes of sulphurous smoke, pierced with forked flame, enveloped the scene, shutting it out from the view of all around. Then there were seen, ejected hundreds of feet into the air, massive timbers, and ponderous cannon, and the mangled bodies of three hundred and fifty men. But thirty of the crew escaped.

The officers' cabin, far in the stern of the boat, escaped the force of the explosion. Though the revellers there were terrified, stunned, almost smothered with smoke, and many of them severely wounded, they escaped with their lives.

Such was the end of the Cerf Volant. This only did Morgan gain by his treachery. " Morgan," says Esquemeling, " had captured the ship. And God only could take it from him. And God did so."

For eight days the bodies of the dead were seen floating upon the waters of the bay. Morgan sent out boats to collect these bodies, not for burial, but for plunder. The pockets were searched. The clothing, when good, was stripped off. The heavy gold rings, which nearly all the sailors wore, were taken, and then the bodies were abandoned to the sharks and the carrion birds.

Morgan, upon a review of his forces, found that

he had fifteen vessels, large and small, and eight hundred and sixty men. With these he set sail for Savona. Head winds impeded their progress. Three weeks had elapsed ere they reached the eastern extremity of Hispaniola. Eight hundred hungry men consume a vast amount of food each day. Their provisions ran short. They chanced to meet an English ship which had a superfluity for sale. Thus recruited, they pressed on, in a long straggling line, until eight of the ships reached a harbor called Ocoa, on the southern coast of the great island. Here he cast anchor to wait the arrival of the rest of the fleet.

CHAPTER XVI.

The Expedition to Maracaibo.

The Delay at Ocoa.—Hunting Excursions.—The Repulse.—Cities of
Venezuela.—The Plan of Morgan.—Suggestions of Pierre Pi-
card.—Sailing of the Expedition.—They Touch at Oruba.—
Traverse Venezuela.—Enter Lake Maracaibo.—Capture of the
Fort.—The City Abandoned.—Atrocities of the Pirates.

AT Ocoa, on the Island of Hispaniola, the pirates
remained several days waiting for the arrival of the
other vessels, which were unaccountably lagging behind. Every morning Morgan sent a party of eight
men, from each ship, upon the island as hunters, in
search of game. He also sent a body of armed men
to protect them from any attack by the Spaniards.
Though there were many Spaniards upon the island,
they did not feel strong enough to assail so great a
force as the pirates could muster. They, however,
sent to the city of San Domingo for three or four
hundred men, to kill or drive away all the cattle and
game around the Bay of Ocoa. They hoped thus
to starve out the buccaneers, and compel them to
depart.

Goaded by hunger, a band of fifty of Morgan's

men ventured far into the woods. The Spaniards, who were watching them, drew them into an ambuscade. The pirates were outnumbered and surrounded. With cries of " Kill, kill," the Spaniards opened a sudden and deadly fire. But these desperadoes, accustomed to every kind of danger, could not be thrown into a panic. Instantly they formed themselves into a hollow square, and keeping a rolling fire from the four sides, slowly retreated to their ships. Many fell by the way, dead or wounded. Many of the Spaniards were also slain.

The next day, Morgan, rendered furious by the discomfiture, landed himself, at the head of two hundred men, to take dire revenge upon his foes. But no foe was to be met. Finding his search useless, he gave vent to his rage in burning all the dwellings he encountered, from which the Spaniards had fled.

Still the seven missing ships did not appear. After waiting a few days more, he decided to delay no longer. Spreading his sails, he steered his course for the Island of Savona. But none of the missing vessels were there. While waiting, he sent several boats, with crews amounting to one hundred and fifty well-armed men, to plunder several of the small towns upon the San Domingo coast. But in the capital city and all along the shore scouts were on the watch. Sentinels were placed upon every headland. The moment the boats appeared in sight, signals were given. At every point where a landing was attempted such energetic resistance was presented, that the pirates were compelled to retreat.

They returned to Morgan with this discouraging report. He was in a towering rage, and with sneers and curses denounced them as cowardly poltroons. As no longer delay could be safely indulged in, and as the missing vessels did not arrive, he made another review of his fleet and army, and found that he had eight vessels of various sizes and about five hundred men.

Upon the coast of Venezuela there was a large and opulent city, called Caraccas. It was the capital of the province of Venezuela, and had been founded nearly one hundred years before, in 1567, by the Spanish Government. It was a well-built and beautiful city, delightfully situated, in the enjoyment of a salubrious climate, and enriched by extensive commerce. Near by were Valencia, Barcelona, and Cumana, all important commercial ports. The latter place was the oldest city on the continent of South America. It was established in 1523. The plunder of these four cities would indeed enrich the marauders. And Morgan, in command of fifteen vessels, and with an army of fifteen hundred men did not doubt that he could effect their capture, one by one, if he could strike them entirely by surprise. But it was folly to attempt it with eight vessels and five hundred men.

There was a Frenchman in command of one of Morgan's ships, by the name of Pierre Picard. This man, several years before, had been the pilot of Lolonois's fleet, in his capture and destruction of Maracaibo and Gibraltar, of which expedition we have already given an account. During the intervening years those places had, in a very considerable degree, recovered from their disasters. Again they presented riches sufficient to entice the buccaneers.

Picard was a remarkable man, of great resources. He was a bold soldier and a skilful sailor. Familiar with all these waters, fearless and unscrupulous, with French plausibility of address, and speaking the English language with volubility and correctness, he gained great influence over Morgan.

A council of the officers was called. He proposed an attack upon Maracaibo and Gibraltar. A chart was presented exhibiting the course to be run, the channels to be threaded, the forces to be encountered, and the means of overcoming them.

His proposition was received with general acclaim, and the fleet weighed anchor. After several days' sail to the south, they reached an island called

Oruba. It was inhabited only by natives. They had a large stock of sheep, lambs, goats, and kids. Here the pirates cast anchor, to take in water and provisions. For once these marauders seemed to come to the conclusion that honesty was more politic than thievery, and that it was easier to buy a goat with a skein of thread, than to steal it, and thus rouse the hostility of the whole native population. They remained here twenty-four hours, acting as nearly like honest men as such a gang of thieves, drunkards, and desperadoes could do. They filled their water-casks, and laid in quite a store of provisions, which they bought, though without money and almost without price.

They were now within a day's sail of Maracaibo. They were anxious that the natives should not know their destination, lest in some way they might give the alarm. Therefore the anchors were raised and the sails spread in the night. When the morning dawned the islanders looked in vain for the fleet.

During the day the ships came in sight of the cluster of islands which are found at the entrance of the Lake of Maracaibo. A fair breeze from the north had swept them rapidly through the Gulf of Venezuela. Just within the narrows which connected the gulf with the lake, there was a mountainous island called Vigilia. Upon one of its eminences there was a watch-tower erected, where sentinels were stationed, ever on the lookout to give warning of the approach of any suspicious craft.

Just as the fleet reached this point the wind died away into a perfect calm. Though Morgan made every endeavor to cast anchor out of sight of the watch-tower, the vigilant eyes of the sentinels detected him. The alarm was instantly sent up to the city. Twelve hours passed away before there was a breath of wind to ripple the crystal surface of the lake. It was then four o'clock in the morning. All this time had been granted the Spaniards to prepare for their defence.

At a little distance beyond Vigilia there was a narrow channel to be threaded, which was defended by a fort. Not deeming it safe to expose his vessels to the heavy guns of the Spaniards, and knowing that the works would be weak on the land side, he manned his boats, and marching through the woods, struck his foes in the rear. The garrison had made arrangements for the most desperate resistance. They had burned all the huts around the walls of the fort, and had removed everything which could afford the assailants any shelter.

The defenders of the works numbered probably not more than thirty or forty men. Nearly five hundred reckless desperadoes emerged from the woods for the assault. They were all veterans, and all sharpshooters. Not a hand could be exposed but a bullet would strike it. Such a storm of balls were thrown with unerring aim in at every embrasure, that the guns could not be worked.

When the pirates, in their large numbers, first appeared emerging from the forest, the fort opened a fire so intense and continuous that it resembled the crater of a small volcano in most rapid eruption. But the pirates, who could return ten bullets for every one received, and who were careful that every bullet should accomplish its mission, soon caused the fire to slacken. Still the fight continued for many hours, till night came, with no apparent advan tage on either side.

With the darkness the conflict ceased. Morgan sent a party cautiously forward to reconnoitre. No light was to be seen. No sound was to be heard. Solitude and silence reigned. The fort was deserted. With shouts the pirates rushed forward to take possession of the works. The loud voice of Morgan arrested them.   He was as cautious as he was brave. A party of engineers was dispatched, led by Morgan himself, to search lest there might be lighted fuses leading to the magazine. Morgan was the first to enter., His quick eye discerned the gleam of a fuse slowly creeping toward the magazine, where three thousand pounds of gunpowder were stored. It was instantly trampled out.

But for this caution, five hundred pirates would have swarmed all over the fort. There would have been an earthquake roar, a volcanic upheaval, and not one of those five hundred desperadoes would have survived to tell the story of the retribution which had so suddenly befallen them.

The fort was a small but strong redoubt, or out-work, built of stone, circular in form, with a massive wall thirty feet high. It was only accessible by an iron ladder which could be let down from a guard-room. It mounted fourteen cannons, of eight, twelve, and fourteen pound calibre. There was also found a quantity of fire-pots, hand-grenades, pikes, and muskets.

The pirates had no time to lose. It was needful to press forward as rapidly as possible, for every hour the inhabitants of the city might be adding to their defences. They blew up a portion of the wall; spiked the cannon, and threw them over the ramparts; burned the gun-carriages, and destroyed all the material of war which they could not carry away with them.

The way was now open for the passage of the fleet up the lake to the very entrance of the harbor. With the earliest dawn the fleet spread its sails, leaving behind the smouldering ruins of the fort. The breeze was light, the shoals many; the channel intricate. It was not until the next day that they came within sight of the city. There was still another fort to be passed at the very mouth of the port. Morgan stood upon his quarter-deck, spy-glass in hand. He could see the Spanish cavaliers at work on the ramparts, and had reason to expect a very desperate resistance. Again he decided not to expose his ships to the cannonade which the heavy guns of the fort could bring to bear upon them.

Casting anchor out of gun-shot, he disembarked his forces in the boats. They were ordered not to meddle with the fort, but to march in two divisions through the woods, and attack the town at points which the artillery of the fort could not protect. The guns of the fleet were brought to bear upon all the adjacent thickets, that no foe might find there a lurking-place.

The landing was effected without opposition. The march, through the narrow mule-paths, was undisputed. The town was reached. But there was no foe there; no inhabitant there. All had fled. Warned by the awful fate which had befallen Maracaibo, but a few years before, when sacked by the pirates under Lolonois, the citizens, men, women, and children, had fled utterly panic-stricken.   It is easy for a man of any ordinary courage to brave death in the performance of duty. But who can endure demoniac torture? Who can bear the idea of seeing his wife, his daughter, his child exposed to every indignity, every cruelty which demons in human form can devise.

Maracaibo was emptied of its population. All had sought refuge in the forest, with speed to which terror lent wings. The aged, the sick had fled. Even the dying were carried away. And it is stated without denial that the ship, the Oxford, which took the lead in this enterprise, belonged to Charles II., King of England. This royal buccaneer had equipped it, had manned it, and was to share in the spoil. And he rewarded the demoniac leader of this demoniac gang with the honors of a baronetcy; and appointed him governor over one of the most important colonies of Great Britain. Such scenes were enacted only two hundred years ago. Surely the world has made some progress.

The fugitives had taken with them everything they could carry. There were no carriage roads in those parts. But there were many narrow mule-paths, leading in various directions. On pack-mules and horses much treasure had been removed. Two days had elapsed since the alarm had resounded through the streets, "The pirates are coming."

The houses were empty. The doors were left wide open. The chambers were stripped of everything valuable. Nearly all the gold and silver and jewels had of course disappeared. There were some houses of much elegance in the place, sumptuously furnished. The pirates rushed through the streets, searching for the richest palaces for their barracks. The churches they wantonly defiled and converted into prison-houses. Not a vessel or a boat was left in the port. All had been used, by the terrified fugitives, to escape far away upon the wide lake beyond.

Morgan, chagrined at the loss of so much anticipated treasure, instantly dispatched one hundred fleet-footed men to pursue the encumbered and heavily laden refugees, along all the trails. Scarcely any provisions could be found in the town. The fugitives had taken the wise precaution to destroy what they could not carry away. The little fort which guarded the harbor was merely a half-moon rampart facing the water, and mounting but four cannon. These works the Spaniards had of course abandoned.

The men who had been dispatched in pursuit of the Spaniards returned the next evening. They brought with them thirty prisoners, and fifty mules laden with valuables. The prisoners were feeble

MORGAN TORTURING HIS PRISONERS.

men and women of the poorest class. The owners of the richly laden mules, seeing the approach of the pirates, had abandoned all, and outstripped the pursuers in their flight. The unhappy captives were put to the torture, but nothing could be wrested from them.

This Morgan, subsequently Sir Henry Morgan, governor of Jamaica, suspended his prisoners by the beard; hung them up horizontally by cords bound around their toes and thumbs; placed burning matches between their fingers; scourged them; twisted cords around their heads till their eyes burst from their sockets, and perpetrated other enormities too horrible to be mentioned.

"Thus," writes Esquemeling, "all sort of inhuman cruelties were executed upon these innocent people. Those who would not confess, or who had nothing to declare, died under the hands of those tyrannical men. These tortures and racks continued for the space of three whole weeks; in which time they ceased not to send out daily parties of men to seek for more people to torment and rob: they never returned home without booty and new riches."

In one of these excursions they captured two negro slaves, who were faint for loss of food. They were both put to the torture, to compel them to reveal where their master was concealed. One, the elder of the two, endured the horrible torment without a word, and almost without a groan, till death came to his release. The other captive, a young man, just emerging from boyhood, bore up bravely until the agony became utterly unendurable. He then offered to lead them to his master. The wealthy Spaniard was soon taken, and with him the exultant pirates seized thirty thousand dollars in silver.

In such days of disaster and woe, families, flying into the wilderness, would cling together. Morgan had gradually captured one hundred of the most prominent families. He had also acquired an unexpectedly large amount of plunder, in silver, gold, bullion, and rich merchandise.

Captain Picard was very exultant in view of the success of the enterprise which he had suggested and guided. He now urged that they should advance upon the city of Gibraltar. It will be remembered that this place was at the head of the lake, about one hundred miles south from Maracaibo. Morgan embarked his prisoners and all of his plunder on board his fleet and spread his sails for this new enterprise.

CHAPTER XVII.

Adventures on the Shores of Lake Maracaibo.

Preparations for the Defence of Gibraltar.—The Hidden Ships.—
The Hiding-place of the Governor and the Women.—Disasters
and Failure.—Capture of the Spanish Ships.—The Retreat Commenced.—Peril of the Pirates.—Singular Correspondence.—
Strength of the Spanish Armament.—The Public Conference of
the Pirates.—The Naval Battle.—The Fire-Ship.—Wonderful
Achievement of the Pirates.

BEFORE Morgan weighed anchor for his expedition to Gibraltar, he sent two Spanish prisoners to
the city to say that if they made a peaceable surrender of the place, without attempting to conceal or
carry off their valuables, their lives should be spared.
But if any resistance were offered, the city should be
laid in ashes and every individual put to the sword.

But ample time had been given to the citizens of
Gibraltar to prepare for a vigorous defence. The
garrison from Maracaibo had also fled to her forts.
The troops were landed a mile and a half from the
town, and marched through the woods to attack the
foe in the rear. The Spaniards had anticipated this
movement and were prepared to meet it. Still they

12*

were baffled by the strategy of Morgan. Instead of advancing by the regular route, he employed a large party of sappers and miners to cut a new path through the woods. Thus he approached the city without exposing his men to storm ramparts bristling with artillery and musketry.

The Spaniards had no time to throw up new intrenchments. It was evident, even to the most unintelligent soldier, that all was lost. Their hearts sank within them, and soldiers and citizens fled with the utmost precipitation. So general was the flight that the pirates, when they entered the streets of Gibraltar, found but one single man there, and he was a semi-idiot. Even that weak creature they tortured. The poor wretch cried out:

"Do not torture me any more, and I will show you my riches."

The pirates thought, or pretended to think, that he was some rich person assuming the disguise of poverty and semi-insanity. He led them to a miserable hovel containing only a few earthern pots. He dug up, from under the hearth, three dollars which he had buried there. Still they affirmed that he was a grandee in disguise, and commenced torturing him anew. In his agony he cried out:

" In the name of Jesus; in the name of the Virgin Mary, what will you do with me, Englishmen? I am a poor man. I live on alms. I sleep in the hospital."

He died under their hands. They dragged him aside and covered him with a few shovelfuls of earth. Some of the slaves, who had been inhumanly treated by their masters, now took revenge, and revealed their hiding-places to the pirates. A poor lame peasant, with his two daughters, was brought in. Appalled by the terrors of the rack, he promised to lead them through the woods to a retreat where several of the Spaniards were concealed. But the Spaniards, vigilantly on the watch, fled. The pirates, in the rage of their disappointment, hung the poor peasant. What became of his daughters we are not informed.

But I cannot torture my readers with a narrative of these horrors. They were dreadful beyond all powers of description. It seems inexplicable that God could have permitted such awful deeds.

Parties, thoroughly armed, were sent out to explore the region for many miles around. One of the slaves promised to conduct Captain Morgan to a river flowing into the lake, where there was a ship and four large boats richly laden with merchandise, taken both from Gibraltar and from Maracaibo. He also promised to lead a party to the place where the governor of Gibraltar was concealed, with most of the females of the city. The capture of the governor, for whom a great ransom could be expected, to save him from death by torture, and the capture of the females, were deemed matters of the greatest moment by these demoniac pirates.

Morgan himself took a party of two hundred men, with the slave as a guide, and set out on an expedition to capture the governor and the women. At the same time he dispatched another party of one hundred men in two large boats, to seize the ships. They were to coast along the shores of the solitary lake until they reached the mouth of the river where the vessels of the refugees were concealed.

The governor was on the alert. His scouts watched all the approaches to his retreat. It required a very painful and laborious march of two days for the pirates to reach the spot where the fugitives were intrenched. The governor, with much sagacity, had selected a large island in a river. The region was difficult of approach, leading through the roughest paths of tangled thickets and bogs. God seemed to frown upon the pirates. The rain fell in floods upon them. They were drenched to the skin. Many mountain torrents they were compelled to ford, wading up to the waist through the foaming water. They sank to the hips in the softened marshes. Their shoes were torn from their feet. Their clothes were rent and their skin pierced by the thorns.

When they reached the river they found the current rapid and the channel deep. There were no boats with which to cross. These desperate men were provided for every emergence. They soon constructed canoes and crossed the stream. But in the hurried passage many of the canoes were swamped and the men lost. Upon reaching the island they found that the governor had taken refuge on a densely wooded and craggy mountain. The path which led to the summit, winding through the thickets and the immense rocks, was so narrow that it could only be mounted in single file.

In fording the rivers and wading through the bogs, and breasting the rain and the gale, all of the ammunition of the pirates had been injured, and much of it utterly spoiled. The whole party was in such a condition, that Esquemeling writes: ·

"If the Spaniards, in that juncture of time, had had but a troop of fifty men, well armed with pikes or spears, they might have entirely destroyed the pirates, without any possible resistance on their side."

The governor was not aware of this. Prudently he remained upon the defensive. He had several of

the soldiers of the garrison with him, and an ample
supply of ammunition. His men were admirably
posted behind rocks and trees, so that had the pirates
persisted in their endeavor to ascend the mountain,
every man must have perished. And it is doubtful
whether they could have inflicted even a wound
upon their unseen assailants.

Morgan perceived that the case was hopeless.
Discouraged and maddened he commenced a retreat.
Twelve days passed from the time they commenced
their enterprise before Morgan, with his diminished
and shattered party, returned to Gibraltar. They
had, however, captured on the way quite a number
of fugitives whom they had found scattered through
the woods, and also a considerable amount of money.
They took a sort of fiendish pleasure, on their return, in seeing the aged women and the children
swept away by the foaming mountain torrents, which
they forded. They returned to Gibraltar exasperated, and prepared to inflict severer torture upon all
their captives.

The party sent to take the vessels were a little
more successful. The Spaniards had unloaded the
vessels and conveyed to unknown distances much of
their cargoes. Hearing of the approach of the
pirates, they fled precipitately, leaving behind them
all which they had not removed, or which they could

not immediately destroy. Still there were many bales of goods left in the vessels and on the shore. These the pirates seized and carried back to their ships.

When the pirates had been five weeks in Gibraltar, plundering, torturing, carousing, the failure of provisions rendered it necessary for them to depart. But first they sent some of their prisoners back into the woods to find their hidden companions, and to say to them that unless they sent Morgan, as a ransom for the city, five thousand dollars, in gold or silver, he would lay every building of the city in ashes. Those ruined men went forth on this sad mission. After searching every nook and corner for a long time, they came back to state that they could not find anybody. The terrified Spaniards had fled far beyond the reach of a day's exploration.

They said, however, that if Morgan would have a little patience and give them eight days, they would endeavor to raise the money. The pirate replied:

" I am going to Maracaibo. I shall take with me eight of your most prominent citizens, whom I hold as captives. I shall regard them as hostages for the payment of the ransom. If within eight days the money is paid, they will be set at liberty. If the money is not paid, they must suffer the penalty."

And what was that penalty? Death; and probably death by torture. Morgan began to feel a little solicitude about his retreat. In five weeks the Spaniards must have had time to assemble troops from various parts of the province, to repair the fortifications of Maracaibo, and to throw very serious obstacles in the way of his passing through the straits which connected Lake Maracaibo with the Gulf of Venezuela.

Influenced by this consideration, they moved with haste. Weighing their anchors and spreading their sails, with their fleet laden with plunder, they now directed their course toward Maracaibo. Baffled by light or contrary winds, four days passed before they reached the city. Here they found the same silence and desolation which they had left behind them. There was but one person in the place—a poor old man, sick and almost bed-ridden.

He gave them the alarming intelligence that three Spanish men-of-war were cruising off the head of the lake, watching their return. They had also repaired the fort which Morgan had partially destroyed, had mounted the guns anew, garrisoned the works with experienced artillerymen, and placed all things in posture for a vigorous defence. Over the redoubt the flag of Castile was proudly waving.

Morgan sent one of his swiftest boats down the

lake to reconnoitre the state of affairs. The boat came back the next day, confirming the statements. The ships were large and evidently well manned, as well as powerfully armed. The largest mounted forty-nine guns; the next, thirty-eight guns of different calibre; and the smallest, sixteen guns of large calibre, and eight of less. Morgan could not hope to contend successfully against forces so much superior to his own. The commander of this fleet was Don Alonzo Espinosa. He was vice-admiral of the West-Indian fleet. His little squadron had been sent to those seas to protect Spanish commerce, and to put to the sword every pirate he could take. The pirates were thrown into a state of great consternation. Their largest ship carried but fourteen guns. There seemed no possible escape for them by sea or by land.

Whatever might have been Morgan's secret feeling, he assumed an air of the utmost confidence. With audacity most extraordinary, considering the circumstances, he sent a Spanish prisoner to Admiral Espinosa, with the message that unless he immediately forwarded to him twenty-eight thousand dollars, in silver or gold, he would apply the torch to Maracaibo, and every building should be consumed.

The reply of the admiral was dated "On board

the royal ship Magdalen, lying at anchor at the entry of Lake Maracaibo, this 24th day of April, 1669."
In it Espinosa wrote:

" My intention is to dispute your passage out of the lake, and to pursue you wherever you may go. But if you will surrender all that you have taken, with all your prisoners, I will let you pass without molestation. But if you make any resistance, I will send my boats up to Maracaibo, and you shall be utterly destroyed. Every man shall be put to the sword. This is my fixed determination. I have good soldiers, who desire nothing more earnestly than to revenge on you, and your people, the outrages and cruelties you have committed on the Spanish nation."

Morgan, upon the reception of this letter, summoned all his men to meet in the market-place of Maracaibo. He submitted the question to them whether they would avail themselves of this offer, and thus escape with their lives, or run the risk of a battle with the Spanish squadron. The vote was unanimous that they would rather shed the last drop of blood they had, than give up the treasure they had obtained at the expense of so much danger and suffering. One of the pirates stepped forward, and said :

" Captain Morgan, I will undertake, with twelve

men, to destroy the largest of those ships. I will convert the large vessel we captured up the river into a fire-ship. We will fill her full of the most combustible matter. Then we will place images of men around, and sham guns, made of logs of wood, at the port-holes, and unfurl the English flag. The crew of the admiral's ship, not doubting that we are bearing down to give them battle, will not think of attempting to escape. We will run directly upon the Magdalen, throw our grappling-irons aboard, and, when both ships are instantly wrapped in flames, will, in the confusion, take to our boats, and reach some vessel near by."

The proposition was accepted with general acclaim. Still Morgan decided to make one more effort to escape without the peril and inevitable loss of a battle. Even should it utterly fail, he would gain time to prepare for the attack by the fire-ship. He therefore sent two of his prisoners to Espinosa, with this announcement :

"If the vice-admiral will pledge his honor that I may retire without being attacked, I will abandon Maracaibo, without burning the town or exacting any ransom. I will also set at liberty all the Spanish prisoners I have taken. The hostages I hold from Gibraltar shall be sent home, without exacting the ransom which was promised." The admiral replied :

" I will listen to no terms of accommodation different from those which I have proposed. If the prisoners and the booty are not voluntarily surrendered to me within two days, I will advance to your destruction."

In the mean time all hands were at work constructing the fire-ship. All the pitch, tar, and brimstone in the city were collected. Dried palm-leaves were gathered, in vast numbers, and smeared over with tar. Packages, containing several pounds of powder, were scattered through the loose mass. New port-holes were cut to let the air in to fan the flames. Many images of men were stationed along the decks, with caps on their heads and armed with muskets and pikes. The ship was so disguised that no one would doubt that it was a war-ship. From such the admiral of the Spanish fleet would surely make no effort to escape.

All things being ready, Morgan exacted an oath from every man that he would fight to the last drop of his blood ; that he would neither give nor take quarter. The Spanish fleet had passed through the strait to the entrance of the lake, and was riding at anchor just above the fort, which it will be remembered they had occupied, strengthened, and strongly garrisoned. Thus the pirates, before they could escape into the Gulf of Venezuela, must not only destroy the fleet, but also sail by the fort exposed to the terrible cannonade of its heavy ordnance.

On the evening of April 30th, 1669, Morgan spread his sails, and ran down the lake until he came in sight of the foe. Darkness was then coming on, and he cast anchor. The morning of the first of May dawned cloudless, over those vast solitudes of land and water, where a few adventurers from a distance of nearly ten thousand miles had met to crimson the waves with their blood, and to cause forest and lake and mountain to resound with the thunders of their demoniac fightings.

With the first gleam of light in the east, Morgan's fleet weighed its anchors and spread its sails. A fresh breeze from the south swelled their canvas. The fire-ship, with its wooden men and wooden guns, and which was prepared in an instant to flame into a volcano, bore down upon the Magdalen. Promptly the crew cleared the decks for action. Little did they dream of the foe whose resistless fury they were to encounter.

The fire-ship ran with a crash against the Spanish frigate. The boat of escape was ready with the men at the oars. The torch was applied at several places to make certainty doubly certain. The boat pushed off with rapid strokes, and scarcely one single moment elapsed before both ships were enveloped in densest smoke and flashing, consuming flame.

In an instant it was seen by all that the great achievement was accomplished ; that the majestic man-of-war, in all its pride and strength, was doomed to immediate destruction. No escape was possible. No resistance could be of the slightest avail. Not a boat could be launched. There was no time for thought even. Many of the sailors were instantly burned to a crisp as the forked flames encircled among them, wrapping them in its cruel embrace. All, who could, plunged into the sea. Many were drowned. A few strong swimmers reached the other vessels and were saved. Among these was the Admiral Espinosa.

The pirates gazed upon the awful spectacle with shouts of exultation. They had sworn to give no quarter. The drowning wretches presented but attractive targets for their sharpshooters. Boats put off from several of their nearer vessels to knock them in the head.

The second Spanish ship in size, which was called the St. Louis, mounted, as we have said, thirty-eight guns in all. The crew consisted of two hundred sailors. Seeing the utter destruction of the flagship, and that they were exposed to be attacked by the whole force of the pirates, they ran back beneath the guns of the fort. To prevent the ship from falling into the hands of the pirates they ran her ashore, scuttled her, and took refuge behind the intrenchments.

The third ship was called the Marquesas. It carried, as we have mentioned, twenty-four guns, large and small, and a crew of one hundred and fifty men. This vessel was so surrounded by the pirates that she could not escape. Her capture was effected with scarcely any conflict. Infamous as was the cause in which these pirates were engaged, it is difficult to withhold our admiration from the skill and the courage with which the great achievement was accomplished.

In less than one hour these Spanish war-ships, armed with the best Spanish ordnance, and manned by over six hundred combatants, were utterly destroyed or taken by the pirates, now but about three hundred in number, and whose largest ship mounted but fourteen guns. It is one of the most extraordinary feats in naval warfare. One of the historians of the time says: " The fire-ship fell upon the Spaniard, and clung to its sides like a wildcat on an elephant."

But still the pirates were by no means out of their difficulties. Their ships were all in Lake Maracaibo. A narrow and serpentine strait was to be threaded before they could enter the Gulf of Venezuela, by which alone they could gain access to the ocean. Here again the genius of Morgan came to the rescue. In the first place he collected all the prisoners he could, men, women, and children, and had them firmly secured. His plan was to compel the admiral to let him pass the fort unmolested, by threatening otherwise to put them all to death.

Among his captives there was a pilot of one of the Spanish ships. Upon being closely questioned, he made the following statement :

" We were sent by orders from the Supreme Council of Spain, with instructions to exterminate the English pirates. The Spanish court has made many complaints to the King of England of the hostilities committed here by the English. The king has ever replied that he had never given any commissions for such hostilities; that these were individual acts which the Government could not control, and for which they were not responsible.

" Hereupon the King of Spain resolved to protect his subjects and punish the perpetrators of these outrages. He fitted a fleet of six ships. Three of these, after an extended cruise, hearing of the attack upon Maracaibo, arrived here. The vice-admiral took possession of the fort, remounted its guns, adding several of large calibre, and added a hundred men to its original garrison whom he recalled."

Morgan returned to Maracaibo to plan for his escape. The Marquesas, which he had captured, was larger than any vessel of his own, and more heavily armed. He refitted this, making it his flagship. The one he had before occupied was intrusted to one of his captains.

13

CHAPTER XVIII.

A New Expedition Planned.

The Threat to Espinosa.—Adroit Stratagem.—Wonderful Escape.
—The Storm.—Revelry at Jamaica.—History of Hispaniola.—
Plan of a New Expedition.—The Foraging Ships.—Morgan's
Administrative Energies.—Return of the Foragers.—Rendezvous
at Cape Tiburon.—Magnitude and Armament of the Fleet.—
Preparations to Sail.

MORGAN, in the self-assurance of triumph, sent
word to the governor of Maracaibo, that unless he
sent him, within eight days, five hundred beef cattle,
the city of Maracaibo should be reduced to smouldering ruins. They were sent in within two days.
All hands were employed in butchering, salting,
and storing away the meat in preparation for
sea.

Returning with his fleet to the mouth of the
lake, Morgan sent word to Admiral Espinosa that he
had, on board his ships, between two and three hundred prisoners, including one hundred and fifty sailors of the Spanish fleet, who were captured in the
Marquesas. He demanded a free passage, promising,
if that were granted him, he would send all his pris-

oners unharmed ashore, as soon as his fleet was safe on the other side of the fort.

If this free passage were not granted him, he declared that he would force his way through ; and that he would bind all his prisoners to the rigging, that they might be the most exposed to the shot from the fort ; and that having passed by, every one who survived the cannonade should be killed and thrown overboard. The prisoners, well instructed in the cruelty and the inflexible will of this demoniac pirate, sent the most pathetic appeals to the admiral to save them from this dreadful fate. He, influenced by the pride of the soldier rather than by human sympathies, unfeelingly replied :

"If you had been as loyal to the king in hindering the entrance of these pirates as I shall be in hindering their going out, you would never have caused these troubles either to yourselves or to our whole nation, which hath suffered so much through your pusillanimity. I shall not grant your request; but shall endeavor, according to my duty, to maintain that respect which is due to my king."

When Morgan heard of this reply he said : "Very well ; if the admiral will not give me permission to pass, I will find a way of passing without his permission."

Before attempting to run through the strait, all

the pirates landed for a division of the booty. In making an inventory of their effects it was found that they had, in gold, silver, and jewels, two hundred and fifty thousand dollars. They had a still larger sum than this in the vast amount of merchandise which they had gathered from all the ships and store-houses of the two cities. They had also a large number of slaves, who brought cash prices in all the ports of the West Indies.

The escape was effected by the following ingenious stratagem. Morgan filled his boats with men, and rowed beneath the boughs which hung densely over the banks of the river, until he arrived at a concealed spot, where he pretended to land them. He took care, however, so to conduct the movement that the Spaniards in the fort should catch glimpses of it. The landing, however, was merely feigned. The men concealed themselves in the bottom of the boats, and were rowed back to the ships. Not one was left on the shore. In this way, by repeated excursions with the boats, apparently several hundred men were disembarked.

The admiral, well aware of the ferocious courage of the pirates, and not doubting that they would make a desperate assault upon the fort on the land side, immediately, and in the greatest haste, removed their eighteen-pounders to command the approaches by the land. In this way the sea-coast was left almost defenceless.

The ensuing night the moon rose full-orbed over the silent waters of the lake. A fresh breeze sprang up from the south. Providence seemed to be favoring these desperate men. The tide was also in their favor. And there was always a gentle current flowing through the narrow strait from the lake into the gulf.

Thus, with their path illumined by the moon's brilliant rays, and aided by wind, tide, and current, the pirates spread their sails, and, almost as by magic, glided by the fort. Every precaution was taken to protect the crews. No attempt was made to return the fire of the Spaniards. Most of the crews were placed in the holds of the ships. Only enough were left on deck for the purpose of navigation. The Spaniards, astonished, bewildered, and with but few guns at their command, fired hastily, furiously, and with very inaccurate aim at the ships so rapidly passing beyond their grasp. But little damage was done, and but few men were killed.

We are not informed whether Morgan carried out his threat of exposing his prisoners to the cannonade by binding them to the rigging. What became of the one hundred and fifty Spanish sailors, is not known. They were probably all put to death.

The prisoners from Maracaibo he sent ashore. Those from Gibraltar he carried away with him, and probably relieved himself of the incumbrance by throwing them all into the sea. As Morgan again set sail, his crews raised three cheers of triumph, and discharged eight heavy guns, loaded with balls, against the fort, as his parting salute.

But the very next day, heaven's frown seemed to succeed heaven's smile. One of the most terrible of tropical tornadoes assailed the fleet. All were in despair. The sailors threw themselves upon their knees, and called upon the Virgin and all the saints to help them. The gleaming lightning seemed to be the symbol of God's wrath, and the pealing thunder sounded like His angry voice.

Esquemeling, who accompanied this expedition, and to whose pen we are mainly indebted for an account of its events, says that the ship which bore him lost both anchors and mainsail. It was with the utmost difficulty they kept the ship afloat, working at the pumps for weary hours. The thunder he represents as deafening, and the mountain billows, rushing by, threatened every moment to ingulf them.

"Indeed," he writes, "though worn out with fatigue and toil, we could not make up our minds to close our eyes to that blessed light which we might

soon lose sight of forever. No hope of safety remained. The storm had lasted four days, and
there was no probability of its termination. On the
one side we saw rocks, on which our vessel threatened every instant to drive. Before us were the Indians, from whom we could hope for no mercy.
Behind us were the Spaniards, hungering for revenge."

At length the storm ceased. The fleet put into
a harbor, in the Bay of Venezuela, to repair dam-
ages. There seems to be but little reformatory
power in punishment. These wretched men were
not made better by the chastisement which they
had received. All unmindful of their prayers to
Virgin and saint, while some were at work on the
ships, others formed themselves into bands to ravage
the country far and wide, plundering all the Spanish
and Indian villages within their reach, and inflicting
the most atrocious outrages upon the inhabitants.
It is very clear that there is no hope for this lost
world, unless it may be found in that *change in the
heart* of man which the religion of Jesus Christ in-
culcates. "The mind is its own place." The pirates
after the storm were the same men as before.

Morgan, having refitted his ships, and having
added very considerably to his amount of plunder,
again spread his sails for Kingston, the capital of

Jamaica. He reached that port in safety, and was very cordially welcomed by the inhabitants and the British authorities there. They seemed to regard him as one of the heroes of the age, worthy of all honor. The sentiments of the English generally, at that time, in reference to these exploits, may be inferred from the following:

In a book published in London, in the year 1684, and which now lies before me, a glowing account is given of these adventures. The book had then attained to a second edition. The title-page says:

"A True Account of the most remarkable Assaults, committed of late years upon the Coasts of the West Indies, by the Buccaneers of Jamaica and Tortuga, wherein are contained more especially the unparalleled Exploits of Sir Henry Morgan, our English Jamaican Hero, who sacked Puerto Velo, burnt Panama, etc."

At Jamaica new scenes of rioting and profligacy were enacted. The money soon passed from the hands of the pirates to the sharpers in liquor-shops, gambling-houses, and dancing-halls, who were eager to grasp it. Morgan's eulogistic biographer writes:

"Morgan, encouraged by success, soon determined on fresh enterprises. On arriving at Jamaica, he found many of his officers and soldiers already reduced to their former indigency by their vices and debaucheries.   Hence they perpetually importuned him for new exploits, thereby to get something to expend in wine and strumpets, as they had already done with what they got before.

"Captain Morgan, willing to follow fortune's call, stopped the mouths of many inhabitants of Jamaica, who were creditors to his men for large sums, with the hopes and promises of greater achievements than ever, in a new expedition. This done, he could easily levy men for any enterprise. His name was so famous through all those islands, that it alone would bring him in more men than he could well employ."

Morgan scattered his proclamations far and wide through all the English and French ports on the various islands.   He wrote particularly to the governor of Tortuga, soliciting his coöperation. The south side of this island was appointed as a rendezvous, where Morgan, sailing from Jamaica, would meet the pirates of Tortuga who wished to join the expedition. Another and general rendezvous was designated, for adventurers from all the islands, at Port Couillon, on the south side of Hispaniola. And here let me give a few explanatory words in reference to this latter island.

Columbus discovered this magnificent island on the 5th of December, 1495. It was called by the

13*

natives Hayti. Its population was estimated at one million. It was four hundred miles long, with a breadth of from forty to one hundred and fifty miles, covering an area of nearly thirty thousand square miles. Columbus called it Hispaniola, or Little Spain. He established a colony on the northern coast, which he called Isabella. His brother, Diego, was intrusted with its command. This was the first colony planted by the Europeans in the New World.

In the year 1665, the French obtained possession of a large portion of the island, and gave it the name St. Domingo. This was about one hundred and seventy years after its discovery, and about five years before Morgan selected a bay on its southern coast as a rendezvous for his piratic fleet. It is in consequence of these changes that Hayti, Hispaniola, and St. Domingo frequently occupy so confused a relation in the public mind.

Punctuality is an essential element of success alike in good and bad enterprises. With singular promptness, Morgan sailed into the harbor of Couillon, in a large ship which he called the Flying Stag. It was crowded with pirates, or buccaneers as they would perhaps prefer to have been called, whom he had taken from Tortuga. It was the 24th day of October, 1670. He found twenty-four vessels already there, and sixteen hundred men. Almost every hour there were new arrivals of both ships and sailors. Morgan had selected for his flagship a large vessel, which mounted twenty-two guns. His arrival was greeted with shoutings, cannon-firing, flag-waving, and the most boisterous drunken revelry.

With energy and administrative ability characteristic of this very able and yet infamous man, he dispatched four vessels to the mainland, to cruise along the coast and plunder Spaniards and Indians of provisions, of corn, poultry, swine, and beeves, to victual his ships. They were also to sack such small towns as they were able to capture. All this was merely in preparation for the great enterprise before them.

While the four vessels were absent on this foraging expedition, Morgan kept his men busy careening, rigging, and calking their vessels, so as to be ready, immediately upon the return of the foragers, to put to sea. The magnitude of the enterprise in which this arch-pirate was engaged may be inferred from the fact that wide regions were to be devastated, and several towns sacked, merely to gather provisions for his army.

Hunters were sent into the woods of St. Domingo in search of game. All cattle and swine were considered fair booty, no matter to whom they might belong. Each hunting party had a certain region allotted to it. Portions of the crews were engaged in salting down provisions for the voyage. There were many swine roving through the woods. Frequently a hunting party would bring in as many as twenty or thirty men could carry. The most admirable discipline marked all these arrangements, over which Morgan presided.

The expedition sent to the continent reached its destination in six days. Fortunately for the Spaniards, just as the ships arrived within sight of land, they were becalmed. This gave the Spaniards time to conceal their treasures and to throw up intrenchments. The little fleet was at anchor just off the mouth of the river De la Hacha. There was in the river a large ship from Carthagena, laden with corn. The vessel, with all its cargo, fell into the hands of the pirates.

The next morning, just at break of day, a gentle breeze sprang up, and the ships ran in toward the shore. A landing of the men was effected, notwithstanding a valiant resistance by a small party of Spaniards. The pirates drove their foes from behind intrenchments which they had suddenly reared, and pursued them toward a strongly fortified town in the vicinity, called Rancheria. Here the Spaniards rallied again, and a desperate battle ensued. Many fell on both sides, for the Spaniards were by no means cowards. But the pirates were the victors, though at a heavy loss. They drove their foes into the woods, and took possession of the town. Several of the Spaniards were captured. As usual, they were exposed to the most diabolical tortures to compel the confession of where they had concealed their goods. The pirates remained here fifteen days. During this time, they were actively employed in taking captives and collecting booty. Just before their departure, they sent a number of prisoners to the fugitives dispersed through the woods, with the message that unless they sent, within a certain number of days, four thousand bushels of corn, they would destroy the town. The corn was sent in. The pirates sailed, greatly enriched with booty, and with all their ships heavily freighted with provisions.

They had been gone five weeks. Morgan began to despair of their return. The pirates had no confidence in each other. Morgan knew full well that if they had been triumphantly successful, amassing large quantities of gold and silver, they would prefer to go to some port where they could squander all their gains in every species of sensual indulgence. He also knew that there were large towns, like Carthagena and Santa Maria, in the region the ships were sent to plunder. There was no little danger that they might have been cut off by these combined garrisons,

Great, therefore, was his joy when, from the lookout, the returning ships were discerned in the distance. The provisions were divided among the fleet. The other booty, of precious metals, jewels, and goods, was awarded to the plunderers.

Morgan personally inspected every vessel. He then set sail for Cape Tiburon, at the west end of Hispaniola. This was a convenient spot to lay in wood and water. Here he was joined by several ships, which had been refitted at Jamaica to join the expedition. Morgan now found himself in command of a fleet of thirty-seven vessels, manned by two thousand two hundred sailors. The admiral's ship mounted twenty-eight guns, large and small. Many of the others carried twenty, eighteen, and sixteen guns. The smallest vessel had four. He had an abundant supply of ammunition, of fire-balls, hand-grenades, and pots which, upon being broken, diffused an intolerable suffocating odor.

The fleet was divided into two squadrons. The second squadron was placed under a vice-admiral. To every captain he gave a commission to practise every species of hostility against the Spanish nation. "You are to seize," he said, "their ships, wherever you can, whether at sea or in harbor, just as if they were the open and declared enemies of the King of England, Charles II., my master."

He assembled all the captains in his cabin to sign certain articles of agreement. It was stipulated that Morgan should have one hundredth part of all their booty. Every captain should draw the shares of eight men. The surgeons were to have two hundred dollars each, besides their regular share. The loss of both legs entitled one to an addition of fifteen hundred dollars; both arms, eighteen hundred dollars; one hand or one foot, six hundred dollars; an eye, one hundred dollars. Whoever should first pull down a Spanish flag, and raise the English in its stead, was to receive fifty dollars.

For a little time, it was debated whether they should attack Carthagena, Vera Cruz, or Panama. The lot fell upon Panama. It was the richest of the three. Though this city was situated on the western or Pacific shores of the Isthmus, and though it would be necessary to leave their fleet in some harbor, and march for several days over an unknown country, still there would be no difficulty in finding guides, the Spaniards would be but poorly prepared for so unexpected an attack, and the amount of booty, particularly in gold and silver, would be immense. Morgan proudly unfurled from his squadron

the royal English flag. Upon the other squadron
he spread to the breeze the blood-red banner of
the pirate ; and, strange to say, upon that piratic
banner he placed a white cross, the emblem of the
religion of our Lord and Saviour Jesus Christ, who
came to this lost world proclaiming " Glory to God
in the highest, and on earth peace, good will toward
men."

CHAPTER XIX.

Capture of St. Catherine and Chagres.

The Defences at St. Catherine.—Morgan's Strategy.—The Midnight Storm.—Deplorable Condition of the Pirates.—The Summons to Surrender.—Disgraceful Conduct of the Spanish Commander. —The Advance to Chagres.—Incidents of the Battle.—The Unexpected Victory.—Measures of Morgan.

On the 16th day of December, 1670, the piratic fleet weighed anchor from Cape Tiburon. They first directed their course to the recapture of the Island of St. Catherine upon the coast of Costa Rica. This island had become a penal colony, the Botany Bay, of Spain. The malefactors from all the Spanish dominions in the West Indies were transported here.

Four days' sail brought the fleet within sight of the island. The settlement was near the mouth of one of the rivers. Morgan sent forward one of his best sailing vessels to reconnoitre the defences. The river emptied into a large bay or harbor called the Grande Aguada. Upon the shores of this harbor the town was beautifully situated, surrounded by massive and well-garrisoned forts. Several of

Morgan's desperadoes had been there before. With his whole fleet he entered the harbor in the night-time.

Guided by instinctive military ability, with his usual promptness he landed one thousand men. Instead of marching directly upon the batteries, a corps of able engineers, with their axes, cut a new path through the tangled forest to the residence of the governor. Here they found a small rampart which was abandoned. The Spaniards, not being able to cope with so large a force as Morgan led, had retired to a stronger position. The pirates pursued. Soon they came upon a massive fort so fortified with encircling batteries as to seem impregnable. As soon as the pirates arrived within gun-shot the Spaniards opened upon them so deadly a fire from their heavy guns, that they were compelled to retire beyond reach of the bails, and take a position upon the grass of the open fields.

Night came. The pirates were weary and hungry. No food had been brought from the ships. It was supposed that food would be found in abundance. But the Spaniards had destroyed all which they could not remove; and it took a very large quantity to satisfy the appetites of a thousand hungry men. Faint from hunger, they threw themselves unsheltered upon the grass to sleep.

At midnight a tropical tempest arose. The glare of the lightning and the crashing peals of thunder were terrific. The windows of heaven seemed to be opened, and the flood fell in sheets. The sailors had left the ships with no clothing but their trousers and a shirt. In one moment they were drenched. And yet, hour after hour, in blackest darkness, the deluge descended, smothering them with its volume and flooding the fields. Notwithstanding all their efforts, nearly all of their powder was injured, and much was utterly destroyed.

In the morning, for an hour the rain ceased. They had just begun to flatter themselves that a pleasant day was opening upon them, when the clouds again gathered blackness, and the tempest assailed them with redoubled fury. It did seem as though they were exposed to the frown and the chastising blows of an indignant God. They found in the fields a poor old sick horse, " which was," writes Esquemeling, who was present, "both lean and full of scabs and blotches, with galled back and sides. This horrid animal they instantly killed and skinned, and divided into small pieces among themselves as far as it would reach ; for many could not obtain one morsel. This they roasted and devoured without either salt or bread, more like unto ravenous wolves than men."

They were at that time, Esquemeling says, in so
deplorable a condition that had the Spaniards fallen
upon them with one hundred men they might have
cut them all to pieces. The rain fell in such blind-
ing torrents that the pirates could not even retreat.
At noon there was another lull. Morgan, assuming
an air of great boldness and confidence, sent a flag
of truce to the governor, with the following summons to surrender:

" I solemnly swear unto you, that unless you immediately deliver your works, yourself, and all your
men into my hands, I will put every one to the
sword."

The governor was appalled. A piratic fleet of
thirty-seven vessels of war, manned by over two
thousand of the most fiend-like desperadoes earth
could furnish, presented a force greater than the
governor thought he could withstand. He sent
back a request that two hours' time might be
allowed him to deliberate with his officers, when he
would return a decisive answer. At the appointed
time he sent to Morgan the following humiliating
proposal:

" The governor is willing to surrender the island,
as he has not sufficient force to repel the English
fleet. But for the saving of his reputation and that
of his officers, he begs that Captain Morgan would

attack him by night, with all his marine and land forces. The governor will feign an attempt to escape from one fort to another, when Captain Morgan's troops can intercept and capture him. There shall be a continued firing on both sides, but without bullets."

To these terms, so degrading to the governor, Morgan rejoicingly acceded. Thus, from apparently hopeless defeat, his sagacity won a signal and bloodless victory. The sham fight took place according to the programme. That night there was a great and ridiculous roar of all the big guns in the fort and on the ships. Powder was burned freely. The white flag was raised by the governor, the surrender made, and the island, with all it contained, passed into the hands of the pirates.

The buccaneers were half starved. Several days were spent in feasting. The island was well stocked with beef cattle, swine, and poultry. Recklessly they were destroyed. The houses were torn down to build their fires. Two thousand men, by day and by night, indulged in the wildest orgies of revelry. Many of the people of the settlement fled into the woods. But the pirates counted four hundred and fifty captives. The women, who were subject to every indignity, were imprisoned in a church.

Morgan, upon inspecting the works, was astonished at their strength and at his own victory. The main fort, or castle as it was called, was very strong, built of stone, and surrounded by a wide ditch twenty feet deep. Heavy guns commanded the port. There were other supporting batteries which mounted nearly sixty guns. An immense amount of ammunition, including thirty thousand pounds of powder, were found in the fort. These were all transferred on board the ships. The guns were spiked, the gun-carriages burned, and the pirates, with shouts of victory, again spread their sails.

Among the prisoners there were three desperadoes, notorious robbers, who professed to be familiar with the route to Panama, and with all the region around. Eagerly they joined in the expedition with the promise of sharing in the spoil. Esquemeling, speaking of the proposition made to these wretches by Morgan, says:

"These propositions pleased the banditti very well. They readily accepted his proffers, promising to serve him very faithfully; especially one of these three, who was the greatest rogue, thief, and assassin among them, and who deserved, for his crimes, to be broken alive upon the wheel. This wicked fellow had a great ascendency over the other two, and could domineer over them as he pleased; they not daring to refuse obedience to his orders."

The Isthmus of Panama was then celebrated for its gold and silver mines. It was the seat of a very extensive commerce, and was perhaps more strongly fortified and more populous than any other of the Spanish colonies. This narrow tongue of land, which separates the Atlantic and Pacific oceans, is about three hundred miles in length, and from thirty to forty in breadth.

Chagres, on the Atlantic coast, was a very strongly fortified settlement at the mouth of the Chagres River. On the other side of the isthmus, on the Pacific shore, was Panama, a far more important place, abounding in wealth. Morgan's plan was to capture Chagres; leave his fleet in the harbor there ; ascend the river in his boats as far as the stream was navigable, and then to march to the doomed city. With his two thousand well-armed desperadoes he doubted not his ability to crush any force which might be brought against him.

Morgan sent, in advance, four ships and a large boat to capture Chagres. The expedition was intrusted to the vice-admiral Bradley, the same one who had so successfully led the foraging party to Rancheria. He was a notorious buccaneer, renowned for his exploits. Three days' sail brought his squadron to Chagres. Upon an eminence, commanding the entrance to the river, there was a strong fort, called Castle Lawrence. As Bradley approached the harbor, he unfurled at his mast-head the blood-red flag of the pirate. The garrison immediately displayed the royal banner of Spain, and foolishly saluted them with a volley of shot which did not reach their ships.

The buccaneers, according to their usual stratagem; instead of bringing their wooden walls up to be battered by the guns of the fort, cast anchor about a mile from the castle, and landing, cut a path with hatchet and sabre through the tangled forest, to attack the works upon their weakest side. Early in the morning the landing was effected. By the middle of the afternoon they had reached a hill, from whose summit they could throw their shot into the fort, could they but have drawn their cannon to that spot.

But the marshy ground would not admit of this. The garrison had brought their guns to bear upon the eminence, and opened a fire before which many of the pirates fell. Bradley was greatly disheartened. The fort proved to be of very unexpected strength. It was surrounded by two high parallel walls of timber, filled in with earth. Well-constructed bastions were at each corner. The works were enclosed by a ditch, thirty feet deep. There was but one entrance, and that was by a drawbridge across this ditch. The north side of the castle was washed by the broad and rapid river. On the south there was a precipitous inaccessible crag. Strong batteries guarded the approaches to both the other sides.

Even the most desperate of the pirates recoiled from the idea of attempting to carry works so formidable by assault. But Bradley could not endure the thought of the scorn and rage he would encounter from Morgan should he retreat without making the attempt. After much perplexity and disputing it was resolved to hazard the assault. They hoped with hatchet and sabre to cut down the timber, and then to clamber over the crumbling earth. The interior of the works was all of wood. There were barracks and huts, which, beneath the blaze of a tropical sun, had become dry as powder.

Cautiously the buccaneers descended the hill, throwing themselves upon their faces as the explosions of the massive guns showered the balls around them. Their sharpshooters threw bullets through the loops of the walls, and through the embrasures, to strike down the artillery-men at the guns. This skirmishing was continued until night, but nothing was accomplished. Many of the pirates were killed, and Bradley himself had one of his legs broken by a cannon-ball. The reckless men charged up to the very walls, threw over fire-balls, and hacked at the timbers.

The pirates, as darkness approached, began to retreat. The Spaniards shouted to them from the walls:

"Come on, you English devils; you heretics; the enemies of God and of the king. Let your comrades, who are behind, come also. We will serve them as we have served you. You shall not get to Panama this time."

This shout alarmed them. It revealed the fact that, in some way, the Spaniards had been warned of the expected attack upon Panama, and would prepare for resistance. As a group of the pirates were conferring together, in the dusk, an arrow from the castle struck one of them in the shoulder. He coolly drew the point from the bleeding wound, and addressing his companions, said:

"Look here, my comrades, I will make this accursed arrow the means of the destruction of all the Spaniards."

He then drew from his pocket a quantity of wild cotton, which the buccaneers carried with them as lint to staunch their wounds. This he wound around the head of the arrow. Charging his musket with powder only, he inserted the arrow and fired it back into the castle. It lighted upon a roof of thatch. The powder set fire to the cotton, and the cotton to the dry leaves. They roof was instantly in a flame.

The Indians had aided the garrison, and their arrows lay thick around. Instantly the air was filled with a shower of these flaming meteors. They fell upon the thatched roofs, and tongues of fire flashed in all directions. One chanced to fall upon a large quantity of powder, and a fearful explosion followed. A terrible conflagration blazed forth. A scene of shrieks, confusion, and horror ensued which is indescribable. The inmates of the fort found themselves in the crater of a volcano in its most violent state of eruption. It was in vain to attempt to extinguish the flames. No one could live in such a furnace.

The night was dark, moonless and starless. The bodies of the Spaniards were clearly defined against the glowing background of flame. The pirates, with unerring aim, shot them down. Every bullet struck its target. The Spaniards, in the horrible tumult, could make but little resistance. They still, however, taking refuge as they could in different parts of the fort, fought with impotent desperation. Oexemelin relates an incident illustrative of the indomitable fury of the assailants.

One of the pirates was pierced in the eye by an

Indian arrow. In terrible agony he came to Oexemelin to draw it out. Its barbed point had sunk deep in the socket of the eye, and could only be withdrawn by cruelly tearing it out. Oexemelin hesitated; he had not sufficient nerve to inflict such torture. The pirate seized it with both hands, tore it out with its mangled and bloody adhesions, bound a handkerchief over the wound, and with a curse rushed forward again to the assault.

The fire raged through the whole night. All the wood-work was consumed. The walls of earth crumbled down. The pirates, mounting upon each other's shoulders, climbed the ramparts and threw down hand-grenades and fire-balls, and pots of suffocating odors upon the helpless garrison. "The armor had fallen piecemeal from their giant adversary, and he now stood before them bare, wounded, and defenceless."

Still, in one corner of the fort, the heroic governor rallied the few survivors, twenty-five only in number, resolved to fight to the bitter end. They were slightly protected from a charge by a deep ditch, which ran directly before them. This, however, afforded them no shelter from the bullets of their foes. A dreadful storm of fire-balls and lead fell upon them. They had no hope of victory—no hope of escape even. Their only desire was to kill as many of the pirates as they could before they should die themselves. At last a shot pierced the brain of the governor. The feeble remnant was easily overpowered.

The garrison had consisted of three hundred and fourteen men. All of these, excepting fourteen, were either killed or helplessly wounded. Not a single officer was left alive. The governor had previously dispatched a courier to Panama to alarm the city. In this sanguinary conflict the pirates had lost very heavily. One hundred were killed and seventy grievously wounded. A large pit was dug and the one hundred dead bodies of the pirates were thrown in and covered up from sight and smell. The prisoners were compelled to drag the bodies of the dead Spaniards to the cliff, and cast them into the sea. A large amount of ammunition and provisions were found in the fort.

Morgan, informed of the fall of Chagres, devastated the Island of St. Catherine as much as possible, so as to render it quite indefensible. It was his intention to return and recover the place, so as to make it a rendezvous for his fleet in future operations. On the cruise to Chagres a violent storm arose. His fleet was scattered, so that they were detained many days at sea. But as ship after ship entered the bay, and the crews beheld the English flag floating from the blackened walls of Chagres Castle, the bay resounded with their cheers, and with salutes from their cannon. So eager was the admiral and some of the others in their heedless joy, that, without waiting for a pilot, his own and three other vessels were driven upon sunken rocks, where they broke to pieces. The crew and cargoes were saved.

Morgan immediately set to work with great energy, employing all his force of engineers, carpenters, and laborers in repairing the castle. Here he stationed a garrison of picked men, storing the magazines with provisions and ammunition, as a refuge from any possible disaster at Panama. The fortunes of war are proverbially inconstant. The pirate Morgan was a very able general. His plans were generally well formed to meet adversity as well as prosperity.

CHAPTER XX.

The March from Chagres to Panama.

FROM the prisoners Morgan learned that three weeks before their arrival the garrison at Chagres was informed, by a message from Carthagena, that the English were equipping a fleet at Hispaniola for the capture of Panama. The governor immediately sent one hundred and sixty-four soldiers to strengthen the garrison at Chagres, which had previously numbered but one hundred and fifty. Morgan was also informed that the governor of Panama had placed several ambuscades along the Chagres River, and that a force of three thousand six hundred men was awaiting his arrival at Chagres.

These were tidings sufficient to appal any ordinary mind. But the pirates were accustomed to triumph over vastly superior numbers.   There were several large Spanish boats at Chagres, adapted to river navigation.   All these Morgan seized.   They generally mounted two great iron guns and four smaller ones of brass.   These vessels, with those he took from his ships, made a flotilla of thirty-two gunboats.   They were manned by twelve hundred sailors.   Five hundred were left behind to garrison the castle.   One hundred and fifty had charge of the ships.

On the 18th of August, 1670, Morgan put his fleet in motion to ascend the Chagres River on his advance to Panama.   His boats were greatly crowded, and so heavily laden with men, ammunition, and arms, that he could take but a small supply of provisions.   He expected to provide himself abundantly from the supplies he should find in the Spanish ambuscades.

The first day the little fleet ascended the river but eighteen miles, to a place called Bracos.   The men on board his boats were greatly cramped in their limbs, having but little room to move, and none in which to lie down.   They therefore found it necessary to land for the night, that they might enjoy a few hours of sleep.   They also hoped to rob some of the neighboring plantations.   Nearly all their food had disappeared in this one day's sail.

The cheer of camp-fires seems to be essential to all bivouacs. The gloom of the dense tropical forest was soon illumined by the flames around which twelve hundred men were congregated. Most of them went supperless to their mossy beds, consoled only by their pipes of tobacco. In the morning they ranged the country in vain for food. The planters had fled, taking with them or destroying everything that could be eaten.

Again they repaired to their boats. Hungry, disappointed, and murmuring, they ascended the river about twenty miles farther until they reached a place called Juan Gallego. Here they were compelled to leave their boats, as the river was so shallow from want of rain; it was also much impeded by decayed and fallen trees. Thus ended the second day.

There was no road for an army through the rough, miry, tangled maze. They were told by the guides that, at the distance of two leagues, they would find the country more favorable. With sabre and hatchet these half-famished men hewed a narrow path for themselves. They fed upon berries, roots, and leaves. One hundred and sixty men were left to guard the boats, and to feed themselves as best they could by hunting or plundering, or obtaining supplies from the fleet.

14*

Morgan had advanced but a mile or two when the gigantic growth and interlacing vines seemed to render the forest impenetrable. The river also deepened a little, so that some of his boats would float. There was imminent danger every moment that he would fall into some ambuscade. He sent back for some light canoes to be brought up. This was accomplished with great labor. He then embarked his men, taking a part at a time, and thus, ascending the river a few miles farther, reached a place called Cedro Bueno. To accomplish this, the canoes made several passages. The pirates were very eager to encounter the Spaniards, as their only means of obtaining any food. But the Spaniards wisely left them to the hardships of their march and to the pangs of starvation.

The morning of the fourth day dawned upon these wretched marauders. Most of them struggled along the banks of the river, led by one of their guides. Others toiled against the stream, in the canoes, being often compelled to alight in the water, to cross sandbars or surmount rapids. To guard against ambuscades the guides were kept a quarter of a mile in advance. The Spaniards had sent forward their Indian scouts, and kept themselves informed of every movement of the foe. About noon of this day they reached a place which from its extreme ruggedness was called Torna Cavallos.

Here the guides came rushing back to the main body with the announcement that they had discovered an ambuscade. The half-starved men were delighted. They knew that the Spaniards, on all their expeditions, provided themselves luxuriously with food. Examining their muskets, their priming, and their sabres, that they might be prepared for a resistless charge, they pressed eagerly yet cautiously forward. They soon came in sight of an intrenchment, which was shaped like a half-moon. Their practised eyes told them that it would protect a garrison of about four hundred men. Twelve hundred men, impelled by rage and hunger, with hideous yells rushed upon it. Bitter was their disappointment when they found no foe there. They had captured but an abandoned and crumbling rampart. There were some coarsely tanned, hairy leather bags scattered around. Their hunger was so great that these were cut up, cooked, and eaten. We have a minute account of the cookery of these unsavory morsels.

First they took the leather and sliced it in pieces. Then they beat the pieces between two stones rubbing them and dipping them in the water, to render them supple and tender. Lastly they scraped off the hair, and roasted or broiled the pieces upon the fire. Being thus cooked, they cut it into very fine pieces, which "they helped down with frequent gulps of water, which by good fortune they had nigh at hand."

"I can assure the reader," writes Oexemelin, "that a man can live on such food, though he can hardly get very fat."

Esquemeling adds, "Some who were never out of their mothers' kitchens may ask how these pirates could eat, swallow, and digest those pieces of leather so hard and dry? Unto whom I would answer that could they once experience what hunger, or rather famine is, they would certainly find the manner, as the pirates did, by their own experience."

On the morning of the fifth day the weary march was resumed. Having had but little food, save the leather bags, they were in a deplorable condition. The pirates were not amiable men. They staggered along, in their weakness, over the rough ways, murmuring, quarrelling, and cursing each other. As night approached they came to a place called Barbacoa. Here they found another abandoned ambuscade. Not a particle of food was to be obtained. Loud and bitter were their oaths against the Spaniards. Dreadful would have been the fate of any of them who might have fallen into their hands. Esquemeling says that they were so consumed by hunger, that if they had caught any of the Spaniards they would certainly have roasted and eaten them.

Parties were sent out to explore the woods in search of habitations. But none could be found. The inhabitants, in all directions, had fled, carrying with them their provisions. The day was spent here. It was a day of dreadful suffering. Life was preserved by devouring berries, roots, and leaves. Several plantations were discovered, but there was generally not an individual, an animal, or a kernel of corn left behind. In one place they found concealed two sacks of wheat, two jars of wine, and a few plantains. These Morgan divided among those who were nearest to perishing of hunger.

The sixth day they continued their march, still along the banks of the Chagres River. Such as could not walk were paddled along in light canoes. At night they came to a plantation, which, as usual, was entirely abandoned. Their supper consisted mainly of leaves and grass.

The next day, at noon, they discovered a barn, full of Indian corn in the husk. They fell upon it and devoured it dry, with the rapacity of a herd of swine. Having satiated their hunger, each man loaded himself with as much as he could carry. With renovated spirits, they pressed on their way. After journeying along for a couple of hours, they came upon a band of about two hundred Indians, who fled with the utmost precipitation. They were far more fleet of foot than the exhausted pirates, and not one of them was shot or captured. In their flight, the Indians threw back a shower of arrows, which wounded several of the pirates, and killed three of them. They shouted out in Spanish: " Ha! ye dogs, go to the plain, go to the plain."

They now reached such a bend in the river that it was necessary to cross it. They therefore bivouacked for the night. This place was called Santa Cruz.

Loud murmurings filled the camp. Morgan was denounced in unmeasured terms. They were indeed involved in gloom. To go back was certain starvation. And destruction seemed equally to threaten them in a farther advance. There were some, however, who still kept up their courage, and shouted, "Onward! onward!"

The morning of the seventh day they crossed the river. As it was supposed that they must soon meet the Spaniards, every man was required carefully to examine his musket and pistols, to be ready for any engagement. The guides told them that they were approaching the important town of Cruz, where they would find provisions and other stores in abundance. This was called the halfway house between Chagres and Panama, though it was sixty-eight miles from the former place and but twenty-four from the latter. To this point the Chagres merchandise was taken in boats, when the river was full, and, being landed, was conveyed to Panama on the backs of mules. To give the reader some idea of the style of Esquemeling's narrative, written two hundred years ago,* I will quote his graphic description of what ensued:

"While yet at a considerable distance from Cruz, they perceived much smoke to arise out of the chimneys. The sight thereof afforded them great joy, and hopes of finding people in the town; and afterwards what they most desired was plenty of good cheer. Thus they went on, with as much haste as they could, making several arguments to one another upon those external signs, though all like castles built in the air. For said they, 'There is smoke cometh out of every house. Therefore they are making good fires for to roast and boil what we are to eat,' with other things to this purpose.

"At length they arrived there, in great haste,

* His account was written in Dutch, but translated into English and published in London.

all sweating and panting; but found no person in the town, nor any thing that was eatable, wherewith to refresh themselves, unless it were good fires to warm themselves, which they wanted not. For the Spaniards, before their departure, had every one set fire to his own house, excepting only the storehouses and stables belonging to the king.

"They had not left behind them any beast whatever, either alive or dead. This occasioned much confusion in their minds; they not finding the least thing to take hold of, unless it were some few cats and dogs, which they immediately killed and devoured with great appetite. At last, in the king's stables, they found, by good fortune, fifteen or sixteen jars of Peru wine, and a leather sack full of bread. But no sooner had they begun to drink of the said wine, when they fell sick, almost every man.

"This sudden disaster made them think that the wine was poisoned, which caused a new consternation in the whole camp, as judging themselves now to be irrecoverably lost. But the true reason was their huge want of sustenance in that whole voyage, and the manifold sorts of trash which they had eaten upon that occasion. Their sickness was so great that day as caused them to remain there till the next morning, without being able to prosecute their journey, as they used to do, in the afternoon.

" Here Captain Morgan was constrained to leave his canoes and land all his men, though never so weak in their bodies. But lest the canoes should be surprised, or take too many men for their defence, he resolved to send them all back to the place where the boats were, excepting one, which he caused to be hidden, to the intent it might serve to carry intelligence, according to the exigency of affairs. Many of the Spaniards and Indians, belonging to this village, were fled unto the plantations thereabouts. Hereupon Captain Morgan gave express orders that none should dare to go out of the village except in whole companies of one hundred together.

" The occasion hereof was his fear lest the enemies should take an advantage upon his men by any sudden assault. Notwithstanding, one party of English soldiers stickled not to contravene these commands, being thereunto tempted with the desire of finding victuals. But these were soon glad to fly into the town again, being assaulted with great fury by some Spaniards and Indians, who snatched up one of the pirates and carried him away prisoner. Thus the vigilancy and care of Captain

Morgan was not sufficient to prevent every accident which might happen."

On the morning of the 8th, Morgan reviewed his troops. He found that he had still eleven hundred resolute men at his command. He selected a band of two hundred of his best marksmen as an advance guard. They were to watch vigilantly for ambuscades. The path they were to traverse was very narrow. At many places but two could pass abreast. Cautiously they proceeded for ten hours, encountering no sign of an enemy.

At length they reached a dark wooded gorge, which the sunlight could scarcely penetrate. Apparently no one could enter the dense thickets around, of bushes, thorns, and intertwining vines, but by hewing his way with the hatchet. A high mountain rose before them. But nature had tunnelled it, so that there was a narrow path through. This remarkable place was called Quebrada Obscura.

Suddenly, from the impenetrable forest which enveloped the mountain, a shower of arrows fell upon them, like hailstones from the clouds. They probably exaggerated the number in estimating them at between three and four thousand. They came rushing, as by some supernatural impulse, through the leaves. No hand was seen. No sound was heard. No movement was perceptible. There was but that one flight of arrows and no more. Those who, with sinewy arms, had thrown them, in some mysterious way escaped—as it were, vanished.

This singular and inexplicable assault threw the army into great confusion. For a moment, these reckless men were staggered. It seems strange that but eight of the pirates were killed and ten wounded by this shower of arrows. After a few moments' delay, the pirates moved cautiously forward, threading the narrow tunnel, through which but two could walk abreast, until they came out upon a very rough plain on the other side, encumbered with huge rocks and a growth of gigantic trees. To this vantage-ground the Indians had retreated, and here they seemed disposed to make a stand.

Quite a fierce battle ensued. The Indians could be seen, in large numbers, dodging from rock to rock, and from tree to tree. They fought with great bravery. Their chief was a very handsome young fellow, gorgeously dressed, and with a very brilliant coronet of variegated feathers. He seemed to have no fear. At length, in his zeal, he plunged headlong upon the pirates, utterly regardless of numbers, and endeavored to thrust his javelin through one a little in the advance. The blow was parried, and he was instantly shot down.

As he was seen to fall, there was a loud cry from

his followers, and, without discharging another shaft, they all fled. The pirates impetuously pursued. The fugitives could not be overtaken. A few of the boldest concealed themselves behind trees and thickets, whence they could make good their retreat, and worried the pirates with a random fire, which sorely wounded a few, without accomplishing any important results.

The buccaneers entered soon upon a broad, treeless prairie. Here they halted to tend the wounded. At some distance before them there was another rocky and wooded eminence. The Indians, who seemed to be swarming there, were evidently preparing for another battle. A party of fifty men was sent, by a circuitous route, to attack them in the rear. Their watchful eyes detected the movement. With nimble feet, they fled, shouting to their assailants, "To the plain, to the plain, you English dogs."

The pirates rightly interpreted these words to mean that on the plain before Panama a large body of Spaniards was assembled, and that there the great struggle was to take place. Many Spaniards were with the Indians. At this point, which was but a few miles from Panama, they disappeared. The next night there came one of those flooding rains with which tropical lands were so often deluged. The pirates in vain sought shelter from the drenching storm. There was the blackness of darkness, with thunderings and lightnings, and the howlings of the tornado. There were many plantations on the route where houses and huts had been reared. But the Indians had applied the torch. Every building was in ashes. The cattle were driven away. All provisions were removed or consumed. These wretched men, on their fiend-like mission, were still starving.

The next morning, which was the ninth of their journey, the rain ceased. Heavy clouds floated through the sky, darkening the sun, and thus enabling them to march sheltered from its scorching rays. A well-mounted troop of twenty Spaniards appeared at some distance in the advance, watching all the movements of the invaders. During the day they came to quite a high mountain, which it was necessary to cross. From its summit they first caught sight of the Pacific Ocean, and of the Bay of Panama, upon whose shores the city of the same name was situated. In the bay there was a large Spanish ship riding at anchor. Six boats were under sail, directing their course toward the islands of Tavoga and Tavogilla, which were about eighteen miles distant.

At this sight the pirates raised shouts of joy Never doubting their own prowess, they considered their toils as ended, and the city, with all its treasures, as already in their possession. At the foot of the mountain there was a large grassy plain, over which thousands of cattle were grazing, cows, horses, bulls, mules, and donkeys. With a rush, the piratic gangs descended the mountain, and, with the voracity of famished wolves, fell upon the cattle.

"One shot a horse. Another felled a cow. But the greater part slaughtered the mules, which were most numerous. Some kindled fires; others collected wood; and the strongest hunted the cattle, while the invalids slew and skinned and flayed. The whole plain was soon alight with a hundred fires. The hungry men cut off lumps of flesh, carbonaded them in the flame, and ate them half raw, with incredible haste and ferocity. 'They resembled,' Esquemeling says, 'rather cannibals than Christians, the blood running down their beards to the middle of their bodies.'" *

* Monarchs of the Main, vol. ii. p. 114.

CHAPTER XXI.

The Capture of Panama.

First Sight of the City.—The Spanish Scouts Appear.—Morgan's
Advance.—Character of the Country.—Fears of the Spaniards.—
Removal of Treasure.—Capture of the City.—The Poisoned
Wine.—Magnificent Scenery of the Bay.—Description of Panama
and its Surroundings.—Wealth of the City.—Scenes of Crime
and Cruelty.

MORGAN was an extrordinary man. Fear never
appalled him. He was never discouraged by disasters. Passion was never allowed to throw him off
his guard. He shared, in full, all the hardships of
his demoniac crew. Though hungry and weary himself, and sympathizing with his starving men in their
sufferings, he did not in the least degree remit his
watchfulness or lose his self-control.

Perceiving the danger that his men, in their
famished condition, indulging in such reckless gluttony might induce sickness which would incapa-
citate them for battle, he ordered a false alarm to be
sounded. Instantly every man seized his musket
and ran to his appointed place in the ranks. Morgan had taken the precaution, before descending

the mountain, to order every musket to be discharged and loaded afresh, from fear that the powder might have become damp.

There were several miles yet to be traversed, over plains and through forests, before the pirates could enter the streets of the city, which they had discerned in the distance. Cautiously they continued their march until the approach of evening, when they ascended an eminence which commanded a perfect view of the city, with its steeples, houses, and streets all aglow with the rays of the setting sun. Here the shouts of exultation were renewed. The pirates, strengthened by their feast, danced for joy, beating their drums, sounding their trumpets, firing off their muskets, and exulting as in the hour of perfect victory. Here they encamped for the night, waiting impatiently for the morning, which would usher in the decisive battle.

In the evening two hundred mounted Spaniards rode out from the city, dashed along until they came within hailing distance of the pirates, and shouted out to them words which could not be understood. Morgan established double sentinels, and all his men slept upon their arms.

At daybreak on the tenth day the Spaniards, from their walls, sounded with bugle-peal and drum-beat a challenge to their foes. The pirates were equally eager for the fight. Rapidly they advanced into the plain. The Spaniards, on horseback and on foot, crowded out to meet them. In glittering battalions they were drawn up upon the plain, outnumbering the pirates three to one. There were two squadrons of cavalry, four regiments of foot, and, most singular to relate, "a huge number of wild bulls, roaring and tossing their horns, driven by a great number of Indians and a few mounted matadores."

It is recorded that the pirates were surprised and alarmed in view of the force thus to be encountered. Many of them wished they were at home. No quarter was to be expected. There was no hope for them but in fighting with the utmost desperation. All were conscious of this. They therefore bound themselves, by the most solemn oaths, to conquer or to spend the last drop of their blood.

Morgan formed his men into three battalions, after selecting a band of two hundred sharp-shooters to skirmish in the advance. Many of the Spaniards were armed in glittering coats of mail. Their silken banners, richly embroidered, presented a beautiful appearance as they fluttered in the rays of the morning sun. The Spaniards sent forward a squadron of horse. As they came galloping over the plain, Morgan's skirmishers fell upon one knee, in the tall grass, and opened upon them a very destructive fire. Several riders dropped from their horses. Several horses, struck by the bullets, and appalled by the sudden explosion of two hundred guns, became uncontrollable, and rushed wildly over the plain in all directions.

"The bulls," writes Thornbury, "proved as fatal to those who employed them as the elephants to Porus. Driven on the rear of the buccaneers, they took fright at the noise of the battle, a few only broke through the English companies, and trampled the red colors under foot; but these were soon shot by the old hunters. A few fled to the savanna, and the rest tore back and carried havoc through the Spanish ranks."

The plain was rough with ravines and quagmires, so that the cavalry could not operate to advantage. The desperate pirates were all reckless in their courage, and nearly all unerring in their aim. The Spaniards were also men of war and blood, who had been guilty of the greatest atrocities as they had cut down and robbed the native tribes. They fought with ferocity equal to that of the pirates. In this battle it was, in reality, fiend against fiend The Spaniards were as bad as the pirates.

For two hours the battle raged with intensest fury. There was neither tree, stump, nor rock to protect either party from the bullets which with deadly velocity swept the plain. On the one side there were eleven hundred pirates. Esquemeling estimated the force of the Spaniards at four hundred cavalry and two thousand four hundred infantry. There were also one or two hundred Indians and negroes to drive the wild bulls through the English camp, hoping thus to break their lines and throw them into confusion. The Spaniards had also dug trenches and raised batteries to arrest the advance of their foes.

Morgan, as usual, ordered his men to approach the city by a circuitous route, so as to avoid the batteries. In preparation for this movement he ordered a review of the troops. He concealed from his troops the number of pirates who had fallen, but announced, probably with some exaggeration, that six hundred of the Spaniards lay dead upon the field.

It would seem that the Spaniards had not been very sanguine as to the result of the battle; for they had shipped to the Island of Tavoga much of their portable wealth and all of their women. In the battle thus far, the Spaniards had been so decidedly beaten that they had abandoned the field, and horse and foot had taken a new stand behind the ramparts. Many prisoners had been taken, including quite a number of Catholic priests. Morgan, not wishing to be encumbered with prisoners, ordered them all to be pistolled. The pirates had lost heavily, but their loss exasperated instead of disheartening them.

Esquemeling writes: "The pirates were nothing discouraged, seeing their numbers so much diminished, but rather filled with greater pride than before, perceiving what huge advantage they had obtained against their enemies. Thus, having rested themselves some while, they prepared to march courageously towards the city, plighting their oaths to one another that they would fight till never a man were left alive. With this courage they recommenced their march either to conquer or to be conquered.

"They found much difficulty in their approach unto the city. For within the town the Spaniards had placed many great guns at several quarters thereof, some of which were charged with small pieces of iron and others with musket bullets. With all these they saluted the pirates at their drawing nigh unto the place, and gave them full and frequent broadsides, firing at them incessantly. From whence it happened that they lost, at every step they advanced, great numbers of men.

"But neither these manifest dangers of their

lives, nor the sight of so many of their own dropping down continually at their sides, could deter them from advancing farther and gaining ground every moment upon the enemy. Thus, although the Spaniards never ceased to fire, and act the best they could for their defence, yet, notwithstanding, they were forced to deliver the city after the space of three hours' combat. And the pirates, having now possessed themselves thereof, both killed and destroyed as many as attempted to make the least opposition against them.

" The inhabitants had caused the best of their goods to be transported unto more remote and occult places. Howbeit, they found within the city, as yet, several warehouses well stocked with all sorts of merchandise, as well silks and cloths as linen and other things of considerable value. As soon as the first fury of their entrance into the city was over, Captain Morgan assembled all his men, at a certain place which he assigned, and there commanded them, under very great penalties, that none of them should dare to drink or taste any wine.

" The reason he gave for this injunction was because he had received private intelligence that it had been all poisoned by the Spaniards. Howbeit it was the opinion of many that he gave those prudent orders to prevent the debauchery of his people, which he foresaw would be very great at the beginning, after so much hunger sustained by the way; fearing withal lest the Spaniards, seeing them in wine, should rally their forces, and use them as inhumanly as they had used the inhabitants before."

Morgan was now master of Panama. The city, with nearly all of its wealth, had fallen into his hands. And still the vanquished Spaniards could rally a force greatly outnumbering his own. The Bay of Panama is one of peculiar beauty. At that time its shores were fringed with luxuriant groves of oranges, figs, and limes. The feathery tops of the cocoanut trees towered over all the rest, rivalled only by the lofty tamarinds. Through the rich foliage there peeped, in much picturesque beauty, numerous cane-built huts. Indian children, entirely unclothed, were running about upon the beach, while birch canoes, light as bubbles, were skimming the placid waves.

The islands of Tavoga and Tavogilla appeared in the distance as masses of foliage. The mines of Mexico and Peru had emptied their floods of wealth into that port. Many of the mansions were architecturally magnificent. They were adorned with the richest paintings and with the most costly furniture. The Spanish grandees had hung upon their walls the masterpieces of Titian, Murillo, and Velasquez.

The streets of the city were broad, an unusual circumstance in Spanish cities, and were lined with the most beautiful and ever-flowering of tropical trees.

Within the walls of the city there was a cathedral of imposing magnitude and towering splendor. There were also eight monasteries, massive buildings, occupied by the religious orders, and abundantly supplied with works of art. The broad avenues were lined with two thousand mansions of the wealthy; and five thousand smaller houses and shops crowded the more busy streets. The most imposing block in the city was what was called the Genoese Warehouses. These belonged to a company who had enriched themselves by the slave trade. An immense number of horses and mules were used in transporting goods across the isthmus, from one ocean to the other. These were kept in long rows of stables admirably arranged. The products of the mines of gold and silver were melted down into solid bars called plate or bullion, and in that form were sent to the Old World. The city was surrounded with rich plantations and highly artistic gardens.

" Panama was the city to which all the treasures of Peru were annually brought. The plate fleet, laden with bars of gold and silver, arrived here at certain periods, brimming with the crown wealth, as well as that of private merchants. It returned laden with the merchandise of Panama and the Spanish main, to be sold in Peru and Chili ; and still oftener with droves of negro slaves that the Genoese imported from the coast of Guinea to toil and die in the Peruvian mines.

" So wealthy was this golden city that more than two thousand mules were employed in the transport of the gold and silver from thence to Porto Bello, where the galleons were loaded. The merchants of Panama were proverbially the richest in the whole Spanish West Indies. The governor of Panama was the suzerain of Porto Bello, Nata, Cruz, and Veragua. The bishop of Panama was primate of the Terra Firma and the suffragan to the archbishop of Peru. The district of Panama was the most healthy of all the Spanish colonies, rich in mines, and so well wooded that its ship-timber covered with vessels both the northern and the southern seas. Its land yielded full crops, and its broad savannas pastured innumerable herds of wild cattle." *

Such was the city and province which had fallen into the hands of this gang of pirates. They found the booty, notwithstanding all the Spaniards had removed, rich beyond their most sanguine expectations. The stores were still crowded with goods of great value. Wine, spices, olive oil, silks and cloths

* Monarchs of the Main, vol. ii. p. 159.

of every variety of fabric were found in great abundance. The magazines were amply supplied with corn and other provisions.

Morgan himself was surprised at the grandeur of his capture. He was also alarmed in view of his own peril. The force which could still be arrayed against him was far greater than he had anticipated. He was in imminent danger of being cut off from his return to the ships. There were several Spanish vessels aground in the port. Morgan seized them. With the high tide they were floated. He manned them with the most desperate of his gang and sent them to the islands, and to pursue the vessels which had escaped with treasure along the coast.

There was one royal Spanish mercantile vessel, in particular, of four hundred tons, which had escaped, laden with church plate and jewels, and the richest merchandise. It had put to sea in the greatest haste, with but seven guns and but about a dozen muskets. It was poorly supplied with food and water, and had only the uppermost sails of the mainmast to spread. All the females of the nunnery were on board this ship, with the most valuable ornaments of the church.

Morgan was anxious to make an immediate pursuit of this vessel. Had he done so the vessel would easily have been captured. But for a time he lost

15*

the control of his demoniac crew. Inflamed with wine—for Morgan's prohibition had no effect—and rushing into the most pitiless debauchery, they spent many hours in scenes which neither Sodom nor Gomorrah could ever have outrivalled. Thus the ship escaped. It is said that it contained gold and silver of greater value than all the treasures found in Panama.

Morgan probably foresaw that unless he could destroy these liquors, with which the city was filled, his men would become entirely disorganized, and the Spaniards, falling upon the drunken rabble, would easily cut them to pieces. He could not destroy liquors before the eyes of the pirates, for they would not permit it.

He set fire to the city in various quarters, carefully spreading the report that the conflagration was kindled by the Spaniards themselves. The fire spread with such rapidity that, in a few hours, nearly all of the business portion was laid in ashes. Most of the humbler buildings were of wood, with thatched roofs. They burned like tinder. Two hundred stores, with all their contents, were destroyed. The Genoese Warehouses were burned. There were many poor slaves imprisoned in them. They were consumed by the all-devouring flames.

This energetic commander, as pitiless as any

beast which ever howled in the jungle, had accomplished his purpose. His troops were driven out of the flaming streets into the fields, and there they were compelled to encamp. These wretched men, satiated with gluttony, drunkenness, and debauchery, began now to awake, with new eagerness, to their old passion for plunder.

Four vessels were dispatched to visit the islands and to cruise along the coast in both directions. One hundred and sixty men were sent back to Chagres to convey supplies to the troops in garrison there, and to inform them of the great victory. Daily companies of two hundred men, one party relieving another, were sent out to explore the region around. They returned every night with a group of pale and trembling prisoners, and with mules laden with treasure. These unhappy captives were tortured to compel them to reveal where treasure, of which they knew nothing, was concealed. The father, the mother, the maiden daughter, and the child were alike stretched on the bed of torture. Neither innocence, beauty, nor virtue afforded the female captive any protection.

A pauper Spaniard, not much more than half-witted, wandered, during the confusion, into a rich man's house, stripped off his rags, and clothed himself in costly linen with breeches of bright red taffeta and a coat of silk velvet. As he was foolishly strutting about admiring his finery, the pirates broke in, and seized him as their prize. They believed, or assumed to believe, that he was the master of the house, and demanded that he should inform them where he had concealed his treasure.

In vain he pointed to his rags and protested, by all the saints, that he had lived upon charity. There was nothing he could reveal. These cruel men stretched him on the rack. They dislocated his joints. They twisted a cord around his forehead, " till his eyes appeared as big as eggs, and were ready to fall out." They hung him up by the thumbs and scourged him. They cut off his nose and ears and singed his face with blazing straw. Then with the thrusts of their lances they put him to death.

" After this execrable manner," writes Esquemeling, " did many others of these miserable prisoners finish their days; the common sport and recreation of these pirates being these, and other tragedies not inferior to these."

CHAPTER XXII.

The Return from Panama.

Return of the Explorers.—The Beautiful Captive.—Sympathy in her
behalf.—Embarrassments of Morgan.—Inflexible Virtue of the
Captive.—The Conspiracy.—Efficiency of Morgan.—His Obdu-
racy.—The Search of the Pirates.—The Return March.—Morgan
Cheats the Pirates.—Runs Away.

THE vessels which Morgan sent out to the islands,
and to cruise along the shore, all returned within
about eight days. They came laden with merchandise and with captives. The fate of the female captives was dreadful. In this treatment none of the
men were worse than Morgan himself. In one of the
shiploads of captives there was a Spanish lady of
exquisite beauty. She was quite young, and the
wife of a wealthy merchant, then absent in Peru.
She is described by both Esquemeling and Oexemelin as a lady endowed with such loveliness as is
rarely seen upon earth. Esquemeling writes:

"Her years were few, and her beauty so great as,
peradventure, I may doubt whether, in all Christendom, any could be found to surpass her perfections,
either of comeliness or honesty."

Oexemelin gives a more detailed account of her charms. He says that her hair was in glossy, silken ringlets of jet black. Though a brunette, her complexion was of dazzling purity. Her large, lustrous black eyes beamed with a peculiar expression of tenderness, which won the admiration of all who beheld her. The roughest pirates were subdued and softened by her presence. To them she presented almost the image of the Virgin Mary, and they regarded her charms as angelic.

The moment Morgan cast his eyes upon her he was overawed and captivated by her beauty, and was inspired with the most intense desire to win her love. Others had been his slaves, subject to his brutal will. But this lady, with her beauty, her grace, her accomplishments, her virtue, so far vanquished him, that he could not approach her but as a suppliant for her favor.

Love, the essence of the deity, is, under some circumstances, in its legitimate bearing, the most purifying of influences. Under other circumstances it is the most debasing and brutalizing of passions. It was observed that the demeanor of Morgan became quite changed. He became more social, more gentle, and was particularly attentive to his dress, clothing himself in his richest attire. He ordered his beautiful captive to be separated from the other prisoners, appointed a negress to wait upon her, sent her delicate viands from his own table, and treated her, in all respects, with the greatest consideration. The negress was instructed to do everything in her power to convince the captive lady that her captor was not a beast and a heretic, as she had been taught to believe, but a gentleman, and a Christian, a man of polished manners and cultivated mind. Esquemeling writes :

"This lady had formerly heard strange reports concerning the pirates, before their arrival at Panama, as if they were not men, but heretics, who did neither invoke the blessed Trinity, nor believe in Jesus Christ. But now she began to have better thoughts of them than ever before, having experienced the manifold civilities of Captain Morgan; especially as she heard him many times swear by the name of God and of Jesus Christ, in whom she had been persuaded that they did not believe.

"Neither did she now think them to be so bad, or to have the shapes of beasts, as she had often heard. For as to the names of robbers or thieves, which was commonly given them, she wondered not much at it, seeing, as she said, that among all nations there were to be found some wicked men who naturally coveted to possess the goods of others."

Morgan visited the lady with smiles and bows

and costly presents. He flooded her chamber with robes, jewels, and perfumes. She was not deceived. And when he ventured to propose that she should abandon her husband, and become virtually his wife, and accompany him to the home of splendor with which he would provide her, she repelled him with indignation and loathing. Replying to him with all the eloquence of impassioned innocence, she said :

"Sir, my life is in your hands. But sooner shall my soul be separated from my body than I will surrender myself to your demands."

This repulse stirred up the rage of the infamous pirate. He stripped her of her rich attire, left her only the coarsest garments, and threw her into a dark and loathsome dungeon. She was supplied with only enough food to support life. By these brutalities he hoped to break her spirit, and to compel her to acquiesce in his wishes.

Even demons can appreciate true nobility of character. The beauty and virtues of this lady had won, in some degree, the sympathy of the vilest of these wretches. Morgan could not conceal his treatment from them. They began to murmur, to denounce him, to curse him as a brute.

"I myself," says Esquemeling, "was an eye-witness of the lady's sufferings, and could never have believed that such constancy and virtue could have been found in the world, had I not been assured thereof by my own eyes and ears."

Morgan became alarmed by the threatening aspect assumed by his men. Various causes had been for some time undermining his authority. He knew full well that there was not one of these desperadoes who would hesitate, for one moment, to thrust a poniard into his heart, or to pierce his brain with a bullet. These pirates were all consummate villains. There was no sense of honor among them. There was no crime from which they would shrink did they deem it for their interest to commit it. Even their sympathy for the beautiful captive lady resolved itself mainly into jealousy of the captain. Had they seized her unprotected in the halls of a nunnery, she would have experienced no mercy whatever at their hands.

The pirates, flushed with their great victory, and the vast amount of wealth, of every kind, at their disposal, had formed a conspiracy, in which more than a hundred were implicated. Their plan was to get rid of Morgan, then to seize one of the islands in the neighborhood as their rendezvous, and to make it their stronghold. With the vessels they already had, and the ships they would soon capture, they would have an invincible fleet. Then they would sweep the Pacific Ocean, and ravage all the coasts of Chili and Peru. After they had acquired sufficient plunder to make them all millionnaires, they would return to Europe, by the way of the East Indies, picking up ships by the way, and would then disperse to seek new homes and riot in luxury for the remainder of their days.

In preparation for this movement they had secreted several of the large guns of the town and an ample store of ammunition. But Morgan was equal to this emergency. One of the conspirators betrayed the rest. The first intimation the conspirators had that their design was discovered was in seeing every vessel and boat in the harbor in flames. Every piece of artillery in the place was spiked. Thus they were entirely frustrated in their plan. Orders were then given to pack the mules with treasure, and to make immediate preparation to return to Chagres.

The plunder of Panama had not yet been divided. Though every pirate had taken the most solemn oath that all the booty should be thrown into common stock, and that he would not secrete anything, no one had any confidence in the oath of another. Morgan ordered every man to be searched, from the crown of his head to the soles of his shoes. Though Morgan himself submitted to be first searched, they were all exasperated by this. Every man was compelled to discharge his musket to prove that no jewels were hidden in its barrel.

The French portion of the pirates were especially enraged against Morgan. Many oaths were uttered that they would put him to death before they reached Jamaica. In a few days all the treasure was packed in convenient bales, and placed upon the backs of the mules. The church plate was beaten into shapeless lumps for more convenient stowage. The treasure which could not be removed they wantonly destroyed. One hundred and fifty men were sent to Chagres to bring the boats as far up the river as the stream was navigable. He informed the prisoners that he should take all, as slaves, to Jamaica, who did not, through their friends, obtain an ample ransom.

For the ransom of his beautiful captive, from whom he now rather desired to be relieved, he demanded thirty thousand dollars. Two of the ecclesiastics were permitted to go to her friends to obtain this money. It was immediately furnished them. They returned with it, and treacherously, instead of ransoming her, employed the money for the ransom of their own particular friends.

This treachery was known throughout the army. Even the pirates denounced it. The murmurs in the camp were so loud, that Morgan was compelled to heed them, and he gave the lady her liberty.

On the morning of the 24th of February, 1671, these robbers set out on their return to Chagres. Many of the captive women implored Captain Morgan, upon their knees, with loud lamentations, to permit them to remain with their husbands and their children.. Unfeelingly he replied :

" I did not come here to listen to the cries of women, but to obtain money. Bring me money, and you shall be released. If you do not, you shall surely go to Jamaica."

" When the march began," writes Esquemeling, " those lamentable cries and shrieks were renewed, insomuch that it would have caused compassion in the hardest heart to hear them. But Captain Morgan, as a man little given to mercy, was not moved therewith in the least."

The line of march was as before. First there were scouts a quarter of a mile in advance of the troops. Then followed the advance guard in great strength. The prisoners came next, with the heavily laden mules. The remainder of the pirates formed the rear guard. They goaded forward the fainting, tottering, despairing captives with push of javelin and prick of sabre.

When they reached the blackened ruins of the

town of Cruz, which was at the head of boat navigation, the mules were unloaded, and their burdens
were placed in the canoes. There was a necessary
delay here of several days, and quite a number of
the prisoners, who had written agonizing letters to
their friends, received their money and paid their
ransom. Morgan still had with him many woe-
stricken Spaniards, and one hundred and fifty negro
slaves. These last he deemed cash articles, for they
would bring the money in any of the ports of the
West Indies.

From Cruz the pirates advanced in two parties,
one in the boats, and another on the land. Chagres
was reached without any event occurring of special
importance. Immediately after his arrival, Morgan,
with his characteristic energy, sent some of his prisoners to the important town of Puerto Velo, frequently called Puerto Bello, with the announcement
that if the citizens did not forthwith send him a large
ransom, he would utterly demolish the castle and
lay all the works there in ruins. As Chagres was
the all-important port of entry for the whole province,
he thought that this threat would bring the money.
They, however, paid no heed to it.

The booty was now divided. The pirates were
bitterly disappointed in finding that the whole estimated value amounted to but about two million

dollars. Probably ten times that sum, which they could not remove, had been destroyed in their rapacity. Every man had expected at least ten thousand dollars. When they found that but one thousand was their share they were greatly enraged. This pittance was scarcely sufficient for the carouse of a single week.

Loud and threatening murmurs rose from nearly all lips. They accused Morgan of cheating them. The consummate knave with great adroitness had done so. Many of his men had conspired against him. With far greater ability he was now conspiring against them. He had taken a few into his confidence to share the spoil which they were to steal from the rest. The common sailors had no idea of the value of diamonds and other precious stones. His partisans bought them up at not one hundreth part of their real value. Massive bars of gold were easily concealed.

Morgan endeavored to engross the attention of his men in plundering, burning, and destroying Chagres. While apparently his whole force, in the delirium of intoxication, were engaged in this work, Morgan and his accomplices repaired on board the ships, quietly in the night weighed anchor, and taking advantage of a fair wind, before the morning were out of sight with all their treasure. Their dupes, consisting of nearly one-half of the piratic crew, were left on the shore amid the ruins, without food, without a boat, without shelter, in utter destitution. What ultimately became of them is not known. Probably some starved; some were shot by the Spaniards; some were caught and hung. "Vengeance is mine; I will repay, saith the Lord."

We have no more details respecting the final career of this very able, sagacious, and infamous man. We simply know that he reached Jamaica in possession of an immense fortune. There he was honored as one of the great men of his age. Charles II., King of England, whose accomplice he is said to have been in his piracies, rewarded him for his achievements, appointed him governor of the island, and conferred upon him the honors of a baronetcy. We know not when he died. But we do know that, however Sir Henry Morgan may have escaped the penalty of his sins in this world, he has long ago appeared before the tribunal of that God "who will render to every man according to his deeds."

CHAPTER XXIII.

Montbar the Fanatic.

Partial Solution of a Mystery.—Montbar's Birth.—His Education and Delusions.—Anecdote of the Dramatic Performance.—Montbar Runs Away from Home.—Enters the Navy.—His Ferocious Exploits.—Joins the Buccaneers.—Desperate Battles on the Land and on the Sea.—His Final Disappearance.

IN reading the narrative of the cruelties practised by the pirates upon the Spaniards, the mind is often oppressed with the thought that a God of infinite love and power should have allowed such scenes to have been enacted. There is nothing conceivable, in intense and protracted torture, which was not inflicted upon men, women, and children. There is no satisfactory explanation of this great mystery of earth. Still there are considerations which may perhaps point in the direction of a solution.

The pirates seem to have been permitted to revenge upon the Spaniards the awful sufferings which they had inflicted upon the Indians. The Spanish armies of Cortez and Pizarro ravaged the homes of the innocent native inhabitants of those countries with ferocity and cruelty which Satan and his legions could not possibly have surpassed. The Spaniards had thrown the Indian into the flames of the most awful misery. And then God allowed the pirate to throw the Spaniard into the same flames.

There was a celebrated pirate by the name of Montbar, who seemed to have been inspired with fanatical frenzy approaching maniacal fury against the whole Spanish nation. He was the child of one of the most opulent and respected families in Languedoc, in France. He had received all the advantages of education which wealth could afford. In the process of this education he had read the account of the atrocities practised by the Spaniards in their conquest of the islands and the continents of the New World.

The blood of this ardent young man seemed to boil in his veins, while pondering these fiend-like crimes. As a child he brooded over these tortures until he became almost insane. Soon he devoted himself to all martial exercises, that he might avenge the wrongs of the Indians. This generous but cruel determination grew rapidly into monomania. The animal forces of a mind of unusual energy were all concentrated in this direction. Revenge for the wrongs practised upon the Cubans, the Peruvians, the Mexicans occupied his thoughts by day and

his dreams by night. This became the all-absorb-
ing passion of his soul.

Even when a child, practising with his cross-bow,
he said, "I wish to shoot well, only that I may
know how to kill the Spaniards." George W.
Thornbury, in his sketch of this singular man, allud-
ing to the Spanish enormities in the New World,
writes :

"Fanaticism, avarice, and ambition had ruled like
a trinity of devils, over the beautiful regions desolated and plague-smitten by the Spaniards. Whole
nations had become extinct. The name of Christ
was polluted into the mere cipher of an armed and
aggressive commerce. These books had impressed
the gloomy boy with a deep, absorbing, fanatical
hatred of the conquerors, and a fierce pity for the
conquered.

" He believed himself marked out by God, as the
Gideon sent to their relief. Dreams of riches and
gratified ambition spurred him unconsciously to
the task. He thought and dreamed of nothing but
the murdered Indians. He inquired eagerly from
travellers for news from America, and testified pro-
digious and ungovernable joy when he heard that
the Spaniards had been defeated by the Caribs and
the Bravos.

" He indeed knew by heart every deed of atro-

city that history recorded of his enemies, and would
dilate upon each one, with a rude and impatient
eloquence. The following story he was frequently
accustomed to relate, and to gloat over with a look
that indicated a mind capable of even greater cruelty,
if once led away by a fanatic spirit of retaliation.

"'A Spaniard,' the story ran, 'was once upon
a time appointed governor of an Indian province,
which was inhabited by a fierce and warlike race of
savages. He proved a cruel governor, unforgiving
in his resentments, and insatiable in his avarice.
The Indians, unable any longer to endure either his
barbarities or his exactions, seized him, and showing
him gold, told him that they had at last been able,
by great good luck, to find enough to satisfy his demands. They then held him firm, and melting the
ore, poured it down his throat, till he expired in torments under their hands.'"

The peculiarities of this young man were singularly exhibited on one occasion, which showed
that his mental operations were so deranged that he
could not calmly reflect upon anything connected
with the Spanish nation. At one of the college
exhibitions, a comedy was to be enacted by the
students, in which Montbar was to take a part.
During the performance there was a dialogue to
take place between a Spaniard and a Frenchman.

Montbar represented the Frenchman, and one of his companions the Spaniard.

The Spaniard appeared first upon the stage, and began to utter a tirade of extravagancies against France, denouncing and ridiculing the French in unmeasured terms. Montbar listened, with ever-increasing excitement, until he lost all self-control. The mimic scene in his mind became a reality. In a perfect fury he broke upon the stage; assailed the representative Spaniard like a maniac; called him a liar and a murderer; knocked him down, and would inevitably have killed him, had he not been dragged away by the terrified bystanders.

The boy developed a very active and powerful mind, and his wealthy father was very proud of him. His eccentricities did not alarm him, as he thought that contact with the world would soon remove them all. He wished his son to study some profession. But Montbar insisted upon entering the army. "I wish to learn to fight," said he, "that I may kill the Spaniards."

As his friends opposed his entering the army, he ran away from home, and found his way to Havre. Here he had an uncle who was in command of one of the king's ships. France was then at war with Spain. The ship was just entering upon a cruise against the Spaniards. The uncle, pleased with the enthusiasm

of the boy, and with the intensity of his desire to
join the expedition, wrote to the father, and obtained his reluctant consent. In a few days the ship
sailed.

The young fanatic kept a constant watch for the
foe, evincing the most intense eagerness for an engagement. The moment any sail appeared, he
armed himself, and seemed overjoyed with the
thought that he might soon wreak vengeance on the
Spaniards. At length, a Spanish ship appeared.
Soon they met and exchanged broadsides. Montbar was quite intoxicated with joy. He was perfectly reckless. Not a thought of danger entered his
mind. When the order was given to board, Montbar, sabre in hand, led the party, and was the first
to leap on board the Spanish ship. He seemed to
bear a charmed life, and to be endowed with her-
culean strength. He sought no assistance from his
comrades, but plunged into the thickest of the
enemy, hewing on his right hand and his left, with
marvellous strength. Twice he rushed from end to
end of the vessel, mowing down all who opposed
him. He would give no quarter.

The Spaniards were overpowered. Their slaugh-
ter was awful. Montbar, dreaming that he was
God's appointed minister of vengeance, was in an
ecstasy of exultation, as he cut down some, ran his

sabre through the heart of others, and drove others into the sea. His spirit inspired the rest. Nearly every Spaniard was killed. His uncle succeeded in saving one or two.

The prize was found to be of immense value. The hold was crammed with riches. There was one casket of diamonds of almost priceless worth. While the captain and the crew were examining these treasures, and rejoicing over them, Montbar regarded them with entire indifference. He was counting the dead. Blood, not plunder, was what his soul craved.

As there was now war between France and Spain, the French buccaneers, even when acting without any formal commission, were regarded by the Government as engaged in legitimate warfare. The buccaneers of England, robbing Spanish commerce and Spanish colonies, were encouraged and aided by the French navy. The conflict we have described took place near the shores of St. Domingo. Montbar's uncle learned, from his prisoners, that the ship he had captured had been separated by a storm from two others, and that they were bound to Port Margot on the island.

He immediately sailed to the vicinity of that port, where he kept watch. The vessel he had captured was used as a decoy. He placed French soldiers on board, unfurled the flag of Spain, and stood off and on, waiting the arrival of the two vessels. While thus on the watch, some buccaneers, from the shore, came on board in canoes, with provisions to sell. They had been wrecked upon the coast ; and while a part of their number had been at a distance from the camp hunting, the Spaniards had fallen upon them, put them to flight, and plundered their stores.

"Why do you suffer this ? " exclaimed Montbar, indignantly.

"We do not mean to suffer it," they replied. "We know what the Spaniards are, and what our power is. We are collecting our forces, and will soon take signal vengeance upon them."

"Let me go with you," said Montbar. "I do not ask to be your leader, but I will go at your head. I will be the first to expose myself, and will show you how I can fight these accursed Spaniards."

Gladly they accepted his offer. His ardor and energy inspired them with great confidence in him. His uncle very reluctantly allowed him to go, cursing him as a foolish, hair-brained madcap, ever eager to push his head into danger. Yet the uncle was very proud of him. As young Montbar descended the side of the ship into a canoe, the captain said exultingly to one at his side, "There goes as brave a lad as ever trod a plank."

The buccaneers returned to their camp, and immediately, in a strong war-party, set out in search of the Spaniards. They threaded intricate paths through the woods, until they opened upon a small treeless prairie, which they called a savanna. Just before entering this field, which was surrounded by hills and woods, they saw, in the distance, a mounted party of Spaniards who were evidently on the march to attack them.

Montbar was transported with rage at the sight of the Spaniards. He was ready, single-handed, to rush upon them at once—he alone, against several hundred, regardless whether the others followed him or not. But an old, experienced buccaneer, who led the party, held him back.

"Stop," said he; "there is plenty of time. If you do as I tell you, not one of those fellows shall escape."

These words, "Not one of those fellows shall escape," arrested the impetuous young man. The buccaneers halted, pretending not to have seen the Spaniards. They allowed one or two of their number to exhibit themselves, as if belonging to a hunting party. They then pitched their tent of linen, apparently entirely unconscious that they were near any foe. Drawing out their brandy-flasks, they feigned a great revel, singing songs, shouting, and passing the flasks from one to another, as if in the wildest of drunken bouts. This was done by a small portion of the company, while most of the buccaneers were hidden in ambush.

The Spaniards, having secreted themselves, watched all these movements. They supposed that the buccaneers, stupefied with drink, would ere long fall helplessly asleep. The Spaniards would then creep cautiously upon them, and kill them all. But the cunning old buccaneer had taken good care that the brandy-flasks should all be empty. Not a single drop of intoxicating drink had the feigned revellers taken.

As soon as darkness veiled the scene the buccaneers all assembled in ambuscade, anticipating a midnight attack. Every musket was in order, and their brains were cool and uninflamed with drink. The Spaniards delayed their attack until daylight. As the hours lingered away, Montbar was restless, and chafed like a caged lion, saying that they would never come, and imploring permission to march out and attack them.

At daybreak the buccaneers discerned a dark line moving noiselessly over the ridge, and descending into the plain. They knew full well what this

16*

meant. Every movement was watched by the ambushed buccaneers. Cautiously the Spaniards advanced. They crossed the prairie, and entered the forest, intending to encircle the tent, which they supposed held the sleeping buccaneers.

Suddenly the woods seemed to burst into volcanic flame. The report of the musketry was followed with shout and yell, and the storm of lead swept through the ranks of the Spaniards, striking down scores, either in death or grievously wounded. The buccaneers rushed instantaneously upon their bewildered, staggered, bleeding foe. Montbar seemed animated by demoniacal frenzy. He rushed upon the Spaniards in utter recklessness, regardless of their numbers, or of the support he should receive from his comrades. His heavy sabre flashed in all directions, as if wielded by tireless sinews of steel.

Soon he was quite in advance of his companions, and was alone in the very thickest of the Spanish squadron. He would inevitably have been cut down, had not the other buccaneers, astonished at his audacity, rushed to his rescue. Montbar's sword was dripping with blood. He was in a frenzy of joy. Every blow he struck cut down a Spaniard. He exulted in the carnage, and ever after declared that this was the happiest day of his life. One wounded Spaniard clung to his knee begging for mercy. Montbar brought down his sabre upon his head, splitting it from crown to chin, fiercely exclaiming, "I wish that you were the last of this accursed race." An eye-witness of the battle describes the carnage as horrible. Nearly every Spaniard was destroyed. The victors, all absorbed in their bloody work, stumbled over the dying and the dead, deaf to every cry for mercy.

The buccaneers were astonished and delighted by the prowess which Montbar had displayed. They entreated him to remain and become their captain. But a signal gun, fired by his uncle, called him back to the ship. Montbar was placed as captain on board the large ship which his uncle had captured. Many of the pirates eagerly engaged to serve under him.

After a sail of eight days these two vessels encountered four Spanish war-ships, each one larger than either of those commanded by Montbar or his uncle. One of the most desperate of naval battles ensued. The elder Montbar was attacked by two of the ships. For three hours they struggled, grappled together, receiving and giving the most terrible broadsides. At last the three sank together in one watery grave. The uncle, it is said, rejoicing to drag the two other ships with him, went down laughing.

Montbar, with his crashing shot, succeeded at length in sinking one of the ships assailing him, and then he boarded the other. The terror-stricken crew threw themselves into the water. The floating bodies presented targets for the buccaneers. No quarter was shown. Montbar rushed up and down the decks killing all he could reach. His courage and accomplishments were so marvellous, that his comrades regarded him with superstitious reverence, as endowed with more than mortal powers. He himself ever averred that he was God's appointed messenger, to avenge the wrongs the Spaniards had inflicted upon the Indians. It is not known that a single individual escaped from these four Spanish ships.

Montbar had now two vessels at his command. He engaged many other buccaneers in his service, and soon had an army of nearly eight hundred men ready to follow him to the death. He swept the seas, and, often landing, ravaged the coasts. We have no detailed account of his subsequent career. One of his biographers writes:

" And this completes all that history has preserved of one of the strangest combinations of fanatic and soldier that has ever appeared since the days of Loyola. In another age, and under other circumstances, he might have been a second Mohammed. Equally remorseless, his ambition, though narrower, seems to have been no less fervid. If he was cruel, we must allow him to have been sincere even in his fanaticism. Daring, untiring, of unequalled courage and unmatched resolution, the cruelty of the Spaniards he put down by greater cruelty. He passes from us into unknown seas, and we hear of him no more. He died probably unconscious of crime, unpitying and unpitied.

" Oexemelin, who saw Montbar at Honduras, describes him as active, vivacious, and full of fire, like all the Gascons. He was of tall stature, erect and firm, his air grand, noble, martial. His complexion was sunburnt, and the color of his eyes could not be discerned under the deep, arched vaulting of his bushy eyebrows. His very glance in battle was said to intimidate the Spaniards, and to drive them to despair."

THE END.